HIGH HAND

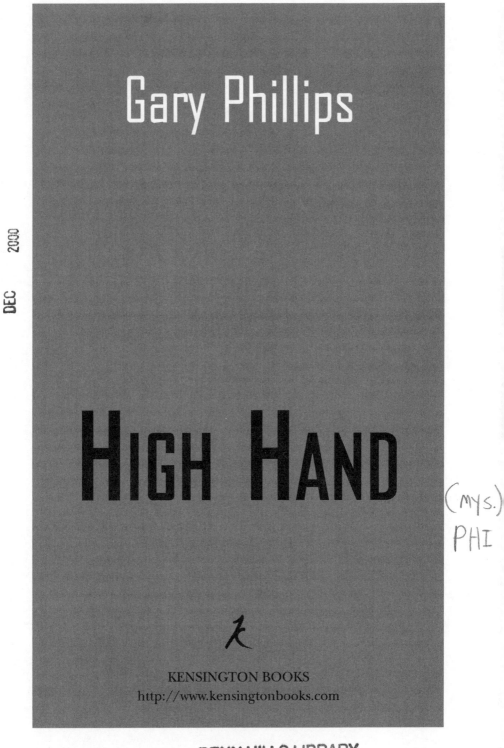

Gary Phillips

HIGH HAND

KENSINGTON BOOKS
http://www.kensingtonbooks.com

KENSINGTON BOOKS are published by

Kensington Publishing Corp.
850 Third Avenue
New York, NY 10022

Kensington and the K logo Reg. U.S. Pat. & TM Off.

Library of Congress Card Catalogue Number: 00-105318
ISBN 1-57566-616-2

First Printing: November, 2000
10 9 8 7 6 5 4 3 2 1

Printed in the United States of America

*To all the squares, players, shot callers, and eight ballers
who ever made it off of Flower Street*

"You face reality, not the lights.
The lights go off as quickly as they come on."

—James Baldwin

HIGH HAND

CHAPTER ONE

The dual sets of legs jutted from the floor of the Amargosa Desert like some kind of forgotten pop-art project. One pair was stouter than the other. The thicker legs had shit-kicker boots on the end of them that weren't just fancy, Saturday-night line-dancing numbers. These were broken-in, scuffed-leather, chipped-heel beauties that had seen many a rocky trail and weathered planks in a bar.

The other pair of legs wore tasseled loafers on the feet. These shoes had expensive sewn stitching details and appeared as if the pair had just been plucked from the showroom window. Both legs were clad in jeans. The boots led to the Wrangler's brand, and had seen plenty of washings. The second pair, to go along with the fine loafers—which subsequently turned out to be Ferragamos—were tailored bluish-white jeans prewashed for subtle comfort.

Not that the men the legs belonged to cared for such fashion niceties now. The owners of the legs were of course dead. Each man had been buried head first to mid-thigh in the warm earth. For it was a typical mild evening after another blast furnace of a day in the desert. Ironically, this part of the Amargosa Desert, located on the Nevada side of the border, lay against the Funeral Mountain Range that spilled across to California.

But again, this was a bit of circumstance the two unfortunates who had their legs stiffening in the night air were not in a situation to appreciate. A coyote was prowling around the two, each set at an angle to the other, sniffing at one of the men's kneecaps. The coyote had crossed Highway 95 at a slow trot; not much in the way of traffic happening at this time of the night.

The coyote had waited and watched from a clump of sickly cholla cacti on the other side of the stretch of the road, the hint of ripening flesh having held her interest for some time. A big Lincoln had barreled by as she started her journey toward the source of the odor. The car drove steady on in a northern direction. Its vermillion taillights were like receding gargoyle eyes as it disappeared in the dark, away from the coyote and the men planted among the rocks and brush. Their legs not easily seen from the road.

The woman at the wheel of the Lincoln wasn't doing much sightseeing anyway. She hadn't picked this road for the view. Martha Chainey stretched in her seat, tightening her long fingers around the steering wheel, her arms rigid as she arched back against the car's seat. Highway 95 was not the most direct route to where she was going, but it was the smartest approach. She glanced in the rearview mirror, catching a glimpse of an animal slipping across the road.

She thumbed the eject button on the car's tape player. The cassette of Casandra Wilson slid out partway and she removed the tape, tossing it beside her on the bench seat. Deftly, she opened another tape box beside her with one hand and held the new selection to her eyes briefly to see who the artist was. She smiled, hoping to crank it up some in the confines of her sealed retro wagon.

The gruff delivery of Sweet Pea Atkinson of the Boneshakers emanated from the front and rear speakers as the ex-showgirl guided the sleek, 1979 jade green Givenchy-accented car toward her destination. In those days, Mercury had tried to boost sales of Lincolns by introducing a collector series of sedans. The idea was to use noted fashion designers to work their runway magic on steel as they had done for cloth.

Bill Blass came up with nautical-inspired themes, while Emilio Pucci went in for maroon and gunmetal grays. Even Cartier, the jeweler, got in the act and provided Continentals with touches of foreign elegance and champagne-colored bodies. Much the same as one could nowadays buy Eddie Bauer Ford Explorers.

The Givenchy Lincoln she was driving had been restored to assembly-line freshness, replete with butter soft-turquoise leather interior and black highlights on the dash and trim. There was a gas-gulping 400 V-8 under the hood, and the vehicle's suspension system provided for smooth riding over the terrain like it was a sled over new-fallen snow.

The crafters who'd worked on the car had done an award-winning job on the vehicle. The thing was a throwback to an era when American car companies operated as if fossil fuels would never end. And it was our birthright to use whatever means to keep the black gold flowing in the engines of big, impractical cars like this Lincoln.

Chainey considered such an outlook; the belief that the product of the petroleum tap would always be ours got shattered in 1979, when another fuel shortage hit due to Middle East unrest and, some speculated, chicanery by multinational oil companies. Apparently sales of Lincolns had remained brisk; people were going to have their luxury cars even if they had to be hitched to a team of horses. Even now, decades later, you had sales of bigger and bolder SUVs at an all-time high, countering the dictates of common sense. Ah, the American spirit, she reflected, yawning loudly. Folks wanted what they wanted and when they wanted it. Certainly that axiom was embodied in Frankie Degault.

Degault was not a man one could charitably call patient. He enjoyed his fits of pique, and being able to exercise his caprice on those who depended on him for their paychecks. With his more reasonable sister, Victoria, he ran the Riverhead Casino on the Strip in Vegas. It was a bright and shiny construct of tri-level gaming floors, restricted rooms for the whales—the high rollers—and a mere 728 rooms for guests. Sneering at tradition, and maybe fate, Frankie Degault had insisted the elevators have a button for the thirteenth floor. If you were going to romp in Frankie's playground, then you did so by his rules.

And rule number friggin' one, he was inclined to remind you in that fake wiseguyese he'd adopt, was not to fuck with his money. If you owed, you made your marker good. If you borrowed, you paid on time; no whining, and preferably grinning as you handed over the vig too. When discussing the subject of money, Degault would hunch his shoulders a lot and work his neck like he had a crook in it. He manifested all sorts of tics and irritating mafiosi behavior he'd gleaned from TV shows and movies.

He was connected, that was true. But like many of the third and fourth generation of the original Mustache Petes, Degault learned to use a calculator much more adeptly than the business end of a crowbar. Getting his MBA from Smith had prepared him for what he was—a spoiled brat who had benefitted from the pernicious labors of his forebearers.

Yet like the needs of those gents from the halcyon days of Vegas's ascendancy, there were still situations when substantial amounts of cash were generated off the books, as it were. In the past those funds had been the skim money from the slots and crap tables, whore dollars and heroin profits. These days Vegas offered thrilling roller-coaster rides that slammed your stomach against your spine, galleries of high-brow art and knights having a joust while the kids ate chicken diners. Beneath that patina of family friendliness, and beyond the climate-controlled board rooms, the methods of the old school prevailed.

How one got the scratch was more sophisticated, but sex and drugs remained the basis upon which millions could be realized. And the fact that these moneys were obtained through nefarious means meant you had to hide it from a plethora of authorities and agencies that were forever probing the doings of the movers and shakers on the Strip. So there was an ongoing industry in moving the moneys from one spot to the next, for one reason or another.

A jackrabbit hopped across the road in front of Chaney as

the Lincoln approached Tonopah. This town was where the highway teed, and she'd take it west, then jog back north on into Carson City. The glow of the sun was hinted at over a low rise to her right. Idly, she glanced at the clock on the dash. She'd been driving steady for the last five hours and wanted to stop and get something to eat. Her plan was to rest sometime in the midday hours after she'd crossed over to California. Afterward, get back to it as early evening came on. Working at night, she faintly smiled to herself. Always working at night.

Frankie Degault had demanded to know the route she was going to take, and she'd told him flat that wasn't a good idea. Even if was just her and him who knew, that was one too many. Of course he'd sputtered and thundered, how dare she question his professionalism. Doing his I'm-the-man shtick. Calmly, enunciating and using precise words, she'd explained her reasoning.

Say he's on the phone—and he let slip a word or phrase that indicated which way his shipment was coming in. Bad enough, she'd continued over his gesticulations, there was a time certain the freight would be delivered. Why take a chance and possibly give his enemies any other information that might jeopardize his plans?

He'd finally nodded his head, stroking his chin with the ends of his manicured fingers. If you wanted to get Frankie to stall out the chatter, wind the conversation back to him. Make it so it was only his well-being you were concerned with. As if Chainey shouldn't be worried for her own butt. She was riding on seven million change in neat, nonconsecutive one-hundred-dollar bills. And like that wasn't a siren's call to every strong-arm goon or rival of the Degaults should they hear a rumor of such a transport.

Frankie had shaken a finger at her as they stood in his cherry-wood- and burnished-aluminum-paneled office on top of the Riverhead. He'd said that was smart thinking. He didn't say for a broad, but she knew it was on his mind. Just as every time she had to interact with the guy, she noticed his eyes regarding her six-foot frame as if measuring her for a suit—a skintight one. Last year on her birthday, he'd sent a bottle of white Chardonnay and a single blood red rose to the Truxon Ltd. office. His note said: "The moon and you."

She'd split the bottle with her friend Rena Solomon, a reporter for the Las Vegas *Express*. The *Express* was a twice-weekly tabloid run by a former Free Speech Movement Sixties radical, ex-est counselor and hot air balloon salesman, Anson Hiss. The publisher was a relative of the late Alger Hiss. In the fifties Alger had been the head of the Carnegie Foundation and a former State Department employee, who Communist-hunting Senators Joseph McCarthy and Richard Nixon would politically crucify to further their own careers. Hiss's *Express* could hardly be termed competition for the establishment *Review-Journal*. But given the boom in population growth of Vegas and its environs, the alternative paper in town was gaining a steady readership.

Chainey's car approached a cluster of neon and reflective surfaces off to the left about sixty yards away. Blinking tubes of purple and white angled high on a pole announced the Dirty Foxx 24 Hour Coffee Shop. In a neon circle seemingly superimposed on the sign in one corner, the jaws of an anthropomorphic fox in a snap brim hat opened and closed. Several cars, SUVs and big rigs were scattered about the gravel parking lot in a haphazard fashion.

She pulled in, parked and entered. Inside, she half-expected to see photos of the late comedian Redd Foxx along the walls. When he played and lived in Vegas, she'd attended several of his parties. But the bawdy Redd was nowhere in evidence. The walls were bland, with Auto Club–type pictures of sunsets and landscapes in inexpensive frames. Truckers, retirees, and young couples were eating and talking. She caught the loser's look in more than one pair of eyes as she took a booth to the rear.

A young man in a canary yellow sport coat and rings on all five fingers of his left hand was in a booth in a direct line from hers. He had his arm around a girl, a hammerlock around her neck. Canary Coat was whispering to her and she was giggling. The girl looked like she should be at home catching some sleep before another day of high school. Coat looked up while he nibbled the girl's ear. He locked on Chainey, raw desire evident on his face.

Chainey shifted her gaze. Through the window, she could see the Lincoln. She hadn't brought her purse in, preferring to keep her piece strapped on her side beneath her jacket.

"Coffee and . . . ?" the young waitress with the big hair asked. A nostril of her nose was pierced by a stud with the club card suit on it. She wore stacked tennis shoes and her pen was poised to take the order.

"Chicken salad sandwich on toasted wheat and a glass of water."

"Sure thing, doll." The kid even smacked on gum to complete her punk/hip/retro getup. She sashayed off.

A trucker in a quilted vest was walking back to his cab out in the lot. He slowed as he got near the Lincoln. It could be innocent enough, somebody pausing to appreciate a cherry seventies vehicle. Or it could be something else. That was the problem with Frankie Degault and his goddamn goodfellas image he was so in love with. He wouldn't listen that the best way to ferry his money around wasn't in a conspicuous road hog like the Lincoln. A nice sedate MPV soccer mom van, now that was the way you did it. But Frankie wasn't going to heed common sense in that regard. He was going to show whoever it was she was delivering to that he was all style, all the friggin' time.

The trucker ran a hand along the hood of the car like he was in the middle of foreplay. He stared at the car for several moments. Time went into slow motion for Chainey, her senses sharpened to movement and sound. The trucker could be a diversion, and she was tensed to push back from the table, kicking it over in the same movement. Her gun would be in her hand as she dove to the floor, ready to pop whoever the threat was.

Her food arrived. The trucker got in his rig and cranked the engine over. She smiled thinly and took a bite as the eighteen wheeler turned toward the highway. Discernable under the lights of the lot, she could make out a plate on the rear door of the truck's trailer. The plate read: THINK SAFETY.

"Amen," she said, taking another bite.

After paying her bill and leaving a tip, Chainey went to the ladies' room. Coming back out, she wasn't surprised to find Canary Coat pretending to be talking on the phone in the alcove between the rest rooms.

"You in the business, huh?" Coat hung up the undialed phone. A toothpick bobbed in his slack mouth.

Normally she ignored moronic come-on lines. Normally she ignored all come-on lines. She wasn't going to have fun; she wanted to make sure he wasn't anything more than the pushy prick he seemed to be.

"What business is that, slick?" She put her back to the ladies' room door. There had been no one else in the toilet when she was in there. But that didn't mean someone hadn't managed to come through the window she'd latched inside.

He flashed evenly spaced teeth. "The way you move, my mahogany Xena. The way you take everything in, looking casual as you do it. I've seen you at the MGM or Luxor, haven't I?" Coat snapped his fingers with many rings. "The Luxor, right? You run that review with the dancers all spray painted in gold in Egyptian getups."

He was shaking his head, pleased with himself. Chainey summed him up as a civilian and was moving past him when he got cute.

"Aw, come on, Cleopatra Jones, don't be like that." The man moved to block her way, his face close in on hers. She hadn't noticed it before, having concentrated on the wider surroundings. Focusing on him now, she knew now why his eyes had that gleam in them. The pupils were constricted, the veins marbling the whites thin and gnarled like withered stalks.

Chainey looked past him at the girl. She was giggling some more, one hand up to her mouth. Her eyes were also glimmering like 200-watt bulbs. This game was a tag team effort.

"I'm going, and you will get out of my way."

"Oooh." He turned to look at the girl, wiggling his hands and body in mock fear. He leaned back toward Chainey. "Be nice."

He slipped a hand in the side pocket of his coat. Chainey remained placid. As she expected, he came out with something other than a gun. He produced a wad of bills.

"I know what it takes, okay." He cocked an eyebrow and couldn't help the quivering smile bracing his lips. He watched her while he separated three one-hundred-dollar bills from the roll. "This is just so we can have a conversation, see how we vibe, all right?"

"The three of us, huh?"

"Most definitely."

"I've got to run, darlin'. We'll have to explore your *Hustler* fantasies later." She patted him on the cheek and started to step past him again. Chainey expected him to make a grab for her arm and that was when she was going to slam the ridge of her palm into his sternum. He didn't do squat. He looked truly regretful as she marched to the door.

"Come back, y'hear?" her waitress said, balancing three plates of food on her arms.

Chainey curtly saluted and stepped into the humid night.

"Yo, z'up, huh?"

The girl had followed her out and had yanked, hard, on Chainey's arm. The taller woman allowed herself to spin around, looking for lover boy. He was at the glass door of the Dirty Foxx, his eyes iridescent in their sockets. He was biting on a knuckle as he watched his sweetie go into action.

"Yes?"

"Yeah, like you all that." The girl was effecting a *vata loca* accent. She was as white as a bar of Ivory soap. "You rude like that all the goddamn time?"

Girlfriend was swaying, arms loose at her sides like she was Lennox Lewis warming up for a thirteen-rounder.

"Don't think I won't drop your ass 'cause you're young and stupid," Chainey warned.

"Aw shit." She did a fake like she was going to walk off, then whirled back, a vicious right whizzing over a ducking Chainey's head.

The other woman effortlessly stepped inside the next swing and then she brought a swift elbow against the younger woman's windpipe. She faltered back, her breathing temporarily interrupted. Chainey grabbed her by the arms to keep her from falling. Canary Coat was still at the door, gnawing his knuckle and getting his kicks. The waitress and a patron were behind him, their mouths open.

"What ever flips your flapjacks, I'm not in the mood, feel what I'm sayin'?" Chainey shook her and the other one giggled, spittle gathering on her lips. She sagged in her grasp.

Chainey let her drop to the gravel. The younger woman swore and laughed louder. Chainey got in her Lincoln and drove away from the roadside café and its customers. Kids today; she shook her head in disbelief. It wasn't the pros messing everything up. It was the wannabes and posers. The amateurs who spent too much time playing video games and watching nihilistic movies where the body count was a ratio for the box office gross. And then acting on their head trips, trying to make the world conform to their narcissistic viewpoint.

Of course, who was she to condemn, she concluded as the Lincoln powered across the border. She'd made her peace, or maybe it was a detente, with her psyche about what she did for a living. Still, there was something to be said for conducting oneself in a proper manner. Not that Chainey had anything against kinky sex. Yet she didn't go around imposing herself on strangers in the wee hours. How declassé. She laughed to herself and dropped the subject in her musings. Chainey put in a tape of the late jazz vocalist Joe Williams singing "Everyday I Have the Blues." The sun was up and she didn't try to dwell on how many people like Williams and Foxx she'd met over the years in Vegas who'd died in the natural course of life—as well as those by another's hand.

Around 2:00 A.M. she got bored with tapes and switched to the radio. Fifteen minutes later the signal carrying Tom Jones's voice faded out as the ageless crooner sang "Thunderball." The hurried monotone of a newscaster could be discerned through a static crackle as the new station replaced the Welsh Wastrel.

". . . report of Highway Patrolwoman Amy Florence's startling discovery in the early morning hours. Two pairs of legs were discovered by this observant law enforcement officer at approximately twelve-oh-five this A.M. She was out on routine patrol on the lonely stretch of the roughly ninety miles between the outskirts of Las Vegas and the beginning of the Amargosa Desert."

The last line of the newscaster caught her interest. She fooled with the digital setting of the car's stereo in an attempt to bring the voice in clearer. The Lincoln would have to have a high-tech stereo unit rather than its original dial radio. The earlier sets were much better at nuancing the between spaces of the airwaves to bring in a troublesome program. These new gadgets were supposed to be superior, given their internal electronic antenna and all, but at the moment Chainey was gritting her teeth at their inefficiency.

Presently, a woman's flat voice could be heard again through the hiss and pop of the interference. ". . . never seen anything like it in my eight years on the job." That voice ended and then the newscaster was back. "The authorities have yet to start excavating the bodies. They want to make sure they've canvassed the area throughly before beginning that process. Stay tuned throughout the day to K-ZAN for more developments in this matter. And now to Len Shockman—"

Chainey wasn't empathizing with the two unfortunates found in the desert she'd come through hours earlier. Whoever they were, either they'd settled accounts on this side of the grave or come up craps like the rest of us, she reasoned. Either way, they were dead. What mattered to her was whether those deaths had some bearing on her gig now. Were the bodies planted there for her to see, or at least to hear about? Had security been so compromised that the opposition could afford to screw around with her like it was a game?

Had someone snatched Frankie and sweated him to talk? And she had no illusions that Degault wouldn't fold like a pensioner from Dubuque at the two-dollar table if it came to saving his skin. The self-important punk. No, get real, girl. She knew this was just her superstitious side acting up. Unconsciously, she touched the horseshoe earring in her left lobe. The rough-hewn silver earrings were studded with small diamonds and rubies and had been given to her a long time ago. They'd been with her through a lot of situations. She quit touching the earring and got her mind back on her work.

To satisfy her insecurity, she pulled the car over to the side of the road. From a sports bag in the trunk, she extricated a device that looked like an ohm meter. With the instrument humming, she walked around the car, checking for bugs. She popped the hood as the day heated up. The thin membrane of invisible tape she'd adhered to the hood and the body was still intact until she'd disturbed it. There were no surveillance apparatuses in the engine compartment. Chainey completed her check, gliding the scanner slowly below the vehicle's undercarriage. She paid particular attention to the disguised areas where the money was tucked away.

Everything was negative, which was good. She didn't like the coincidence of her passing by the bodies in the desert, but there was nothing to be done about such things. Life was full of weird shit like that. She took off the jacket, then placed her gun and holster on the bench seat, the jacket on top of the piece. Her rayon/silk blouse was wet across the back and stuck to her as she got in behind the wheel and joined the morning flow. She notched the air conditioner to three. KZAN was now coming in with crystal clarity.

Chainey recognized the voice of Shockman, the on-air personality. He was a self-appointed arbiter of ethics and values. The man had held a position in a recent Republican president's administration. He'd written several books, and his lectures commanded big fees and many attendees. He'd brought his road show to Vegas, the citadel of sin, to admonish and cajole his audience. There was good money to be made, albeit taking the sucker's money and then flagellating him for being weak in the first place.

She settled in and drove steady, only stopping for gas, until midafternoon and fatigue began to overtake her. She pulled off the highway and prowled along various streets until she'd traveled several more clicks of the odometer. Eventually she parked at a deteriorating motor court place called the Lucky Eight.

An older gent in a Hawaiian shirt gave her a measured study from behind the lopsided counter in the prison cell of a lobby. The front of the counter was painted with a large pair of dice showing four dots apiece. The art had yellowed and portions of it had chipped with age. It looked like the image hadn't been retouched since the Harding administration. A lone old-fashioned slot machine resided on a circular table. Sitting next to the one-armed bandit was a woman in sweatpants, top and heels. She was perched sideways on the edge of her seat, working the machine's handle and feeding it coins.

The man read the registration card again, slowly. He rechecked the information Chainey had written on it against the driver's license the tall woman had offered. The license and the written information were consistent, but both were false.

The man leaned out across the sloping counter to glare at the Lincoln. Chainey watched him, a bland look on her face. The proprietor scrunched up his features and slid a key across.

"Cash, huh?" he groused, holding her twenty and ten close to his nose.

"That can't possibly be a problem in this place, can it?"

The man blinked and turned his sourness on the slot machine operator. "You might as well rest up from pulling on that thing. It must be filled up with your quarters by now anyway."

Chainey walked out as the woman ignored the advice and continued her Sisyphean task. She moved the Lincoln in front of her room, number 12. She secured the car, including setting a localized motion detector. If it went off, a monitor in her purse would screech her awake.

Inside the dank room she took off her shoes. The air conditioner rattled but functioned. She unbuttoned her shirt and lay on the bed. The upper part of her body was propped against the pillow and the headboard. Sleeping like this wasn't natural to her, but in her line, it was the surest way to get moving if she needed to. She shut down, letting the hum of traffic and the clacking air conditioner soothe her to a state of sleep.

Too soon her eyes came open. The room had deeper shadows but wasn't completely dark. Chainey remained motionless, letting her body come fully awake. Her watch read 6:09. She got up and moved back the curtain at the window to look at the Lincoln. It was where she'd left it. Her cell phone rang in her purse.

"Shit," she cursed, punching the phone on in the middle of the second ring. "This better be important," she said.

"I'm just checking on you," Frankie Degault remarked enthusiastically.

"Check out," she clipped. "Emergencies only." Chainey shut the cell off and considered throwing it against the wall. If the call had been picked up, they'd come here and get a description of her car. It would be a pain. She'd have to segue to North Hollywood in L.A. and see some guys she knew there to switch the cars. That meant more exposure, but only if it came to that. Of course, the only way to know if she'd been made was to hang around and see who showed.

Goddamn Degault, why didn't he pay attention to his sister more? She knew the answer to that. Why didn't any man listen to a woman? Chainey was moving, buttoning her shirt, gun from underneath the pillow. She went out into the tepid late afternoon, sweeping the area, prickly alert for anything. Inside the Lincoln, the engine caught on the second crank and she eased the car into reverse. In the side mirror she could see the hombre from the lobby hobbling up, a worried look on his face.

The car idled in neutral. She waited, the gun close. He kept going to frantically knock on the door of number 9. Putting the car into drive and aiming it back toward the road, Chainey adjusted the rearview mirror. She caught a glimpse of a man in striped boxers and a fez in the crack of number 9's door. Chainey kept on the pedal till she got to Carson City. She took a rest room break, gassed up, got a cup of coffee to go and hit it again. She whipped past the WELCOME TO CALIFORNIA sign after midnight.

Chainey wasn't drowsy and kept plowing highway. Maybe she was overreacting, but something since the first mile she'd taken on this job was crawling under her scalp. It wasn't just Frankie, though that was a factor. In the rearview mirror she took a glimpse at herself. There were new crow's feet at the edge of her eyes. Relatively speaking, she was still young, not creaking just yet. But that ancient drum beat about marriage and helping raise a passel of kids wasn't a rhythm she resonated with—yet. Or could be she knew but wasn't ready to admit to herself that the future of being a freight manager for Truxon Ltd. had a finite point.

Whatever. The job was the job. All this introspection, she reflected, made for slipping, and that was definitely not an option.

Chainey was on schedule as she pulled to a stop one house down from her destination. It was nighttime, and in this section of the residential hills of pricey Mill Valley in Marin County, even the bull frogs understood that it was inappropriate to croak too loud. She'd driven past the place a couple of times to make sure there weren't any surprises. The house at which she was to make her drop was a large, two-story Victorian with Japanese touches reflected in the trim. The mansion had an overhanging balcony, and she could see a birdcage up there too. Paper lanterns marked with individual ideograms hung from the balcony's canopy, each lit with inner fires. The house was partially hidden by an array of colorful plants, flowers and shrubbery. The rear of the house abutted a hill that rose into more greenery.

There was a high stone wall topped with metal spires surrounding the house. Or rather, she assumed the wall went all around, given the overgrowth of topiary and what portions of the wall could be seen. She stood at the gate and pressed the announce button on the intercom box. Overhead a closed-circuit camera attached to the wall swung into position to focus on her.

"Yes?" came the voice through the intercom.

"I'm here from Degault." She looked up at the lens rotating in on her.

"Please keep looking at the camera."

Chainey did as asked. Several moments went by.

"Very good," the detached voice said. The gate clicked open

and she walked inside and up a curving pathway. A series of floodlights lined the pathway, casting the area in pale yellow tones.

The door to the house opened, revealing a dark-skinned man, probably East Indian. He was tall and lean, dressed suburban casual, complete with a sweater with a crest on it. His sleek black hair fell to his shoulders, and in one hand he held on to a chunky, amber-colored Persian cat. His eyes were the same hue as his cat.

"Chainey," he said, scratching the cat on its head.

"That's me. Want to help me unload?"

He stepped back, allowing her inside. "Would you like to relax first, a glass of juice or something with more bite?"

She smiled, briefly touching one of her good-luck earrings. "That'd be nice, but business first." They stood in a foyer with a large, ornate mirror on the wall and a huge standing vase filled with sprays of wheat stalks. There were stairs leading upward to her left.

"Of course." He let the cat go, revealing the pistol he'd been hiding underneath the animal. "You must want to be rid of that burden after such a long ride."

"You have a duffel bag or two?"

He turned his head and called into another part of the house. "Buchanan."

Chainey heard footsteps. "Coming, McLaughlin." A muscular blond-haired man appeared. He was heavier but the same height as the other man. Buchanan was dressed in shorts, an athletic T and sandals. His bronzed deltoids were solid but not bulky. He carried two empty canvas bags. When he reached the man, the two kissed quickly on the mouth.

So much for that fantasy. "Shall we get busy, gentlemen?"

Chainey was directed to pull the car around the corner into a garage set perpendicular and built into the house. The garage was well-equipped, with a large rollaway tool box, a creeper and various other car-related items. From inside the empty trunk, the carpeting was pulled back so as to access a panel. Chainey removed wrapped plastic packets of bills. Then she lifted the side of the car with a floor jack. McLaughlin stood guard with a pistol as she and Buchanan used screwdrivers and pliers to pop coverings in the undercarriage loose. From those hidden compartments, more wrapped plastic packets of bills fell out. Buchanan let the car down as Chainey and McLaughlin finished filling the bags. Straightening up, she jerked her head in the direction of the rise behind the house.

"Something?" McLaughlin asked, a bemused look on his face.

"I don't know," she said.

Buchanan pointed to three monitors on a shelf. On each screen was a green image of a different section of the hillside. "We've got infrared sensors, night vision optics and motion detectors that can pick up a mouse moving through the brush. If there's anything out there, we'd know about it."

"A drink before you get back on your horse?" McLaughlin asked.

"A quick one," Chainey said, finally relaxing.

The three went back into the house through the garage. In the den, crowded with antique furnishings, they stood around, toasting each other with Napa Valley wine. On a Shaker-style desk in the corner was an array of computer and other types of electronic equipment. The coffee table, a stressed antique, contained a set of blueprints held open by books stacked on the edges. On top of the blueprints were a digital camera and a partially disassembled toaster. At least Chainey guessed it was a toaster.

"Curious?" McLaughlin offered more burgundy to Chainey.

She put a hand over her glass. "I better stay sharp. No, I'm not curious. I've done my job." The cat came scurrying into the room. "What the money is for is not my concern."

McLaughlin shook his head and opened his mouth. "Yes, I supp—"

Suddenly he was up on his toes, bending forward. The handsome man's eyes bugged from their sockets. Chainey dove and reached for her gun. Shit. Stay calm, put all your energy and fear into going on automatic, as an old friend and mentor had taught her.

The three point knife off-center in McLaughlin's back quivered like a thing alive. Chainey landed next to a large trunk that seemed right out of a pirate movie. McLaughlin's body convulsed, reversing its arc, and he pitched forward, crashing to the floor.

Bullets dug into the thick carpeting as she sighted on a brief flash of gray. She tore off two shots from her pistol. Glass crashed and the Persian yelped. *Come on, Chainey, don't shoot just to be shooting, make it count.*

McLaughlin was still alive, still holding on to his glass of wine. He blinked rapidly, trying to talk. Chainey rolled, winding up on her back as more bullets hissed and sparked, ripping through the trunk she'd been using for cover.

"McLaughlin, McLaughlin," Buchanan wailed. He now had a gun and was shooting from behind the desk with its collection of electronic gear and computers. His pistol clipped off rounds in quick succession, some kind of auto job Chainey registered as she ran toward the darkened hallway leading to the kitchen. The kitchen they'd come through into the hallway, then the den. Had this been the same route of the invaders?

One of the shooters had stepped into the den. The attacker was dressed in gray overalls and was wearing a tight-fitting mask. The robber raked the area where Buchanan was crouching down. The sound suppressor on the end of the gun's barrel smoked. Methodically, he used the automatic assault weapon. The hallway where Chainey hid was at an angle to the invader. He must have calculated that she had continued running, to be caught by his pal or pals outside, she concluded.

As he turned, she pumped two into him and he fell to the floor. Her breath caught up short in her throat. She'd shot at people before, but this was the first time she'd actually hit someone. No time to dwell on that, she scolded herself. Her first priority was keeping her firm butt alive.

A nasty stillness descended and made her even more jumpy. She knew at least one more shooter had to be around. *Calm, be calm, girl. Listen. There, a footfall, another and another, creeping, but from where, what direction? Shit. Got to move, can't remain stationary. Which way, Chainey? Come on, make a choice.*

She rushed into the den just as bullets sounding like buzzing wasps tore into the wall and floor of the hallway—from the direction of the kitchen. Chainey was already at the stairs and moving up when someone from the kitchen appeared. This invader too was dressed like the other one. Chunks of wood from the steps, plaster, bits of metal and sections of the railing sailed through the air as the attacker opened up with an assault rifle. Chainey leaped and flopped hard on the landing. She belly-crawled furiously and took the first left available.

She was in a bedroom. There was an armoire, a bed buried in quilts and an exercise bicycle in one corner. It was a bucolic tableau, awaiting owners who'd never return. Chainey kneeled by the doorjamb, holding the door open only a sliver. She had a perfect view of the upper portion of the stairwell and the landing. Nothing. Nothing for several moments. That boy could be playing possum, using a phrase her Grandfather Hiram might.

A voice, calling to her? No, talking, low, to someone else. Okay, at least two and maybe three. Swell. Would they charge or wait her out? Then there was a new sound. Sirens, from not too far off. Their guns had been near-silent, hers and Buchanan's had not. The footfalls this time were quite evident as they ran from the house.

Chainey had to chance big time they weren't pretending to have split. She tore from the bedroom, gun first. She braced for gunfire and none came. The sirens continued their wail. She got downstairs and went directly to the hooded attacker. The ex-chorus girl stood looking at her handiwork, a dead body. She was surprised she wasn't queasy, but she was stunned at how quickly it had transpired. One minute this joker was breathing like she was and now he was growing cold. Unlike people's reactions she'd seen on TV, she wasn't feeling sick, like she had to throw up, or anything.

She did have a brief episode of nausea as she rolled the man over. His mask was like the one you saw on a costumed wrestler.

She hesitated again, then removed the mask. It was a greasy task feeling the sweat in his hair as her fingers worked to untie the mask from the back.

The face she didn't know, not that she expected different. She looked around and again caught her breath. What was left of Buchanan had his body parts intermixed with the trashed electronic stuff. She averted her eyes and spotted on the floor next to him a broken frame containing a *Wired* magazine cover of the two men, arm-in-arm and beaming. The words SMASH GRAPHICS were all she could make out, given the blood covering the fragmented glass of the frame. She forced herself to move quickly but thoughtfully, not in a panic. Chainey saw the digital camera underneath the coffee table. The sirens were damn near up the driveway.

She clicked off three shots of the face. McLaughlin coughed. She'd forgotten about him. Chainey turned to stare down at the handsome man. He was on his stomach, looking up at her. The knife was immobile in his back. Blood dribbled from one side of his slack mouth. Incongruously, he held on to the wineglass.

"The police are coming." She didn't know what else to say. She had to get out of there. She took the disk out of the camera.

"Buchanan?"

She took a silk-covered pillow from the couch, its cotton stuffing billowing out through gunshot holes. She put the pillow under his chin and ran out the back. She didn't bother to wipe her prints off the camera; she'd left them everywhere in the house and garage. Tears had been rolling down McLaughlin's cheeks. The Lincoln was intact in the garage. She couldn't drive it out. The only road leading in would be packed with cops. The door to the garage was wide open. Her prints were all over the car and the house, but there was nothing to be done about it now.

She went outside and around the corner of the garage. Between the rear of the garage and the hill was the wall and the spires sticking out of it. She dashed back into the garage. She retrieved a hammer from the toolbox and a plastic milk crate she spotted in the corner. She also remembered her meter and tools in the bag. She snatched the gear from the trunk.

Back in the rear, she got up on the crate and climbed up the wall. There was just enough space for her feet not to slip if she held on to the spires. The alarm went off, which meant the cops had stormed the front. That was good. The sound would cover her banging on the spires. The bag was tossed over into the dirt. Then she got five of the spires bent over. She latched on to the spires. Fortunately, there was a slat of metal running perpendicular to the spires and welded to them, for stability. The slat allowed her to get a foothold and she was over.

Chainey came down on moist earth. To her right was an infrared sensor, its metal mushroom head a dull milky gray. She looked harder at it; the thing seemed to have been incapacitated. The invaders had planned well. They knew the layout of the grounds, and how to disable the alarms. Very sophisticated and very deadly. She scrambled up the hill with the bag into undergrowth and thickening flora. It came to her that she might run into the remainder of the chill crew, but that wasn't much of a bet. They were too prepared not to have a getaway scenario worked out.

Working through the brush, Chainey was glad she'd left her purse at the hotel room she'd stopped to rent in San Francisco. She'd splurged and gotten a place overlooking the ocean, not too far from the Presidio. Her idea was to go back there after the delivery, eat a nice meal, relax in the tub and sleep between clean sheets before getting back on the road. Now she knew she had to get back there to get her things and be gone.

A shape moved in the forest and she halted. Her gun was out, pointing like it could sniff trouble. That something moved again, and she could see the leaves shaking. A couple of squirrels appeared, gazing at her wide-eyed. They bounded off and she kept moving. Hurried voices came from the house below. She got to a leveled-off spot and took a breath. Below her on the other side she could make out portions of another swank house as its lights gleamed through the trees. She could also hear cars, and that meant an access road at least. That meant the way the others had come and gone.

By paralleling the road and staying in the brush, Chainey made it down to the thoroughfare she'd taken to the couple's house. Out on the main drag there were bars and restaurants open, people queuing up for the latest big-budget movie, and moms taking their kids to the Blockbuster after Little League practice. She'd brushed off dirt and leaves from her clothes. In her faded jeans jacket, khaki pants and work boots, she might just be any other Buppie out for a stroll.

In front of a happening place called the Club Lash, she got a taxi. The cabbie was a big-shouldered woman with a scorpion tattoo on her forearm. She sported an old-fashioned visored hack's cap. The woman took her south on the 101 and then over the Golden Gate Bridge into San Francisco.

"Thanks," she said, rubbing together the bills that Chainey handed her. "You in town long?"

"Sorry, in and out on business."

"Business always demands hurry up, doesn't it?" She let her eyes stay on Chainey's form. "We need time to appreciate one another, don't you think?"

"How true." Chainey shut the door and walked into the hotel. Her rush was wearing off and she wanted to crash. But she couldn't be sure those hitters hadn't somehow stumbled onto where she was staying, so there was no resting now. In her room, she dialed Mooch Maltazar.

"Wha?" His voice was drowsy. Like she figured, he'd probably been taking a nap after a few belts of his Havana Club rum.

"We've been popped, Mooch."

"The whole kit?" He was fully awake now.

"Yeah, three guns. I got one." Did she sound tough enough? Like taking another human being's life, even in self-defense, didn't bother her.

"You in transit?"

"Gonna use the Greyhound route. And I'll need a back story."

"I'll get on that, and let our clients know."

"I'm out."

Maltazar, who never said good-bye, was true to form and merely hung up.

Chainey took another cab to San Francisco International Airport in Burlingame. There she employed another of her fake licenses and rented a car, a one-way she could drop off in Sacramento. She wasn't sure that there wouldn't be shooters waiting for her either. Maybe messengers from Frankie Degault who'd beat down ol' Mooch to reveal what their code meant. Frankie would naturally assume she'd been in on the job and have her iced for betraying him. Or maybe he'd be gracious and have her raped and tortured first, see if she talked, then cut her tongue out for lying.

Yeah, some days wasn't it just great having a job like hers?

CHAPTER TWO

"You were there five months ago, making a delivery of some high-falutin' processor chips from Taiwan. Seems McLaughlin and Buchanan—"

"Those were their real names?" Chainey had more of her cranberry juice.

Ira "Mooch" Maltazar adjusted his thick, oversized glasses. He was a wiry man in his late sixties with bandy legs and a pot belly, and the inseam of his pants always drooped over his shoes. With his index finger and thumb, he rubbed at the nub on the end of his left hand. The little finger had been severed in a childhood accident. As a kid growing up in dictator Batista's Cuba, he'd had to work long hours chopping cane like his father and uncles in Camaguey.

"Legally, yes. At any rate, the two were in that kind of business. They designed those alien shoot-em-up video games, virtual reality spook stuff for theme parks, those kinds of things, *que no?*" Maltazar dismissed such things with a wave of his hand.

"Invoices from us and the factory in Taiwan, receipts from hotels and gas, it's all there in the trail for the cops to discover. And fortunately, Buchanan was into old cars. He's got a garage of 'em in Oakland." He took off his glasses, looking evenly at the woman across from him. "The Lincoln is now registered to him. That was the easy part."

Chainey drained her cup. "I'm supposed to go kiss his ring this morning, Mooch."

Maltazar tilted back in his chair, his eyes glittering. "If you kissed more than his ring, he'd probably be more inclined to forgive you. Well, at least give you more time to even up."

Chainey dramatically rolled her eyes for his benefit. "Even with the gun to my head, I wouldn't give him the satisfaction."

"I seriously hope it doesn't come to that." Maltazar leaned forward, picking up one of the prints she'd made of the dead shooter's face. "So far, none of my usual contacts have been able to make this mook."

"Which in a perverse way is the only reason I'm alive and you're still in business," Chainey observed. "The unknown quantity has to be answered before he acts."

"Up to a point," Maltazar amended. "Frankie Degault is not what one would call a far-sighted thinker."

"That's why I appreciate you putting in the call to make sure Victoria will be there too."

"Sound business practice. I can't go and lose my best courier when it's not her fault." He fiddled with his glasses as he talked. "I am right about that, yeah?"

"None of us are innocents around here, Mooch. But unequivocally for the fourth time, I did not engineer the rip-off, I did not get paid to look the other way to let it happen. If so, why the hell would I drive a rental to Sacramento and take a plane back here?"

"You know why, *chica*. Because you're smart and the way it went down would be the best way to keep some of the heat off you. As it is, you're gonna be the one he sends out there to get his money. Though he might make you take that rascal Baker with you."

Chainey winced. "I didn't want to think about that."

"You got no choice, Chainey. Victoria is more level-headed, but that money is hers too. She'll want insurance."

"And so do you, right, Mooch?"

He splayed his hands like he was throwing in a lousy pair. She knew better. She knew Mooch Maltazar was always working the angles. You didn't survive the days of Moe Dalitz, Tony Accardo, and the old Outfit by expecting grace from the sharpies. He'd only go so far protecting her back. But if it came to it, he'd toss her to the lions if that was the decision. And he liked her.

Chainey left the office and walked downstairs. Truxon Ltd. took up the entire second story of a strip mall on East Bonanza Road. It was an area of town bordering West Vegas, that part of the capital of sin and glitter not usually included in the guide books. West Vegas was black Vegas, though it was less than five miles from the Strip and the action that never stopped.

This was the part of Vegas that had pawn shops, plumbing supplies, nail parlors, the occasional drive-by, and day care for the working folk who did and did not make their living in the casinos. But there was enough spillage of profit and glitz that the rest of the City of Las Vegas benefitted materially, to lesser and greater degrees. Even the Westside was witnessing a spurt or two of progress.

Recently, a Canadian businessman named Bart Maybie re-opened the Moulin Rouge Casino and Hotel in black Vegas. The Moulin Rouge had first opened its doors in 1955, the brainchild of New York restaurateur Louis Rubin. It was the first casino to allow blacks not just on stage, but onto the casino main floor and into the hotel rooms too. And unlike the time Sammy Davis Jr. jumped into the pool at the Strip casino where he was head-lining and the pool was subsequently closed and drained, every-one could swim at the Moulin Rouge. And they did. The third show was added at the Moulin Rouge so that whites who wanted to come there after working on the Strip could. Though many had been forbidden by Strip owners from doing so, they came in droves anyway. There they mingled with celebrities such as Louis Armstrong, Pearl Bailey, Bob Bailey, Hines, Hines and Dad, Cary Grant, Lena Horne, Jack Benny, and, of course, Frank Sinatra.

Rumors abounded as to what led to the demise of the inte-grated casino. Some said the investors expanded too quick too soon. Some said the mobsters running things made it clear to the Moulin Rouge's owners that shutting down would be good for their health, as the casino proved to be a fierce competitor for Las Vegas Boulevard dollars. The place opened a few other times over the years but couldn't hold on. Now it seemed that, like much else of American businesses, foreign capital could make a go of things.

Chainey crossed the hot asphalt of the strip mall's parking lot and reached her car. She didn't look back, but she knew Mooch was watching her go. Could be he was already calculating how to fill her position. She got in her new limited edition two-seater Thunderbird, a down-sized new millennium model that had borrowed some features from the classic '57–'59 T-Birds. Turning the ignition, she was happy the car didn't blow her ass into the morning air. After all, she had more payments to make on the car.

She considered putting on an appropriate song from the rack of CDs in the car, but canceled the idea as too morose. As she drove to the Strip, the massive edifice of the Riverhead came into view.

The casino/hotel/amusement park was one of the newest and brightest baubles of the constantly evolving Las Vegas. Sprawling over seven acres off Flamingo Road, the Riverhead cost a mere $570 million to construct at the turn of the new century. Smaller than the recent Bellagio, New York, New York or Paris, the Riverhead, like the Venetian, was intended for the more serious vice indulger. The hotel contained a paltry 728 rooms—small by modern standards. But each room was large and airy, and there were Starbuck's coffee machines on each floor next to the ice machines.

The whole of it was designed with an Indiana Jones/Doc Savage motif. The architecture was a mix of Aztec, Sumerian and Gothic. The gigantic entrance was made like a series of interlocking temples that led to a tower that itself rose nine stories. Inside the tower were an arcade and virtual reality rides. A roller coaster that looped-the-loop encircled the perimeter and also went through the mouths of three large heads based on the famous statues sculpted of volcanic rock on Easter Island. Even hard-core gamblers wanted something to distract the rest of the family.

Arriving at the VIP entrance to the Riverhead, she was recognized and comped for valet parking. At the private elevator, located inside the entrance to the kitchen, the guard unlocked the elevator and brought it down. Upstairs, the door opened on Baker.

"Miss Chainey, always a pleasure."

Baker was originally from South Africa and he particularly delighted in thickening his Afrikaans accent when he saw her. He was big, with fleshy trunks for legs and arms, and a full mustache going gray quickly. He favored the late English bad boy actor, Oliver Reed. Degault's bruiser maintained the close cut he'd favored when he was in the Security Forces, and was partial to three-piece suits with an open collar.

"It would seem," she replied dryly.

"Consent to a search, lass?"

"Not while I'm breathing."

He laughed at his joke, and jerked his head toward wide double doors. "You know the way."

"Thanks."

"Ungh," he grunted, allowing what might have been a leer to form beneath his mustache. "I never get over how much you remind me of that lass, Halle, whatsername? Only taller and more, shall we say, voluptuous."

"Let's not say, shall we?"

She pushed through the polished redwood doors. Each was inlaid with large gold representations of the four suits of cards lined up vertically. She expected Baker to be coming in too. But he went back through the unmarked door to his office.

"Chainey," Victoria Degault greeted her when she'd entered. "Care for anything?" She was dressed in a dark gray DKNY skirt and matching jacket, her black hair pulled back in a ponytail. She was standing at one of the windows, which offered a panoramic view, including the roller-coaster cars whipping by.

"I'm fine." She also remained standing.

Frankie Degault came in through a side door. He was carry-

ing a sheaf of papers and reading them. He was in rolled up
shirtsleeves and leather suspenders. His longish black hair was
in need of a trim. Nonetheless, he was the picture of the young
exec on the go. He stooped, looked at his sister, then folded the
papers in half. Degault sat on the edge of his massive desk.
Victoria Degault crossed her arms and remained motionless at
the window.

Frankie tapped the folded papers against a knee. "I don't
have to explain the consequences, do I?"

He sounded so goddamn condescending, she felt like slapping him. "I'm not new to this."

The double doors opened and Baker finally showed up. He
carried a file folder that he opened, standing legs apart. From it,
he extracted a photo of the shooter Chainey had tagged. "No
known associates." He addressed no one in particular but
handed the file to Frankie Degault.

The rhythm of Frankie Degault tapping the sheets against his
knee continued in the silent room. His sister kept her arms
folded. Baker's glacier blues slid up then down Chainey—not in
his usual sexist way. He was looking for a twitch, a shifting of
feet, any sign, any smell of weakness. She wasn't in the mood to
give it to him or anybody else in the room.

Chainey put her hands on her hips. "How much time do I
have?"

"What makes you think you have any?" Baker slurred.

"We're wasting time with this Clint Eastwood bullshit,"
Chainey countered. "You want your seven large back and I want
to keep shopping at the A & P."

"You don't have the high hand here, Chainey," Victoria admonished.

"I don't have shit, Victoria, but a short leash, I know that.
There's no sense in me making excuses 'cause that won't make
a difference." She glanced at Baker, who was stone. "What I do
need to know is what the money was for."

"Why?" Frankie Degault stopped tapping the sheets and was
doing his chin stroking bit.

"It might provide a direction for me to go in."

"Baker's on that angle," Frankie Degault answered.

"So I should just go home and sit around and wait for Black Jack Tar over here to tidy up everything?"

"You could wait for me at my place, Chainey." Baker worked his tongue in the side of his mouth.

"I could wrestle gators, but to what end?"

"Oh, it wouldn't be that bad."

"If we might stay on point," Victoria Degault interjected.

"That would be nice," Chainey countered.

Frankie stood up, making his shoulders bob like a fighter's. "You're kinda flip for someone in your spot."

"How much time, Frankie? How much time do I have until you drop the hammer? Because I intend to find that swag and bring it back. But you got me operating at a handicap." She quickly jerked her head at Baker. "He knows what the money was for and that gives him an advantage. What about me?"

Degault came closer to her. His sister unfolded her arms. "I still don't know your sweet black ass wasn't the brains behind this, Chainey."

"Yes you do, otherwise we wouldn't be having this meet."

"Chainey's right. She's got to know if she's going to have a chance at delivering," Victoria Degault advised.

Her brother puffed out his cheeks and glared hard at Victoria. His expression was a mixture of emotions. "I guess," he eventually admitted.

There was a wetness across the back of Chainey's neck and she hoped it wasn't spreading, hipping Baker to how nervous she was. She willed herself not to turn his way.

Victoria Degault sat down behind the desk. Her brother took the file folder from Baker.

"The money was an investment," Victoria said, spreading her green-nailed hands on the desktop in front of her. "As you probably know by now, Buchanan and McLaughlin were computer gurus."

"Multimillion-dollar company the two gay geeks started in one of their parents' garage in San Leandro." Degault sounded bitter, as if the men hadn't deserved such good fortune.

"Poofters," Baker snorted.

"This transaction wasn't about anything legit, otherwise why the cash?" Chainey added. "What was the scam?"

Frankie Degault looked at his sister, who returned an even look. He said, "A hedge fund angle."

Chainey frowned. "I thought those were played out."

"People wanting to get something for nothing is as old as Cain and Abel, Chainey, you're hip to that." Victoria Degault crossed her well-proportioned legs, moving back and forth in the swivel. "Offshore hedge funds are the new, if supposedly insider knowledge, rage. By their nature such funds are more risky because of the possible maximum profits. Hedging on shorting stocks, utilizing what they call puts, and other methods."

Chainey filled in. "Basically, a hedge operates because the manager of the fund is allowed to use a variety of investment techniques not usually allowed in other types of investments."

"Suckers think they can cut out the middle man all of a sudden 'cause they've read a book or talked to some clown on the golf course, and whammo, they know how to do their own stock investing over the Internet." Frankie Degault was getting excited, his voice rising and falling.

"McLaughlin and Buchanan had it all worked out. They had the fronts and cutouts, it would have looked like extraordinary gains could be had via up-and-coming investment engines. The beauty was, you could only find it online through actually wanting to find it. They had it set to plant rumors and hearsay among the right types to whet everyone's whistle." Greed made her mouth form an ugly smile. She caught herself and soon replaced the real her with the tranquil public face she worked hard to maintain.

"Do you know if there were other investors in this effort?" Chainey asked.

Frankie Degault scratched at his eyebrow. "How do you mean?"

"Your assumption is that you were the only ones allowed in on this money-making machine. Maybe that wasn't so, you know."

"Maybe you better stop using so much brain power on what we got going and what you better get on to, you know, Chainey?" Frankie Degault handed the file back to Baker. "You're on the clock now, Chainey."

"When's quitting time?" She wasn't about to do the back down, not to this bunch.

The brother inclined his head at his sister. "Victoria's got the big heart, let her decide. A woman-to-woman consideration."

Chainey wasn't looking, but she knew Baker had a huge crocodile smile splitting his face.

The woman behind the desk uncrossed her legs. She tapped the thumb and little finger of the same on the desk like she was playing piano keys. "Three days. You should have a line on who these hitters were by then. If not . . ." She didn't complete her sentence, nor did she break eye contact with Chainey.

"I don't check in with Baker, or anybody else," Chainey declared.

"Now wait a goddamn—" Frankie Degault began.

"Uh-huh," Chainey objected. "I follow what I develop, no shackle on my ankles."

"I'm pretty spry yet, Chainey," Baker shot back.

"And how do we trust you won't leave town and not look back?" Victoria crossed her legs again.

"Because you know I won't." Chainey returned her stare with a flat look of her own.

"Aw, let her have her head start," Baker piped in. "I can fetch her if I need to."

"Bow-wow, baby." Chainey left the room, putting all her determination into walking slowly and deliberately down the hall, then downstairs, out of the Riverhead Casino. So there it was; despite all the tough talk, it came down to the plain fact that she had seventy-two hours to produce—seventy-two hours and not much in the way of inspiration on which way to jump.

The valet brought her T-Bird around and she tipped him a silver dollar. Out on the Strip the couples and families were walking and gawking, working percentages in their heads of when to bet, when to double down and when to fold. They were playing for excitement, though some might be obsessed and find that luck was not something you could ever appease the same way twice.

Chainey knew better than to start chasing that capricious spirit. Nonetheless, she tugged on one of the horseshoe earrings she'd worn especially for today.

CHAPTER THREE

"Aw shit, Chainey." Horace Lavere clutched his beer belly and staggered back against the wall. A framed photo of two nude women engaged in interposition of the sexual kind fell down on his head.

"Don't be clever, Horace, that's too big a strain for you."

Three of the Rancho Notorious's staff walked by nonchalantly in their bras and panties. "Hi, Chainey," one of the women said. She glanced quickly at Lavere, not making an effort to hide a gap-toothed smile.

"Doris," Chainey replied.

The three went on into the main room to loll around and wait for new customers.

Lavere straightened up. He picked up his Panama from the floor. "I was just horsing around, woman." He jammed the hat on his head.

"I'm never in the mood for your kind of funnin', Horace. And I especially don't have the time for bullshit now." Chainey held up the print of the dead shooter again. "How about a straight answer?"

He squinted at the print. "Why you think I know him?"

"I didn't mean for you to sound as stupid as you look," Chainey answered. "It's as old as the stank on your mama's upper lip that hitters from out of town always visit the local brothels. And from Kalamazoo to Bangkok, the hard boys know the girls at the Rancho Notorious will treat them right or rough, depending on what they want." She didn't mention that the two other cat houses she'd already visited had been a bust.

Lavere squinted at the print. He glared at it, then shook his head from side to side. "Nope, Chainey, I ain't seen this fella and I know you already showed it to the girls." He smiled, and it wasn't pleasant. "What else?"

"*Nada,*" she said sourly. She walked toward the front, all too aware that Lavere was watching her go, almost smacking his lips. Great, not only was she on the hook for seven million, she'd also be the subject of a pervert's wet dreams. She'd known trying the brothel circuit—here in Pahrump, and earlier in Henderson—was a long shot. She was operating on the assumption that the shooters had come through Vegas, possibly dogging her trail all the way to Mill Valley. But the shooters just as easily could have tumbled to the drop on the Northern California end and planned their theft accordingly. But it would burn up too much time for Chainey to go traipsing around for a lead in California, a state where she'd be on unfamiliar ground.

In the spacious front room, which was itself two sections bifurcated by an archway, several of the women hung around. Some were laughing and talking, others watched TV, sitting on the tiger-skin couch in front of the set. Two of the women played pool with a john in the second section.

Doris, the one who had greeted Chainey, was lying on her stomach on the floor in front of the couch. She had on red thong panties and a white satin bra. She was leafing through an issue of *Psychology Today.* Chainey crossed to the door.

"No luck, huh?" she said as Chainey went past.

" 'Fraid not," she said, turning back to look at her. "Thanks for your time, Doris." The pair of nice boots on the TV's screen got her attention. More precisely, it was the legs the boots were attached to that made her interested. The boots were at the end of the body of a man who was being excavated from the desert floor. There was a woman Highway Patrol officer being interviewed in the foreground by a news crew. Chainey went to stand near Doris as the scene shifted to a Latina news anchor in the studio.

". . . Channel Three Headline News has learned that the two men found shot dead and buried head first in the Amargosa Desert have been identified. They are fifty-six-year-old Harry Smith and forty-five-year-old Wellington Delacruz. Both men are believed to be Cahuilla American Indians of the Agua Caliente tribe near Palm Springs. And both were chief personnel of the large casino and hotel the tribe has on their reservation, the Golden Horn.

"As of yet the authorities won't speculate as to the motivation behind these—" One of the girls had gotten up and changed the channel. Rikki Lake was interviewing men who'd left their wives to pursue careers as professional circus clowns.

Doris twisted her neck around to look at Chainey. "What?"

"Saw somebody I knew."

"On 'Rikki'?" she asked, excitedly.

"No." Chainey made for the door again.

"Too bad," Doris said, "I was hoping you could hook me up."

"Fame will be yours yet."

"I'm just a squirrel in your world, trying to get a nut."

An older man in dress slacks and a T-shirt stepped through the entranceway and yelled. "Goddamn, Doris," he hooted, "I've driven a hundred miles to see you again."

Doris stifled a yawn and effusively greeted her client.

Chainey drove off. Punching the speed dial on her cell phone, she rang Rena Solomon at the Las Vegas *Express.*

"Girl, I know you only calling me 'cause of what's been on the news since this morning," Solomon said after they'd exchanged greetings.

Chainey laughed. "Is our relationship so shallow?"

"You forget I sorta know what you do for a living."

"Got time for a late lunch, on me?"

"Sure. Let's meet at the Rye Breaker."

"Forty minutes," Chainey promised and rung off.

The Rye Breaker was a restaurant and nightclub located in

West Vegas not far from the Truxon offices. It had been owned
by a man named Wilson McAndrews, a one-time fixture on the
black scene in town. When you needed a favor, when you needed
something taken care of that the law wouldn't or couldn't do,
you went to see McAndrews.

McAndrews, who had done enforcement work for the mob as
a young man in the seventies, had been killed after pulling off a
heist of one of the big connected casinos not too long ago.
Hipster tourists, and a writer now and then, still came to the city
and made their pilgrimage to the club to rub elbows with the
regulars. The deeds of the man and his time had ballooned into
myth and legend. Like Sinatra on the whiter side of Vegas, a lot
of people claimed to have been pals with Drew, as he was called,
been in a deal with the man, or hung out with him in some after-
hours joint.

Chainey had had a thing with him for a while. McAndrews
had gotten her out of a bad spot in her days as a showgirl.
Afterward, she hadn't gone to his bed out of some misplaced
gratitude. He'd never made a pass, never demanded "payment"
of any kind. Hers had been a genuine affection. Chainey kept
her memories of their time together to herself. They were not
something she'd trade for drinks or mention in a magazine article. She shifted the car easily into fourth as Zack de la Rocha of
Rage Against the Machine blasted his nitro-fueled lyrics from
her speakers.

Inside the cool and dark confines of the Rye Breaker, she saw
Rena sitting in a corner booth. She slid in opposite.

"Harry Smith and his partner Delacruz had been coming
back and forth to town for the last year and a half," her friend
began. She sipped on her tall, slim glass of club soda with lime.
If she drank at all, it was wine, and then not too often.

"That's why I knew his face," Chainey said. "He got into a
shoving match with Degault in the week before last New Year's."

"Hey, what you two having today?" Cleo, the bartender, said to
them from behind the bar.

They gave her their order.

"Anson's got me working on the story," Solomon added, flick-

ing strands of her light brown dreads out of her face. "Seems the
two gents were looking to expand their empire beyond the res.
The profits from the Golden Horn have been very, very good.
And it doesn't hurt that the regulations on Indian casinos are
looser than on those in the white man's world. And what with
those movie star types trying to be new Rat Packers with weekend retreats in Palm Springs, the gay scene, and all them church
groups taking a bus out there to gamble, you couldn't stop the
money rolling in with a tank."

"Asking Jesus to bless the dice," Chainey said flatly.

"So, why exactly are you interested?"

"Please," Chainey said, "I ask and if something comes of it on
the other end, maybe you get a story out of it."

"One of these days you'll come completely clean," her friend
said.

"Not even on my deathbed."

"Hmm, we'll see. Anyway, it wasn't just Degault they'd had a
run-in with. Most of the owners on the Strip were not happy
about our red brothers trying to get a piece of the bigger action.
Look at all the money the Vegas bunch poured into California
to try and defeat the passage of Proposition 5 and 1A, limiting
the kind of gaming Indians could do on the res."

"And pumping more money into repealing Prop 5 when the
voters passed it," Chainey added.

"Though it was overturned by the California State Supreme
Court. But the Indians had made their point; they could flex
with the big dogs and win." Solomon paused. "I'm trying to run
down a story I've heard took place at the Golden Horn. Seems
the security people there busted a crew who were using card
counting and electronic devices in an effort to break the bank.
The rumor is that this crew they ran out were working for the
owners here to create havoc for the Indians."

"So Smith and Delacruz are a message, like in the old days."

"You said that, not me," Solomon replied, finishing her club
soda. "One was shot through the eye and the other, Smith, was
gutted. Oh, stabbing someone is so nasty." She shivered to show
her discomfort.

"It takes a particular kind of mind," Chainey allowed.

Their order arrived and they ate and talked. "All right, what if it's not that?" Chainey speculated aloud. "What if they were bumped off by rivals from another reservation?'

"That's not impossible, just like there used to be that kind of naked competition around here. But why kill them here rather than back home?"

"To throw suspicion onto the Vegas owners." Chainey chewed her grilled chicken sandwich slowly.

Rena Solomon wagged a finger and said over a mouthful of fettuccine, "The other angle I'm looking into is that the Agua Calientes made a deal to become silent partners in an existing casino here. What better way to work your way into the scene than on the down low like? That's certainly been done before."

"And it went south?"

"Or was found out about, and somebody definitely made their displeasure known."

Chainey absorbed this and continued eating. "You ever hear of a video games company called Smash Graphics?"

Solomon indicated ignorance. "Should I have?"

Chainey didn't like drawing her friend into what could easily become a dangerous situation, but she was pressed. She needed information fast, and Solomon was the most expedient source. She was starting to rationalize way too much, she admonished herself.

"I need to know if this is part of what I'm . . ." She paused, suddenly lost for the words. "Part of what I've fallen into, Rena. Like a whirlpool, my raft is going around in circles on the edges of it. And I know if I don't do something, I'll be pulled down into its center, where the deep takes you forever."

"Pretty poetic for an outlaw," Solomon remarked. "Or is it that outlaws are always romantics in their soul?"

Chainey reached out but didn't touch her friend's hand. "I don't mean to—"

"I owe you plenty, you know that," Solomon blurted, cutting Chainey off. "I know you can't really say what your work is, exactly. We've both been in Vegas way too long for either of us to pretend we don't know what the score is. Between what is said and unsaid is the truth, an old hustler told me once." She put her fork down. "What is it you need to know?"

"Whatever you can produce on Smash Graphics."

"Is there a deadline on when you need this?"

Chainey almost laughed at her friend's inadvertent gallows humor. "Let's put it this way. How about I call you in"—she checked her watch—"five hours. Whatever you got is what you got."

"All right." She picked up her fork and went to work on her pasta once more.

After lunch and see you laters, Chainey ran down other possible leads to the dead gunner. She didn't quite buy the Degaults' explanation of their deal with the game designers, but so what? Obviously the gamesters had been up to something crooked, but an online hedge fund grift seemed not to be something that either Victoria or Frankie would find interesting. They were both hands-on managers of the vices they controlled, and these cyber-shenanigans didn't fit. But new times demanded new crimes, so who was she to say what goes?

She burned up more than a quarter tank of gas. And as the orange sun hung low on the horizon, she had nothing to show for all her running around. She decided to head to her condo on the western fringe of Vegas, located in a planned area called The Lakes.

The section where she lived had new town houses for the ever-growing assemblage of lower white-collar types who worked at the twenty-four-hour Citibank Credit Card Center, and construction workers whose wallets and purses were bulging. She found the eight variations on the same basic design of the architecture refreshing in its bucolic complacency. That and the round-the-clock armed patrol. The kind of folks she encountered in her line tended to stick out more in this Spielbergian enclave.

Walking up the driveway to her door, Chainey waved at her neighbor. "Hi, Ronnie."

"Martha, how are you?"

"Fine, just fine."

He was a brother in his early forties, a trademark attorney recently separated from his wife. He was in his khaki shorts and slippers, watering his square of lawn. His upper body was not muscle-mag hard, but it was worth a second look encased in its loose athletic T-shirt.

"The neighborhood association is talking about having a barbecue with another block club. Can you make the next meeting, on the fifth?"

Okay, he was a square, but you couldn't have everything. "Ah, maybe, I'll see. I'll let you know."

"Good." And his eyes lingered while she walked up to her steps and unlocked her front door.

Chainey picked up her mail and punched in the code to deactivate her alarm. By habit, she then swept the small foyer and what she could see of the compact living room. Of course there were no masked intruders or ninjas suddenly diving at her. She poured some Hennessy at her bar and was about to sit down on the couch when she remembered the kit in her trunk. In all the flurry when she got back to town, she'd forgotten to take out the bag she'd transferred to the T-Bird.

She chucked the mail onto the couch and went outside to get the bag. Ronnie was still there, and her mini-errand gave her an excuse to talk with him further. She then went back inside, placing the bag on an end table next to the couch. She took out the meter and clicked it on to make sure the batteries were working. The needle jumped slightly and then settled back to zero. Her eyebrow went up, but she figured it was just excess energy in the device. She turned it back on and nothing happened.

She was about to sit down on the couch when she noticed the impression in the rug. The indentation was next to one of the squat, squarish legs of the couch. The couch had been moved slightly. Chainey didn't have a maid, and she hadn't been home in days. Her eyes narrowed. It could be her paranoia was unfounded. Conversely, she'd been shot at and a death sentence was ticking away on her. The fine hairs on her arms were standing up.

Chainey searched the entire living room, not sure of what she'd find. And then it came to her. Approaching it like it was a sleeping rhino, Chainey walked around the couch, looking hard at the piece of furniture. She got close, examining the cushions for a needle or other object intended to puncture her skin. She got down on all fours, peering underneath the furniture. A blinking green light winked back at her. Her heart thumped loudly in her throat. There was something strapped underneath the couch—a nice, compact mechanism like she'd seen on video in that movie *Blown Away*.

Well, it hadn't gone off when she'd come in, so it must not be activated by motion. She stared at it, then got up. If it was radio controlled, why hadn't the bomber set it off when she'd turned on the lights? Maybe the bomb was designed to go off when she sat on the couch. That could be nasty. The phone rang, startling her. If she picked up the receiver, would that be a signal to the bomber? It kept ringing. "Damn, all right, all right," she blared, picking up the handset.

"Chainey, got some facts," Rena Solomon said euphorically on the other end.

"That's great," she said, trying to sound just as excited.

"Want me to come over?"

Chainey glanced at the couch. "No, no that's all right, Rena. Let's meet at the Atomic Buzz in half an hour."

"On it." Her friend hung up.

She immediately started dialing Mooch but hesitated at tapping the seventh digit. She cradled the handset, chewing her bottom lip. Was he in on it? Or had this been Mooch's way of dealing with an employee who screwed up and exposed him to risk? She picked up the handset again and laughed joylessly. Chainey slammed it home with a deft flick of her wrist.

If she called the law, that would be a hoot. Any attention from them and there would be questions she damn sure wasn't prepared or going to answer. She knew a man who could handle disposing of the bomb on the q-t, only he did work for the buttoned-down wise guys. Hell, he was rumored to be the guy they'd call in to rig the jobs, as much as he was called in to check for explosives.

Chainey weighed her options. She couldn't very well leave and hope the goddamn thing didn't go off. There wasn't much choice. She looked up the mechanic's number and called the man. His line connected, followed by a silence, then a beep. Chainey started to speak but stopped herself; what kind of message was she going to leave? *Can you make a house call and disarm this bomb for me before I have to pick up the kids from swimming practice?* She replaced the receiver and calculated her next steps.

Go see Rena and act like everything was cool. Yeah, handle the bomb situation when she got back home—if there was a home waiting when she got back. She went outside, carefully shutting the door. Chainey imagined the bomber watching her, his thumb depressing the activation button right now. Involuntarily, she held her breath, waiting for the big boom. After several tense moments, she took her hand from the knob and walked to her car. Each step she could feel the concussive wind from the blast lifting her off her feet, the projectiles of metal and wood impaling her back.

She made it to the T-Bird and gunned it to life. Momentarily, she smiled with nervous relief. What if the bomber wanted her to find the device under her couch and had really rigged up her car? Chainey clutched into gear and drove to meet her friend.

"Peep this," Rena Solomon said over her double orange espresso. "According to an article my search engine brought up, Buchanan and McLaughlin had come up with a wing-ding virtual craps game."

Chainey was sipping her café teraza latte, trying to seem at ease. She couldn't shake the feeling she'd be paying a mortgage for a hole in the ground for the next thirty years. "So what? I guess it's new that it's a craps game and not video poker or blackjack, but what's so hot about that?"

She tipped her cup. "Because it was a game designed by Smash Graphics."

Chainey gave her friend a blank look.

"The ancillary angle, honey chile."

"I guess I'm just dense."

"Well, I'm not the one to talk," Solomon guffawed. She produced several color printouts from her soft attaché case. She placed them on the small table they were sitting at.

The reproductions before Chainey included an actor and actress she recognized. The duo in the shot seemed to be slick-dressed cops of some kind, replete with guns, shades and tasteful outfits. Behind them the spike of the Stratosphere Tower could be seen poking the sky. The next print was of some kind of computer-generated character. The illustration depicted a buffed woman in a skintight costume of uncertain ethnicity battling a two-headed beast on a plateau.

Chainey said, "How is all this tied into the game?"

Solomon's finger tapped the actor's chest. "This was a publicity shot from a pilot done here last spring, the 'Wilder Memorandum'."

"Vegas cops?"

"Private eyes or trouble shooters, something like that. In the vein of memorable shows like 'The Strip' and, of course, 'Vegas,' with the redoubtable Robert Urich. Anyway, the deal is, part of the show had the woman character imagining herself as this other character." Solomon shuffled the sheets and placed the 3-D print on top. "This fantastic chick is called Doc Nirvana, and she's a copper-hued titan of strength and courage."

"A fourteen-year-old boy's wet dream."

"And a forty-four-year-old's," Solomon amended.

"Now I'm getting hip," Chainey commented.

Solomon bobbed her head. "Exactly. Smash Graphics was hot; they were the shit, as the kid's say, or used to say. They attracted all this attention with their Foundation City I and II games starring Doc Nirvana, right? It spun off into a comic book, dolls, animated series, a board game, got optioned as a possible movie, she blew up."

"So what does this have to do with the video craps game?" Chainey asked.

"Brand identification, the marketers call it." Solomon had more of her coffee. "The craps game and other Smash Graphics works would feature prominently in the 'Wilder Memorandum' episodes. And when the woman character daydreamed about being Doc, those scenes were done in computer animation. In the course of those scenes, the woman as Doc would encounter some obstacle or do something that helped her figure out whatever case she was working on in the 'real' world."

"So you got hormone-crazed teenaged boys and sagging middle-aged men watching the show. And I guess some of our lesbian sisters too, a 'Xena' kinda happening."

"Yeah." Her friend shook a hand at her to be patient. "But remember, the idea was to somehow include their wares in each show. The pilot episode concerned someone stealing the plans for the video craps machine."

"No," Chainey said.

"For real, girl. The smart money said that not only would the show be a hit, the buzz would get the squares clamoring for the Smash Graphics gaming devices to be in your particular casino. Plus, there were ways you could win prizes if you played one of their machines a certain amount of times and all that."

Chainey scratched a nail on the side of her face. "What's the kicker?"

Solomon smiled sweetly. She looked through the printouts, then showed her one from a magazine article.

Chainey peered closely at it. There was McLaughlin shaking hands with Harry Smith. The caption, dated from last year, indicated that they were at a new technologies expo held in Vegas. The brief article accompanying the photo stated that Smith, representing the Golden Horn Casino, was entering into a partnership with Smash Graphics.

"That's from a trade rag I thought to call on and go through their microfiche," Solomon said proudly.

"Well, well," Chainey commented, trying to keep the eagerness off her face.

"Well, well, my ass," Solomon countered. "You got to be givin' it up, sweetheart. I smell multipart story in this. Might even get me that book contract I've been itching to land."

You can't write from the grave, Chainey reflected. She said, "Like we agreed, Rena, if and when I can tell you something or at least point you in a specific direction, I'll let you know."

Solomon worked her lips into a pout. "Just a hint, huh?"

"I assume other reporters will be following up on the murders?"

"I got a call from the L.A. Bureau of *Newsweek*," Solomon answered. "The style of death smacked of the old days, and nothing beats nostalgia mixed with murder. As you know, Nevada media ain't exactly known for investigating its own backyard. But when the national spotlight swings on us, then the competition for headlines tends to make common sense stand aside."

"But not too far aside," Chainey observed.

"I know what the score is." Some of that ex-junkie toughness came into her face and set her eyes with an arctic calm. Solomon had gotten hooked on smack as a showgirl and Chainey had helped her get straight. "Now you and me go back a ways, Martha. I owe you like I don't anybody else. And one of the things I got from all that was self-respect. Now how can I look myself in the mirror and not follow this up?"

Chainey nodded her head. "You're right, you should follow it up. But be aware that the predators are laying in the cut."

"Are you one of them?"

"I don't know how to give you an answer to that, Rena, I really don't."

"You'd let me know if there was a bullet with my name on it, right?" she pressed.

Chainey was surprised the answer got stuck in her throat. "Naturally, we've been—"

"Or does your career as 'freight manager' leave no room for looking out for anybody else except number one? Trust no one, as the TV show goes."

"No, that's not it, Rena."

"You don't sound too convincing, darling." Frostiness hardened her voice. Solomon got up quickly, leaving the printouts on the table. "They're on me," she said, waving a hand at them and walking out of the coffee shop.

Chainey didn't try to stop her because she wasn't sure what

she was going to say. She sat there, her coffee growing cold, her mind kicked into high gear. A trip to Palm Springs seemed the logical course to pursue. It could be the hitters were working for the Agua Calientes. Looked like California was back on the schedule, she reasoned.

She took the print of the shooter out of her purse, staring hard at it. The man didn't look Native American, but that didn't necessarily mean anything. She'd met American Indians and those of mixed parentage who didn't look like what you'd come to expect if your only reference was Glenn Ford cowboy movies.

She gathered up the printouts and left. Chainey realized on the way home that she still had the little matter of the bomb to take care of. Okay, no way to turn but to call Mooch. Very carefully, she let herself back into her house and shut the door slowly. She dialed and got her boss on the phone.

"Where you going?" he asked incredulously after she'd told him her predicament. "I'm supposed to just stroll over there and disconnect this bomb with my pliers and a flashlight?"

"I'm on deadline, Mooch, or have you forgotten? You know who to call."

"You got an alarm."

"That wouldn't slow him up. 'Course, he might have been the one that set it, but the wiseguys aren't usually this creative with their explosive devices."

Mooch breathed in and out, then said, "Wait there. I'll call back in fifteen."

While she waited for Mooch to get back on the horn, she packed clothes into an overnight bag. From a hidden safe in her closet, she retrieved a Glock and extra clips. She put those in the bag too and the phone rang.

"Mooch?"

"It's me. He can't get to it until tomorrow."

"This isn't a leaky faucet, Mooch. This goddamn thing might go off any time it feels like it for all I know. And I can't wait around, period."

"That's the best I can do, *chica.*"

There was a finality in his voice she didn't like, but there wasn't much else she could do either. "I'll come by the office and leave extra keys and the combination to the alarm."

"That'll work," he said.

He sounded awfully calm, she concluded, hanging up. But then, Mooch's leg could be on fire and he'd ask which one. Anyway, she had almost a five-hour drive ahead of her to Palm Springs, and there was no time for hesitation. She gathered up her stuff and drove over to the Truxon offices.

"I'll handle this, you know that, right?" Mooch jiggled the keys in his liver-spotted hands. An Arturo Fuente cigar smoldered in the heavy glass ashtray on his desk.

"I know that." Were they conning each other, or was it on the square? She couldn't tell anymore. "If you learn anything about who might have planted the bomb, let me know immediately, right?"

"Naturally," he said, a note of pique threading his voice. "Where will you be?"

"I'll buzz you, Mooch."

Maltazar was about to add something when he looked up as Lez, the ex-porn actress who was now his receptionist, stuck her head in his office.

"It's Tony T. on the phone. You said to interrupt you."

"Thanks, dollface."

Chainey was already heading out. "I'm on the trail, Mooch."

"*Buena suerte,* Martha." He picked up the handset and punched his line on.

Chainey lingered for a moment at his door, then left on her road trip. If she didn't find answers at the reservation in Palm Springs, then so be it. There'd be no other hands she could play, her fortune run out. Getting gas at a station on I-15, she played its old-fashioned slot machine. Two cherries and a lemon rolled into place. Good, that meant her luck hadn't peaked—not yet at least.

CHAPTER FOUR

A fragrant wind was blowing in from the desert by the time Chainey pulled into Palm Springs. Not knowing what she might encounter on the res, she figured it was best to get a room in town, then go over there. Things might be jumpy because of the murders of Smith and Delacruz. She checked into a hotel calling itself the Athenian. As might be expected, the facade was done up in the style of ancient Rome.

The decor of the lobby was reminiscent of sets left over from the *Mummy* movie. Consistency of cultural styles or eras wasn't too big a concern, it seemed. Brochures advertising the Agua Caliente's casino were spread over a coffee table and a counter. There was also a flyer announcing a charity golf game to benefit the Eisenhower Medical Center in town.

The room was clean and airy. Chainey showered and powdered up. She put on the silky underwear she'd bought at Macy's and teased out her frizzy hair. She slipped into a red cocktail dress and put some lipstick and a touch of eyeliner on. In the bathroom mirror she assayed the look, patting a hand on her butt.

"Still packed, girl. Still fluctuating between a size ten and eleven." She laughed and put a couple of the printouts of the dead man in her purse and mused whether to take the Glock or not. Too bad she hadn't brought that garter rig for hiding a gun along her inner thigh. Ah well, can't always utilize sex and violence simultaneously, she lamented. She put the gun between the mattress and the box spring and went out.

Fifteen minutes later she walked into the Golden Horn. The layout was the same as most casinos. But on one wall there was a row of framed pictures of the tribal elders and members of the Agua Caliente Cahuilla council. Black bunting had been taped around the photos of Smith and Delacruz. She toured the facility, sizing up the customers and the security. To the left of the bingo area was a bar called the Broken Treaty. She smiled at somebody's sense of humor and took a stool. It wasn't too long before a man offered to buy her a drink.

"Are you alone?" He was white, about fifty, and not too bad-looking. His suit was going to shapeless, and the bags under his eyes were dark.

"I am."

He sat beside her, signaling to the bartender. "What would you like?"

Why not splurge? "A Manhattan would be nice."

The bartender, a young Indian woman with blond highlights in her hair, took the order.

"My name is Tom."

The level of alcohol in him wasn't evident on his breath, but she could see its effects in the glassiness of his eyes. "I'm Martha." They shook hands. The drink arrived and she thanked him, tipping it toward him.

"You're a new face around here," he said, trying to keep the conversation flowing.

A regular—what she was hoping for. "I could become more than a stranger."

Those cryptic words encouraged him. "That might be interesting." He leaned toward her as he spoke.

Chainey turned on her showgirl smile. "You live in town?"

"We—that is, my family—keep a place here." His cheeks got darker from his momentary gaff, then he recovered. "I'm from Redlands. You ever been out that way?"

"Once or twice. Quiet streets."

"Great golf courses," he remarked. "I close a lot of my accounts that way."

She knew it; some kind of middle-management salesman. If encouraged, he'd talk all night about himself. But he was probably the type always sizing up people, gauging what they wanted to hear and when they needed to hear it. Sipping her drink, she noticed his eyes were still roving, still on the prowl. Maybe for the next woman to talk to if she flaked out on him, maybe for some chump to sell whatever it was he hawked.

"I got a question for you, Tom."

"Yeah." He grinned.

"Ever see this man before?" She showed him the print.

Tom took out reading glasses and put them on. "This guy asleep or knocked out or something?"

"A candid shot," she said. "Does he look familiar? Anybody you've seen around here?"

Tom gazed at Chainey, a look of uncertainty molding his features. He took on an edge. "What is this exactly? What are you?" He tapped the printout with his index finger, making it shake as she held on to the sheet.

"It's a long story, but he's got something to do with my sister. She's in a bit of trouble, if you know what I mean."

An odd expression twisted Tom's mouth, like he was chewing on lemon rinds. "No I don't. You come struttin' in here to jack me around about your sister, or we going to get to know each other?"

The smile he attached to the words made them even more offensive. Apparently the booze, and no doubt a losing streak at the tables, had stretched ol' Tom's patience for anything other than money or nookie.

"Look," Chainey said, tucking the printout back in her purse, "I'm sorry to waste your time."

Then he did it; he put the grip on her arm. "Hey, I did buy you a drink. You did cross those legs in front of me and you did seem to enjoy my company."

Sweetly she said, "How about I buy you a drink and we call it square?"

The grip tightened. "What's up with that, huh?"

She probably could have talked him into leaving her alone, but her long drive and the urgency of her business had stretched her patience thin. She snatched his hand with her other hand, and bent his back on the wrist. Her palm pressing against his fingers, she got up fast, using her height and weight to put real force behind the move.

"Fuckin' bitch," Tom wailed, latching his free hand around her arm.

Chainey got the side of her shoe behind his heel and simultaneously drove her elbow into the crook of his arm. This relaxed his hold on her and she shoved, upsetting Tom against the stool. The stool fell over and Tom, his backside to the bar, was at an angle, trying to hold himself vertical. People were gaping.

"As soon as I—"

"As soon as you straighten up, you can leave the bar to go sleep it off, Tom," the man who'd stepped between them said.

He helped the salesman to his feet. "Of course you can have a room on us."

Tom hooked a finger at Chainey. "She's got some kind of scam working, Vern. She tried to snow me."

Vern, who was Native American, had a smile of blunt, strong-looking teeth. "Is that so, ma'am?"

"Trying to find someone, that's all. He just got overheated."

"I see," Vern said. He was about six four, had a hefty torso over sturdy legs. He was dressed in a gray sharkskin suit with an open-collared striped shirt. His hair was military short, with gray flecks throughout.

Chainey showed the security man the digital print. "Family business."

Vern barely looked at the offered photo. Another man had joined him and was standing behind Tom. His attention was on the loudmouth. "Okay, Tom, let's get you some accommodations, how's that?"

Tom's mouth went slack and he seemed to be formulating an argument. Then the man behind him gently put his hand on Tom's shoulder, and his mouth clamped shut.

"Rest, all right?" Vern said. "Leopold here will help you get settled in."

"Sure, Vern, sure," an embarrassed Tom said. He trudged off, the other security man trailing.

"Sorry for interrupting your night." Vern extended a corded hand. "I'm Vern Sixkiller, head of security."

She returned the offered handshake. "Chainey, Martha Chainey."

"I didn't mean to rain on your parade. I could see you were handling matters just fine," Sixkiller said. "But I got to look like I'm earning my pay, right?"

"You stopped it from getting messy."

Sixkiller lightly touched her shoulder. "The drinks are on the house tonight." He looked past her at the bartender and did a little business with his hand. She nodded assent.

"Better than that, maybe you can help me with ID'ing this guy." She showed him the photo.

Sixkiller angled the print to get a better look at it. His eyes seemed to catalogue each segment of the man's face. "This guy is taking a dirt nap, lady." He glanced at her. "You some sort of private eye?"

"Of a kind," she vamped. "This guy is connected to a big robbery and there's an interested party wants to nail him."

Sixkiller balanced the print on the upturned tips of his thick fingers. There was a heavy, pitted gold ring on his middle finger. "You stand to make a healthy recovery fee?"

Recover my life, she almost said. "There might be enough gravy for two plates."

From somewhere in the casino a whooping alarm went off, signaling a winner at the slots. Sixkiller didn't gawk, as everyone else at the bar was doing. "Money shouldn't be one's only motivation." A pause, then, "I don't know this corpse, but if you're gonna be here for a day or two, I can ask around."

"This isn't a convoluted way of getting my phone number, is it?"

"Hadn't even crossed my mind."

"I'm at the Athenian, room four-one-seven. But don't do too much asking; I'll probably be checked out by tomorrow night."

Leopold had returned and was hanging back, waiting for Sixkiller. The security chief folded the printout and put it inside his jacket. "Yes, ma'am." The two men walked away.

Chainey should keep pushing; the sands in the hourglass were inexorably slipping away. Each grain was precious, and so far she hadn't done much to contain them except flirt with one chump and one stud. She damn near laughed out loud at the irrationality of it all. Tired but wired, and needing a sound plan, she sat and had another Manhattan on the house.

Afterward she took a tour around the casino. Out of habit she calculated where the hidden cameras might be and who was and wasn't working undercover on the floor. She wondered where Vern Sixkiller's office might be; was he watching her right now via closed circuit? And was there a picture of the wife and kids on his desk?

Damn, Chainey, you must be getting loopy, thinking about a man at a time like this. Still, she mused, he got her temperature up a might as his big, fine form ambled away. She bumped into a heavyset woman carrying two paper buckets of quarters.

"Don't you think I don't know what you're up to," she bellowed. The woman made a big production of stacking one bucket on top of the other, encircling her arms and hands around her bounty. "I saw about your sort from watching 'Dateline,' yes I did."

"I'm not trying to steal your money, ma'am, really I'm not." She backed off, her hand out in a placating gesture.

"Oh, I know, I know. I'm on to you sharpies, what with that shirt length of a dress and that bad weave of yours."

Chainey was going to make a strong point about the hair being all hers. But she figured making Vern show up twice in one evening wouldn't impress him the right way. "You have a nice night." She walked along, determined to keep her mind on her task.

The tall woman tried the picture on a few others and got a lot of negative headshakes and disinterested glazes in their eyes. Finally, at the blackjack table, where they were playing double down in the early morning hours, Chainey got a nibble. The break came in the form of an older gent in a flannel shirt and a baseball cap with the Broncos logo on its crown. He glanced twice at the shot between bets. "I'm not sure, beautiful, but I seem to recall this hombre was around the res, maybe three, four weeks ago." His breath was heavy with nicotine and his features sagged from fatigue.

Chainey, who'd been sitting in on the game, held up three twenties. "This is to aid you in your next ante if you can remember anything else."

The old man's narrow eyes crinkled in humor. "This must be my night, a good-lookin' gal like you paying me." The dealer dealt a five of clubs and jack of hearts to a busty brunette in a turtleneck and striped blazer. Next to her, a white-haired woman hacked into a handkerchief.

She waved the twenties like a fan.

To Chainey's right was a man with a pushed-in face beneath a snap brim hat. He gave her an irritated glare. Random conversations about anything except the game at a card table was whack, as the kids say.

"I think I saw him twice," the older man said, scratching at his belly with his free hand. The last round of betting finished and the players showed their hands. Snap Brim had an eighteen and a twenty. The brunette had next best, and they split the pot.

"I know for certain I saw him the second time at Mable's," the older man said. Snap Brim hunkered down, grumbling as the talking continued. The brunette smiled slightly as she said "Hit me," and received a nine of spades and an eight of diamonds as up cards.

"That's why I remembered him," the old man went on. "White fellas hanging around here always gets me to thinking they're FBI or survival. You'd be surprised at how many of those nuts we get coming in, thinking they're going to learn some secret about living off the land." The old man snorted through his nose. A new deal was made. He continued. "But this guy was no bureaucrat, I knew that."

Chainey handed him the money. "And Mable's is . . . ?"

"A gift shop; you can't miss it." He touched the brim of his cap as she rose, his eyes following her legs all the way up.

"Oh, yeah," a new player, a young man in shirtsleeves called as he sat down in the seat she'd been in at the blackjack table. Chainey finished half of her third Manhattan and departed. Outside, Vern Sixkiller was smoking a cigarette, leaning on one of the Doric pillars.

"How was your luck?" His fingers pinched the cigarette in his mouth like Bogart in an old movie.

"Could be improving," she said, suddenly very tired.

"Rest easy, Ms. Chainey," he said. The security chief crushed his smoke beneath the toe of a boot and walked back inside.

"Mr. Sixkiller," she said to his broad back. There was something about the way he'd said her name that had made a wiggle go down her spine. Too bad it wasn't a good feeling she noted.

She slept for less than five hours and awoke sharp and ready. She got in her sweats and did a three-mile jog. After showering and getting dressed in jeans, she stopped at the main desk to ask directions to Mable's. Then she headed back to the reservation.

By day the area was bustling with kids walking to school, pickup trucks carrying men and women to work loaded in the beds, and a few men riding along on horseback too. Like other reservations she'd been on, the place had a duality about it. There were activity and new buildings that had to be the direct result of moneys the casino had generated. Yet there were also houses little more than wood and glass slapped together and ruts rather than paved roads. The history of the first people and the occupiers of their land was manifest for all to see even in the new century. As to judgments about how much the government should pay and for what, they were still unresolved. And like any matter of reparations, it would probably never get settled to anyone's satisfaction.

She parked at the gift shop. Mable's was a large single-story building, done on a variation of a miner's shanty. Its roof was covered in galvanized metal. The porch was covered by an outcropping on the roofline and the foundation was raised on concrete blocks. The steps were wood slats and there was a red-brick chimney on the side of the building. Stepping onto the porch, Chainey could see all sorts of gift items displayed in the windows. On an elevated shelf above and behind the knickknaks was a series of shaman figures in snow globes. The shaman's orange eyes were all on her.

The CLOSED card was prominent on the door. There was no time stenciled anywhere to indicate when the shop opened. And there was no response to her knock. Chainey realized her eagerness had thrown off her good sense. It was only a quarter past eight, definitely not tourist-trap time. She walked off the porch, her hands in her back pockets. A large SUV slowed, the men inside looking quizzically at her. She gave them a baleful stare and they drove on by.

Chainey contemplated driving back into town but wasn't hungry or in the need of coffee. She walked around, kicking loose rocks and learning the geography. With no other hot lead, Mable's was the center of her universe. She paced, sat, hummed, walked around and waited. Her patience was rewarded.

A few minutes past nine, a worn Dodge pickup with a miscolored fender arrived at the store. A woman in cords and a sweat top got out of the truck. Her dark hair was braided in a swaying ponytail, and she walked with a noticeable limp.

"Can I help you?" She unlocked the front door, entering the shop without waiting for an answer.

Chainey came in behind her, the photo printout held before her. "For reasons that are awfully complicated to explain, I'm trying to get information about this man."

The woman glanced back, then went on straightening up items on a glass counter. "You a cop?"

Chainey stepped closer. "No, but this is a matter of crime and punishment," she said, straight-faced.

The woman laughed heartily. "Then he must be your deadbeat old man." She crooked two fingers for Chainey to bring the print over to her. She took it and examined the dead man. "He looks peaceful enough, sleeping off a drunk?" She turned the print over, then back to the side with the image. "I have seen this rough boy around, but it's been a while now, if you want to know the truth." She handed the print back to Chainey. "How come you knew to ask me about this joker?'

Chainey explained the reason.

The woman laughed again. "My grandpop"—she shook her head in exasperation—"what a busybody he is."

"You could really be helping me in a tight situation. Did you see him with anybody else?"

"This isn't about a relationship, is it?"

"In a way," Chainey tried.

The other woman notched an eyebrow. The morning light washed across her face, her Asiatic features pronounced in the soft illumination. "I remember him because he came here twice, asking me about what was life like on the reservation, had the casino been good for us, stuff like that."

"That's not out of the ordinary kind of questions," Chainey pointed out.

"True," the other woman said, adjusting some postcards on a revolving rack. "But I could tell he wasn't asking the questions because he was a tourist. Both times he was here he'd be with his back to me, looking out that window"—she pointed to the front picture window—"like he was looking for something."

"Or someone," Chainey added. "You see what he drove up in?"

"Uh-huh, a rental from Costal."

Chainey had seen some of their brochures at her hotel. "You've been a lot of help, Mable, I appreciate this."

"Not a problem, only I'm Kathy."

They shook hands, and Chainey drove back to the Athenian to inquire about the hitter. From the helpful acne-prone desk clerk, who'd rented the man the car, she found out the stranger had said he was from Aurora, Colorado, and had come to do some gambling and sightseeing. The desk clerk didn't recall the man's name and he apologized. But he was insistent that he'd have to get permission from the manager before he let her see the man's rental agreement.

"Don't sweat it," she said. Chainey thanked him and started to walk away. She knew the guy had been a pro, so any information on the agreement was bound to be useless.

"I do remember he asked me about how to find Gemstone Trail. It's an old trail that goes into Tahquitz Canyon, west of here."

Chainey got the same directions and thanked him again. Forty minutes later she was on foot, following an overrun path up a slope. At the crest of the slope was a low-slung structure, its function unknown to her. The building turned out to be made of red bricks and concrete, with an industrial, sixties flair to its design. Layers of graffiti had been applied to the edifice over a period of time, as if they were low-brow hieroglyphics.

The security glass of the double front doors was cracked. One of the doors hung at an angle off its hinges, propped open by a cinder block. On the wall next to the door, what remained of stone letters in script spelled out a title. After a few moments of staring at the letters, she deciphered the name to have once read THE ASCENSION.

She looked up at the roof but could see no cross. Chainey squeezed between the opening in the door and walked around inside. Clearly this building had been some sort of administration facility, as its layout reminded her of any number of state bureaucratic hives. She found a chalkboard stamped PROPERTY OF THE BUREAU OF INDIAN AFFAIRS. That explained the building's original function.

The main building opened onto a courtyard where there was a dried-up stone fountain, a wide swath of concave tile leading to its center. Rising out of the center was a statue of a shapely woman in bronze. She was tastefully draped in sculpted cloth and held aloft not a globe but a nucleus of circling atoms. Chainey couldn't figure out what the hell she was supposed to inspire.

Beyond the courtyard was a black-topped area. Tall upgrowths of weeds sprouted from the asphalt in numerous places. In an arc set to the right of the lot were what looked to be bunk houses. These structures didn't match the architecture of the main building and obviously had been built when the facility had changed hands. Incongruously, a broken-down half-track truck like Chainey had seen on reruns of "Combat" was also on the lot. The truck's treads were separated from its gears, and the thing listed to one side.

There were also numerous cartridges laying on the blacktop near the half-track. Picking up one, she could see no rust or wear from weather on the shell casing. Somebody had been shooting here recently; various nicks and grooves were evident in the body of the military vehicle. Chainey walked over to the bunk houses and could see bulletholes in the sides of several of the facilities. The hitter and his pals had come up here to target practice. Had they also camped up here? Leading down from the opposite way she'd walked up was a paved road that wound around to the blacktop area.

Chainey started going through each bunk house and found empty beer cans, a clean futon, decomposing condoms, old newspapers and the remains of marijuana joints. The Ascension was probably used as a party place by the teenagers on the res. She also found what was left of a gym and some rooms complete with examination tables that had fallen into disrepair. And one could only imagine what the young folk did on the tables as the booze and weed amped up their hormones.

The Ascension, Chainey concluded, must have been some sort of retreat spa, a fat farm, as they called it in the old days. No doubt, given the woman and the atomic symbol and the era in which it had been functioning, the owners had thrown in some hokum about "life is one" and all that. They'd probably also mixed in the top-ten quotes from Timothy Leary and Werner Erhard as the participants slogged through their diet of celery stalks and carrot shavings.

The big clock was ticking, Chainey thought; she knew it was time to leave the rumination for later, if there is a later. She kept searching. On the floor in one bunkhouse next to an upturned crate were some pieces of wiring. In the corner she picked up a piece of an electronic board. In the rear of this bunk house she discovered several of the mushroom sensors buried in the ground she'd seen at the couple's house in Mill Valley. Clearly the hitters had rehearsed dismantling the alarms and worked out the timing of their raid.

They were organized and skilled. There had been at least three in the house, and maybe there was a fourth, the connection between them and whoever hired their services. Chainey felt angry and confused. None of this conjecture got her closer to her quarry. If she was a cop, she could run the cartridges for prints and run them through some computer and get a name, known associates, the whole schmear. She kicked the crate and it clattered against the wall. Chainey snatched the door open and stormed out onto the asphalt.

As she walked across the lot, an anomaly registered out of the corner of her eye. She turned quickly, scanning the area, her ticklers screaming. Simultaneously, she started running. The door that was ajar on one of the bunkhouses had suddenly been thrown open. That was what had alerted her. She'd closed each door behind her.

The burst of gunfire chewed up asphalt and seared the air around her as Chainey reached the relative cover of the half-track. Rapid fire, the sound of its explosive bursts suppressed as they had been previously, pockmarked the sides of the abandoned vehicle. Several rounds ricocheted like blind hornets going everywhere.

The Glock she'd almost left behind this morning filled her hand. Chainey was crouched against the side of the truck, trying to get a look at the door. This shooting might be meant as a distraction, and shooter number two could be working his way toward her at this very moment. She refused to panic, keeping her pulse from racing too wildly. The firing ceased. The birds in the trees kept chirping, but no other sound reached her ears. Chainey jerked around, half-expecting the other hitter to open up on her. There wasn't anybody creeping toward her and she turned back to the most pressing business. She couldn't make out any movement inside the doorway. She ducked her head back quickly. What a time not to be hauling around her purse; the mirror of her compact would sure come in handy.

She waited, tapering her energy down to a manageable level.

The goddamn birds kept chirping, the world kept spinning— and still nothing happened. Chainey couldn't move, and whoever was in the bunkhouse was calculating the odds. Any way you shook the dice, the percentages were in their favor.

A cramp was working its way into her leg. The knotting was getting worse, but she didn't dare stand to relieve it. The pain was spreading up her thigh to her side, and Chainey had to straighten the leg and knead the muscles. She just wasn't as supple as in her dancing days, she lamented. That and getting shot at was definitely starting to stress her out.

She leaned back, letting the leg unfold from under her. Her large muscle was knotted into chords and her fingers would not sink into the flesh. She knew the toe of her shoe and part of her shin were sticking out beyond the edge of the half-track, but she couldn't keep the leg tucked up. She tried to massage the large muscle. Now the back of her calf, the Gastrocnemius, ached terrifically. Funny she recalled the scientific name. Funny, too, she remembered the Nazi Amazon choreographer who used to run the floor show at the MGM, and her insistence that the girls not only learn their routines but the proper names of the muscles of their bodies, too.

"You know the body, then you know yourself," she'd say over and over in that Swiss or Teutonic or whatever the hell her accent was. There was a disturbance of sound, and Chainey came out of her reverie quickly. She stopped fooling with her leg and sat on the ground, her back against the half-track. She turned her head, and a round of fire almost clipped it off her shoulders. She fell back as footfalls sped across the asphalt. *Get up, Chainey, get the hell up or you're not getting up anymore.*

She twisted and went flat on her belly, getting an angle from on the ground, what remained of the tread offering shielding. A shooter was running not at her but away from the bunk house at an angle. He was dressed in casual clothes, but she didn't get a good look at his face. This was due to the fact that another goon was shooting at her from the bunk house, providing cover for the first one. Just to show she wasn't a pushover, Chainey let loose with two shots she knew would have no effect.

The hitter inside the bunk house stepped partially into the light from the gloom of the doorway. Chainey was only mildly surprised to see this one was a woman. You've come a long way, baby. The first one, the man, had gained the safety of the foliage. Behind Chainey and to the left was the main building. Would the man work his way from the side, then try to bushwhack her that way? She looked left, the direction he'd headed. There was the building that had been the gym and examination rooms. To the left of that was open ground before you got to the main structure.

The woman suddenly let loose with another round. The idea, Chainey guessed, was to have her concentrate on this one. The cramp wasn't better, but that was tough. She had to ignore the discomfort. Her leg was throbbing as the woman raked the half-track. A bullet fragment zinged off asphalt, ripping flesh and cloth from across the top of Chainey's leg. She could not notice the new pain, she could not take her eyes off the space between the buildings. It got quiet again. Then the gunfire from the bunk house started up again. That was it, the signal.

The man moved out. Chainey, gun held in the classic two-hand shooting-range fashion, shot at him. The guy who'd sold her the piece had said the Glock was a slick weapon because it had no safeties to be clicked off or on. Just point and pull the trigger. She wasn't sure if she hit him, but he did retreat back into hiding.

His partner didn't fire. The air itself seemed to stop circulating. Chainey had to move, had to get out from under the weight. If the man charged her and the woman too, they'd cut her up. She might get one of them but not both. She decided she'd shoot the woman first. That way she might have a chance at keeping the half-track between her and the man—maybe. She prepared, yet there was no movement, no sound. Finally, from the bunk house, the woman shouted to her partner.

"Are you in position?"

A pause then, "No."

"Is that because you don't have a clear field?"

"Something like that."

More silence. Had Chainey wounded him? Was that why he wasn't moving? Several more minutes dragged by. She knew the woman in the bunk house would have to make a decision.

"I'll come get you."

"Okay," came the reply.

Was it her wishful thinking or did the man's voice sound . . . off? Chainey aimed at the doorway of the bunk house. There was more shooting, but the bullets weren't coming toward her. Then there was the sound of wood being rendered. She assessed the sound and figured out what it was. The woman was shattering what remained of one of the bunk-house windows and its sash. She would climb out the opening, then go down the side of the building, working her way behind the bunk houses to her partner.

Chainey could stand to wait no longer. She got up, stretching her leg and gritting her teeth. She took off and ran and limped as fast as she could toward the main building. No rapid fire came at her and she made it to the building. She went inside and calculated her next moves. The woman would reach her pal and then have to help him get away. Chainey could try to jump them, but that seemed an outlandish and unnecessarily foolish idea. The man might be hurt, but coming full at them could only get her killed. Conversely, the two had backtracked to this location for some reason. Maybe the two knew who she was and had come to eliminate her to wipe their trail clean. Or were they in the employ of the Golden Horn's owners and had been told she was on the scene?

The kink in her leg was better, only to be replaced by a throb from the bullet that had grazed her. The sensation reminded Chainey that this was not an opportune moment for further speculation. *Keep focused.* She crept to the end of the building, crouching low as she got near a window. The window looked out on the area the man had been trying to reach. Beyond that were the trees and growth he had ducked back into. Chainey couldn't see anything. Not too far away was an exit door, partially open. Chainey didn't feel bold enough to chance going through it.

But she couldn't let the two just slip off. They had the money, therefore they had her life in their greedy hands.

She looked around. In a former janitor's closet she found an old plunger. Chainey had to stand close to the door, given the plunger's short shaft—*my kingdom for a broom,* she wished—but it would have to do. She pushed the door open and no shots rang out. Hell, she must have seen this trick on an old "Roy Rogers Show" rerun.

"Fuck it," Chainey swore again. Putting her weight behind it, she kicked the door open and tumbled out, somersaulting. She came up in a firing position, hoping she could take one of them with her before she cashed out, ripped apart by their high-velocity slugs. Fortunately for her, relatively speaking, the couple had fled, so no gunfire slashed into her. She was alive and they were gone.

She went through the brush, which sloped down to a break in its density. Cautiously going through the opening, she came upon the road that led back up to the parking lot. Stopping to listen, she heard cars going by. The road must lead to the part of the highway that led in from town. Trudging back to her T-Bird, Chainey assumed the crew had probably wanted to know about Gemstone Trail in case they needed an escape route.

Chainey drove back to her hotel, every minute or so glancing in her rearview mirror to make sure she wasn't being followed.

CHAPTER FIVE

After a shower Chainey put the pair of Versace jeans that'd been torn by the bullet back on and slipped a purple T-shirt over her head. She dried off her hair, pulling it back out with a natural comb. A knock at the door startled her. The Glock was in the nightstand drawer. It might as well have been in Iowa if they started shooting.

"Ms. Chainey, can I have a word with you?" the voice in the hallway asked politely. "My name is Lizardo; I'm with the tribal police."

"Just a sec, I'm still dressing from the shower." She didn't really think it was the killers, this being daytime and the hotel busy with people. On the other hand, who was going to risk his life to try to stop two armed assailants? She looked out the peephole. At her door was a man with a hawk nose and a black slouch hat. She opened the door.

"Yes?" The man was on the lanky side, with large black eyes that took in everything. He might have been forty or late fifties, his face lined and deep brown. He was dressed in civilian clothes, his shirtsleeves rolled up past his elbows. He was an inch taller than her.

"Here's my ID." He pushed the hat back on his head and with his other hand showed her an open wallet with a badge and photo card. The full name read Martín Lizardo. He was a lieutenant.

"What can I help you with, Officer?"

A man and a woman moved past in the hallway. "If I could step inside for a moment?"

"Of course." Chainey moved aside and let him in. She closed the door.

He took off his hat but kept it in his hand. He pretended not to be looking around the room as he angled to talk directly to her. "What is the nature of your business here?"

"Just an observation, Lieutenant, but aren't you out of your jurisdiction?" She folded her arms.

"The community around here affords us some leeway when the matter originates on the reservation, ma'am."

"What matter?"

Like an old cowpoke, he looked down at the hat in his hand, then back at her. A bemused twist set his mouth. "Since last night you've been hunting for a man who I had occasion to chat with when he was here last. And I understand you were up to see Kathy Mindivile today."

"It's a private matter, Lieutenant Lizardo."

He reared back slightly on the heels of his boots, not once taking his eyes off her. "I'm not looking to detain you or anything like that, Ms. Chainey. I understand you're some sort of employee for an outfit called Truxon in Vegas."

"That's right." Too bad she hadn't had time to create a cover story for him to check up on. "As I said, this is a somewhat delicate matter involving the affairs of my company." It snapped into her head that stonewalling him wasn't the best approach. If she demonstrated that she was cooperating, that might produce a lead. "If you've checked on me, you know that Truxon enjoys a solid reputation with businesses and the authorities in Nevada." It should; Mooch spread around enough gratuity to various city and county commissioners.

"The hombre we're talking about was involved in some knock against one of your casino clients, is it?" He twirled the hat some. "According to what I read, a lot of Truxon's business seems to be centered around the Strip."

Chainey unfolded her arms to give him the impression she was relaxing. "They supply the juice that keeps Vegas lit twenty-four/seven."

"Very true." His eyebrows went up expectantly, but he didn't add anything to his comment.

"As I said, I can't really go into that at the moment. But maybe if you told me why you're looking for him, I could be of some help." She desperately wanted him to say the man's name. And at the same time, she couldn't tip him to the fact that she was making this up as she went along. "Look, I know this man uses quite a few aliases," she said. "When he got involved with our end of things he was using the name of Jursik, Paul Jursik."

"Really?" Lizardo said. He put his hat back on his thinning black and gray hair. "Well, he's not up to any of that now, is he?" The eyes fixed on her.

"Yes, that is so," she confessed, "since I'm told he's dead."

The bemused twist to his mouth came back. "That's the first straight answer you've given me, Ms. Chainey." He adjusted the hat, the gleam in his eyes disappearing into shadow. "I don't know what you sharpies from Vegas are up to 'round here, but let's get clear on something, shall we? You show up not a day after Smith and Delacruz were found murdered in your neck of the woods.

"And among Truxon's steady employers is Francis Degault, who's had run-ins with our tribe. Now maybe what you say, or rather don't say is legit, or maybe it's all wrapped up in this bullshit of how the white boys who run the Vegas gaming want to keep Indians out of the serious end of the money pool."

"I ain't nobody's Aunt Jemima," she barked defensively.

"So you say, Ms. Chainey." He reached for the doorknob. "But why is it when the red man wants to practice a little of the so-called initiative, as the white man's always saying we should, how come we get thwarted for doing so?"

It bothered her that she didn't have an immediate answer.

And it bothered her that his words were backing her into a corner.

"I'll be around if you're still in town," the tribal cop said, opening the door. "And if you're leaving, we're glad you spent some time with us, uh-huh." He smiled effusively and departed.

It took her several moments to realize he hadn't said the name of the dead man. "Shit," she exclaimed, frustrated by her lack of progress and his digs at her. She got on the horn.

"Mooch, it's me," she said after the line on the other end was picked up. "What do you know about a man-and-woman hit team?"

"Yes," she replied at his incredulous statement, " I know it's unusual, but chicks are doing it for themselves these days, haven't you heard?" She paced while holding on to the phone.

"No, they were both white; well, at least he was." She listened some more, then said, "Gee, Mooch, next time I'll see if I can snap a few photos as they're shooting at my ass. But I take your point; I assume the woman is white, though I didn't get that good a look at her. I mean, she sounded white."

She stopped pacing and stood still, listening again. Chainey cut in, "Look, it's all I've got, Mooch. Try the angle they may be husband and wife." He talked and she remained quiet, then, "I'm not sure why I think that, but there was, I don't know, concern in the woman's voice when she called out to the man. Could be they've been together for a while."

Mooch said, "Yeah, I know, maybe they picked up the third player for backup or could be he was the alarm man, since the two in Marin had a pretty sophisticated system." Mooch assured her he'd check it out and clicked off. Chainey stretched on her back across the bed, her feet on the floor. She was stressing out, and that was tightening the muscles in the back of her neck, shoulder blades and spine. Staring at the ceiling, Chainey breathed deep and strategized. It wasn't efficient to wait for Mooch to get back to her. She needed to be moving, always going forward. But what did she have? She could go try to sweet-talk Lizardo, convince him she was on his side. Okay, that wasn't a realistic plan. What then?

She sat up, realizing she did have one other possibility. Had the crew trained for their job at the spa by accident, or was it some other connection? Sure, it was thin, but she didn't have jack all except the couple angle. She got going and went back to see Kathy Mindivile at Mable's.

"I'm not so sure I should be telling you anything else, should I?" Mindivile tossed a book on the countertop. The title of the trade paper edition was *Welcome to the Agua Caliente Reservation.* Two women with backpacks in hiking shorts looked around at the sound.

"Kathy, I'm not here to cause any grief to the tribe. That's not what I'm about."

"What are you about, lady?"

Chainey stepped closer to the angry woman. "Trying to make it the best way I can, just like you are. I don't know what your Lieutenant Lizardo said about me, but I'm not a stalking horse for the Vegas boys."

Mindivile rang up the two women's purchase and they exited. "You know what kind of crap we've had to put up with since the Proposition 5 and 1A campaigns here in California?" She tapped the countertop with the tip of her index finger for emphasis. "The propositions we backed only gave us the right to expand certain kinds of games in our casinos. The same kinds of games you have in yours. But since it wasn't going to be a kickback to the Vegas boardroom gangsters, you fought us hammer-and-claw over it."

"I know, " Chainey said, "Proposition 5 was the most expensive initiative campaign in California history." She didn't go on to remind her that the Vegas crowd also spent millions trying to overturn the vote of the public in court. Though it was eventually ruled unconstitutional, Prop 5 set the stage for the pact the tribes worked out with the governor, and the subsequent passing of 1A by the voters. People wanted to gamble, and they didn't care where.

"That's right," she said. "And don't forget several important black politicians backed our side." She tapped the area between her breasts with her index finger.

"I work for the casino owners, that's true," Chainey explained. "That doesn't mean I share their outlook on everything, and it doesn't mean I always do their dirty work. What I'm after right now is personal, Kathy, I swear to you it is." Chainey's eyes narrowed and her voice got low. "If you can tell me what you know about who owned the spa up there at the end of Gemstone Trail, I'll go away and not bother you again. Promise."

Mindivile looked out her windows at some distant point, then refocused on the woman before her. "I know about broken promises," she began. "But I'll tell you this. What I know is, the spa used to be run by a bunch of hippie types, see? You know, back to the land, don't eat meat and all that," she said in a derisive tone. "Now this was back some time, like the mid-eighties." She laughed suddenly. They even had that old half-track of Vern's towed up there as a symbol."

"Vern Sixkiller?" Chainey asked.

The proprietor nodded her head. "Way back when we were all young, Vern was in AIM, the American Indian Movement. He was organizing and rabble-rousing up in the Central Valley. One time, him and some young bucks broke into a National Guard compound and commandeered the half-track. The militants used it in a rally on the res to demonstrate how the feds have occupied our lands."

"I guess they made their point," Chainey added.

"Oh, yeah. Vern did federal time for the theft but naturally got to be a local hero around here. See, some of the spa people were the sons and daughters of the patricians of Palm Springs, and by extension Beverly Hills, so they came from money—old money, at least. Nowadays Silicon Valley and the gay scene has brought in the new semoleans."

"Any names, Kathy?"

She hunched a shoulder. "The Blanchards were big in the spa. That is the daughter, Zora. She must be in her fifties now. I heard she moved up north, Oakland I think, after the spa closed."

The same silvery-gray SUV Chainey had seen earlier rolled

past the store again, and she could feel the mood shifting in the room. Mindivile's mouth was a straight line and Chainey knew their time was over.

"Thanks for everything, Kathy. Nobody's going to be sorry about this." Was that the truth, or was she getting so good at the bullshit, even she didn't know when she was doing it?

Chainey was on the access road back to the hotel to get her things when a late-model Eldorado veered in from a dirt road leading back to a farmhouse. The Cadillac zoomed in front of her. The car then braked sideways across the road, blocking Chainey's T-Bird. She stopped and got out, not wanting to be too vulnerable. She wasn't surprised to see Vern Sixkiller unlimber himself from behind the driver's wheel. Leopold, his shadow, was getting out on the passenger's side.

"Be cool, man," Sixkiller told the other one. "I only want to chat with Ms. Chainey."

Leopold wiggled broad shoulders and remained stationary in the ride.

"You didn't have to stop to say good-bye, Vernon."

"There isn't an *o* or *n* on my birth certificate, Ms. Chainey. I just wanted to make sure you got all you came for."

"I didn't come for more than I told you last night."

"You been up to the spa."

Were the gunners working for the tribe? Or more likely he'd gotten information from the desk clerk she'd talk to. "That's where the trail took me."

"You got a stiff backbone, don't you, Ms. Chainey?"

"You mean for a girl, don't you, Vern?" A wind had started up and whipped at their stationary forms.

Sixkiller was up on her, his eyes unreadable. "You tell your bosses back in Vegas this isn't over. This isn't the old days when they could piss in our hats and we'd go away happy to have the attention."

"Look, how many times do I have to say—"

She didn't see his blow coming. His fist rocked her gut, and she went sagging back against the fender of her car.

"And here I thought we had something special, big fella," she said hoarsely, refusing to show he'd hurt her.

"You tell Frankie Degault his name is on my mind overtime, understand, Ms. Chainey?"

She met his glare. "Sure, Vernon, sure. After I'm through with my business." *Don't, Chainey, don't put your hand on your stomach.*

Sixkiller sneered and got back in his car. "You make sure your business is somewhere else but here, Miss Melon Balls," he called out, pointing at her through the car's open window. The man drove off as Chainey walked stiff-legged to the door of her car. Fuck him, she wasn't going to show weakness. She got the car going, her stomach coiling from the hit. At one point she hit a bump and had to fight down bile rising in her throat. She got to the hotel, packed and paid her bill. The desk clerk avoided making eye contact.

Out on the highway, Chainey judged whether a trip north was a waste of time or not. If Kathy was telling her the truth about Zora Blanchard, what did it amount to, really? The shooters might have picked the spa for the same reason the young folks in the area apparently did—it was an out-of-the-way place. Yet it seemed no one had stumbled on the crew when they were camped there, so had word spread on the reservation to avoid the place for a certain time? Did the Blanchards carry weight on the res? Chainey hit the steering wheel in frustration. If she hadn't had a fight with Rena, she could ask her to check on this angle. But to call her now would only reinforce her friend's feeling that she only used her when she needed something from her. They'd been through more than that, Chainey told herself. At least that was going to be her argument.

She got her cell phone out of the glove box and it rang in her hand. Crazily, she wondered if Rena had been thinking the same thing as she answered the call.

"*Chica,*" Mooch Maltazar said on the other end.

She masked her disappointment and said, "What's the word?"

"Don't have a lot, but Lemmy in the office here said he heard about a husband-wife team of shooters who're guns for hire."

"They have names?"

"Nothing solid, a handful of AKAs."

"I'm reaching for needles here, Mooch. Throw me something, huh?"

"*Relajar,* baby, *relajar,*" he said, slurring the last syllable of his Spanish in his Cuban accent. "These two go by Mr. and Mrs. North. Sometimes she uses the name Jenny Harlow, him the name Rex Slattery. And Lemmy says he knows one of them used the alias Blanchard on a job in L.A."

"No shit," Chainey said. "You do good work, Mooch."

"So you off to L.A.?"

"Richmond." She'd decided.

"What?"

"I'll call you in a few hours."

"You should know Frankie and Victoria aren't returning my messages."

"How should I interpret that?"

"I'd take it to mean they're doing some moves of their own. I know too that Baker's been scarce."

"Thanks for the warning."

"We have to keep what we can on our side of the table."

"That we do, Mooch. Even though the game is rigged."

CHAPTER SIX

Frankie Degault struck the long-stemmed match on Lucinda's latex-clad butt.

"Ummm," she moaned pleasurably.

It was bullshit, but with what he was paying, it was part of the show he expected. He sat back in the plush club chair, his shirt open to his belly button. She rubbed her multiringed hand on his chest, tweaking his nipples. The match burned down in his hand. Lucinda licked the end of his cigar as if giving it fellatio. She then inserted the Arturo Fuente Gran Reserva torpedo—the same favored by Hemingway—in his accepting mouth.

The match went out and she lit another one, deftly striking it against the front of her latex panties. "Oh, I'm burning up down there," she said in her best rated-X whisper. She made a show of bending over, lighting his cigar while pushing her breasts up with her other hand. "How's that, Frankie?"

"Like buttah," he admitted, puffing away.

Lucinda turned around, her opulent buttocks to him, and then straddled his legs, grinding on his lap. He held on to her flowing black hair by one hand and on to his cigar with the other. Tracy got up from the other club chair at an angle opposite, across the oval throw rug. She was clad in a slit miniskirt

and tube top. Her heels, as per his request, were five-inch stilet-
tos and she moved about in them like they were flats.

The other broad Lucinda used to do the gig with before was
uninhibited, but clumsy. That was the reason he dumped her.
And shelling out five Gs per performance—well, then, a man
like Frankie Degault had a right to demand what he paid for. He
took a deep drag on the stogie and blew a cloud of white smoke
over Lucinda's bouncing form. He was so fascinated it was as if
they were emerging from a dream.

Tracy had removed her tube top and now rubbed it back and
forth between her legs as if it was a towel. "That's it, baby," he
howled. Degault let go of Lucinda's hair. "Get to it. You know
what I want." He choked out the words, excited, yet acutely
aware at the same time. What was it about this special time of his
that he needed? Was Frankie Degault only capable of real thinking while he got off?

He rolled the cigar in his mouth, puffing a few smoke rings at
the girls. So fuckin' what? he figured. Look at that old fuck
Stanley Kabat who ran part of Benny Binion's book. He heard
stories about how the old boy would pay to have hookers and
showgirls line up in stalls just so he could watch them go to the
bathroom. He wouldn't touch himself, wouldn't touch them.
Just this bent-over turtle of a geek with large thick glasses watching the chicks relieve themselves.

Lucinda and Tracy were slow dancing together, kissing and
rubbing each other's firm bodies. Degault watched intently, his
eyes alive behind the haze from his cigar.

He wondered if that ball-buster Chainey would have done the
toilet show for Kabat had she been around then. No, he knew
better. She was an angler. She was out to get her share, but not
like them other flighty broads running around town. New goddamn millennium or not, those kinds of chicks still wound up
here after getting off that bus at Hollywood and Vine and dis-
covering what a pit the supposed tinsel town was. Every step of
the way was either pimps on the sidewalks or in the suites. They
reamed you while you had your head looking up at those movie-

star billboards. That place was the hustle of dreams that would never come true.

He smoked as Tracy, her skirt up over her ample ass, was on her knees doing Lucinda in the other chair. Vegas might be the big neon intravenous spike, but there was more real to be found among the glitter than all the fakery behind the studio klieg lights. Fuck L.A.

Victoria kept a pad out there in the hills. She used it for her— what's she call it?—her retreat to recharge. He laughed aloud, a perfect smoke ring encircling the light fixture above his head. Okay, he copped, he did get the idea for his retreat, his cabin, from all those old gangster flicks he'd watch on TCM. It was an in-town, out-of-town kind of thing. He'd had the walls in this room done in dark paneling, the bar and such along one wall. The light had been installed so as to create a circle of illumination, the faggot interior designer he'd hired had said.

He tapped ash into the old-school free-standing ashtray next to the chair. Well, there was a reason the bungholer had done work on the Venetian. He'd done a good job translating what he'd wanted into reality. And that was the difference to Frankie. You got what you wanted in Vegas. Nobody promised the gold ring on the first grab. But if you hustled and you took advantage when you needed to, you got your piece, baby.

Lucinda and Tracy were dancing, swaying their vaginas in front of his face. He continued puffing his cigar, wondering how best to handle the Smith and Delacruz business. Fucking redskins. They'd felt their oats pushing through the Proposition 5 measure a couple of years ago, then 1A, and now they acted like they were out to get the country back or something.

Contemptuously, he tapped the gathering ash off the end of his Fuente. Those two from the Agua Caliente tribe . . . and what kind of name was that for a fuckin' tribe? Hot Water? Jesus. Anyway, he mused further, Smith and Delacruz had been sniffing around town, making with this talk and that promise. They'd made it plain they were looking to expand into the white man's territory and do it with a vengeance.

Oh, Smith had put on a good act all right. He was the deliberate, methodical one, almost apologetic in his entreaties into Vegas. Delacruz played the stoic red man act in their meetings. And why the hell those punks in the new Gaming Consortium of Nevada had insisted on the meet was another matter. Yeah, this was a new day, but goddamn, this was still our thing, wasn't it? The old crew of Siegel, Dalitz, Green, Moss, Binion and Costello were no more, and that was as it should be. They couldn't hack it nowadays anyway. That didn't mean you didn't follow a certain protocol.

He snorted, liking the sound of that phrase in his head. And it made him smile, the image of those two interlopers being turned into armrests for the vultures. But if . . . hey, what were those crazy chicks doing now?

Lucinda was on her knees, bending backward as Tracy gyrated over her, dipping down rhythmically. Degault leaned forward to get a better look, the cigar comically falling from his open mouth. Satisfied with the view, he picked up his cigar and sat back. Degault resumed wrapping his mind around his current problems and how best to get ahead of them.

So okay, they did a couple of meetings with the Indians to hear them out. To the credit of most of them, they'd only done it to maybe have those clowns tip their hand as to what they were up to. The rumor still persisted after the deaths of Smith and Delacruz that they'd never been about trying to build in Vegas, Reno, Laughlin, or anywhere else outside of the reservation.

Hell, they had it good there. The goddamn Gaming Commission slapped fewer regulations on them 'cause of that sovereign nation bullshit. The word was, they were really sucking around looking for a silent partner. And had in fact found a couple of interested listeners, if not bridesmaids. Nobody was sure who was guilty, but he had his theory. That Yale motherfuck Steinmetz who became the CEO of the King Solomon's Mines casino and entertainment complex after the flamboyant death of Isome Brand.

Now Brand . . . that was a man who understood the score, he reflected. He would have pimp-slapped Smith upside the head and made Delacruz babble like a junkie before he threw them out of town. Not Steinmetz. That cocksucker would make any kind of double-crossing deal as long as his percentage was figured into it. But that episode was over. Though Baker had told him this morning about some big joker called Sixkiller who had shown up on an early morning flight, lurking around.

This Sixkiller and his no-speak-much pal were doing a kind of Smith and Delacruz bit all over again—one who does the talking, the other never saying shit. Only Baker checked and said this dude was supposed to be the real deal, not some chump in a tailored suit just for show. Apparently this Sixkiller, this red man's version of Swarzenegger, made Baker. Sixkiller came up to him as he was shadowing him in the Luxor.

Lucinda was tossing Tracy's salad, each sweating and grinding up a storm. Degault halted in his musings to enjoy their work. This was a big turn on of his. He puffed away contentedly. After a while, the two women toweled off, breathing hard.

"Having a good time, sweetie?" Lucinda asked him.

"Like you wouldn't believe."

"Want me to get you off?" she implored, using her waif-slut voice. She sashayed closer.

"No, I'm fine." He waved her away. "You guys go at it again, okay? Have a fuckin' ball." The two laughed uproariously at his pathetic joke, but he didn't care. In Vegas you got what you paid for. Nobody came here expecting to hit the jackpot on the first throw or flip of the cards. Only an idiot would think that.

You gambled because it was recreation, it was excitement. It got you out of the house and was a diversion from that sucker job you had to go to to feed your ungrateful kids every day till they laid you out in your best duds, arms folded over your chest. That was what Frankie Degault's old man had said, and he was right. About the only fucking thing he said that was right.

The old man; he shook his head slowly. The women moaned and glistened before him. What a mook. He was a second-rate mechanic, a guy who read that goddamn Nelson Algren novel one too many times. He fancied himself a Frankie Machine, able to double deal and switch cards with the best of 'em. Good thing he didn't imitate that other habit of the Machine's and take to junk. That would have done him in way sooner than his bad card-playing had.

The red at the end of the Fuente's ash glowed bright as he drew on it with force. Well, he concluded, the old man had left him with something other than naming him after the favorite, and as far as he knew only, book he'd read. His failings taught him that you didn't believe any dream made up by someone else. You made your own goddamn house on the hill, stick by stick, brick by fuckin' brick.

Yeah, he pondered, he hadn't done too bad for a guy who'd started out as one of the managers of the blackjack tables at the now gone Dunes. After getting the degree his mother had insisted on, he'd parlayed the scratch he'd made in the jukebox trade and bingo skims in Chicago and Cicero. That was done when he was a lieutenant in the Zacks Mahoney crew. Mahoney was one of the largest bookmakers in Illinois, and had ties to the Genovese family. His only goal then was to move up and become righthand to Mahoney.

His cigar burned down, bluish-white smoke ebbing toward the ceiling in lazy swirls. Degault had to admit, though, it was his baby sister Victoria who understood that the future was more than dressing up the old scams in new clothes. She predicted that Vegas would rise again when everyone else was writing it off. The place had seen a severe downturn in the eighties. The Outfit was in disarray, the goddamn feds having crawled all over them like ants on a pile of sugar for decades. The made boys and the ones wanting to be made were looking elsewhere.

Victoria, on the other hand, was reading the *Wall Street Journal* and *Forbes,* not the tout sheet. She had been following the deeds of guys like Ivan Boesky, Mike Milken, Steve Wynn, Maurice Friedman, and bankers like Parry Thomas. She knew the coming of the new thing of arbitraging and junk bonds, and the *nouveau* riche baby boomers arising from the computer age were made for them.

And certainly Wynn and some other pioneers of the new Vegas took advantage. Milken engineered financing for such ventures as the Mirage, and the casino was reborn. It was bigger, more wonderful, a venue that offered entertainment for the whole family. It was not just for men looking to score on the tables and in the sheets over a weekend. Sure, he summed up, stubbing out his cigar, there always had to be that. But the laws of commerce in the remade desert town was that gambling alone was not where all the money could be made.

It was now understood that food and drink and a show weren't just add-ons to fill the time in between making the next bet. The truth was that for some enterprises, damn near 50 percent of the take came from those areas. Like a George Lucas movie, you had to give the customer the special effects and they'd gladly part with their moolah. And so it was that the men with the gold cuff links and mud from Sicily on their shoes were no longer the players they once were in the town that Siegel built.

If you couldn't read a spreadsheet, if you didn't know what was the difference between cash flow and floating cash and you never lifted your head off some chorus girl's chest, then you had missed the friggin' boat, pally. Oh, there was still a role for a guy like that, but it was someone to go to for an unsecured loan—if you considered your life your collateral.

Lucinda and Tracy were finishing up, having now 69'd each other for the second time. Degault clapped with gusto and got up. "That was terrific, girls, a lot of heart."

Lucinda tossed a towel to him. "Dry me off, baby." She pirouetted her nude body around, lifting her long hair out of the way. He complied, enjoying his task as he contemplated his situation.

"Sure you don't want me to stay?" she purred.

He kissed her shoulder. "Later, honey pie. I'll give you a call on Thursday. By then I should have a handle on my current concerns."

She rubbed a hand on his zipper. "I'll be waiting."

The two women disappeared into the bathroom. Degault flicked on the diffused lighting, bathing the room in a warm yellow glow. He went to the window and drew back the curtain, revealing the blistering hot day.

His view was of Boulder Dam, down the slope from where his cabin stood, but his mind conjured up an image outside his office windows off the Strip. There he could see the upper tiers of Turnberry Place. Who'd have imagined ten years ago a condominium project being erected in the heart of the Strip? Or that Vegas would become a place to have a second house, like Aspen and Sante Fe used to be? These were the ones who spent their long green on a pad in the Red Rock housing development or made the Park Towers, luxury condos near the Hughes Center. They had it to spend, and they'd only part with the bread in hopes to make more.

Like day trading, this kind of real estate was another form of gambling. Everybody did it or wanted to do it, and that was why Vegas was respectable and exciting all at the same time. What did that funny man Chris Rock say in one of his routines? men were only faithful because of lack of opportunity? What a fuckin' insight that was. 'Cause now the idea was to create your opportunity and be next door to it, so you could reach out and touch it when you wanted to.

The trendsetters and star fuckers would build in the middle of Kosovo if they thought it was the happening place to be. And Frankie Degault, CEO of Riverhead Resorts, Ltd., made sure he put his hand on what people wanted to be associated with. He gave them something for the entire family, not forgetting that Vegas was still about separating the money from the customer through a means that kept them coming back for more. After all, your fifty bucks spent on the slots or that same amount spent on the kids in the arcade was, at the end of the day, fifty bucks out of your pocket and into his.

It's good to be Frankie Degault, he reasoned. He drew back from the window, adjusting his shirtsleeve. Degault lit another cigar, this one an Upmann Churchill. Yes, this was a different Vegas, but beneath it all, certain aspects were still the same. Like General Motors and IBM and a Hollywood studio, you did your own accounting. You paid your taxes, but there were necessary items to keep out of the ledgers. Liquid funds, by their very definition, had to remain available.

And like the old days, making sure your shit was taken care of meant handling matters off the books, too. He picked up the phone and punched in a number. "Baker, it's me. That Indian Sixkiller still in town playing big red chief?"

He listened. "Good. I want a complete report of who he sees while he's here. But when he leaves, you tail him around. If he goes back to Palm Springs, fine, you come on back. But I got a feeling that might not be the case."

He paused, listening again. "No, of course I haven't forgotten about your fantasy girl Chainey. It could be where Sixkiller winds up nosin' around, your sweetheart will be nearby." He listened, then, "Yeah," he laughed, "that could be. See if you're right. I'm off."

He hung up and struck a pose before the window. He had one hand in his pocket, his head tilted slightly. Yes indeed, it was good to be Frankie Degault.

CHAPTER SEVEN

Chainey didn't have time to drive back to the Bay Area. She parked her car in Palm Springs at a lot near the airport. Luck was with her and she caught a United shuttle flight and got into Oakland Airport before sundown. Using one of her fake driver's licenses and credit cards, she rented a five-speed Activa and worked her way downtown during rush hour on the 580 freeway north. She got off on an exit a little past where the 80 freeway veered toward East Richmond Heights. She remembered the location more by sight than the actual name of the streets.

Once out on the thoroughfares of Richmond, Chainey got turned around as some of the landmarks that had been around last time were gone. The thing about Richmond was, it did not share in the benefits of venture capitalism and the unrealistic rise of housing stock due to Silicon Valley influx, as, say, Berkeley and San Francisco did to the south. The basic landscape remained the same. Some might suggest it had to do with the city being a predominantly black and, increasingly, Laotian enclave, but Chainey wasn't on a sociological fact-finding mission. No, her purpose for being here had a much more prosaic result in mind.

She got to a street where the curbs disappeared and several homeless men and gangbangers hung out in front of a glass and metal recycling center. Past that and the eye-rolling she got from the men, she found the right place. It was near where the street terminated in a dead end. She parked and knocked on a battered and grime-covered glass door. Over the entrance were big letters in faded paint that read APEX PUMP & PARTS X-CHANGE. The letters looked like they hadn't seen a touch-up since the Johnson administration.

"Get the fuck away from here, we're closed," came a raspy voice from somewhere in the bowels of the place. "I got a dog so mean he scares Stone Cold Steve Austin."

"You're never closed, Gilbarth. That's why I called ahead."

"Goddamn, that is you, ain't it, Chainey?"

"Nobody else."

A series of turning locks and the sliding of a bar could be heard as Gilbarth undid his security mechanisms. The creaky door swung inward on the bent figure of an old black man in drooping blue khakis, a tan and red flannel shirt and leather suspenders. His face contained maybe three fewer crags than the surface of Mars. He wore his usual quilted snow cap with ear flaps. An unlit cigar butt dangled from his coarse mouth.

"Gimme a hug." He grinned lustfully, holding his scarecrow arms wide.

"I'm going to give you a kick in the privates unless you let me inside."

"As you wish." He beamed and stood aside.

Chainey entered a long, brightly lit corridor, on either side of which were rows of shelving. On the shelves were various car and truck hydraulic units, power steering pumps and pressure hoses. The parts, as Chainey knew from past experience, were not only for late-model cars; there were some there that were originals for vehicles from the forties and fifties. It was as if Apex Pump & Parts X-Change was from a modern Dickens novel, and the owner was a physical manifestation of the company's function. By extension, Gilbarth seemed to be an organic and machine amalgam of his environs. Yet his true function was as a storehouse of information gathered from a myriad of sources.

The old man led the way around the corner of one of the shelves to a clearing. A younger man in work clothes went past them, holding on to a freshly painted rebuilt water pump. In the open space was an oval throw rug where a pea-soup green Barcalounger and an ancient dog of no certain heredity rested. Next to the lounger was a rickety metal TV tray. On that was a coffeepot first seen new forty years earlier and a mechanical adding machine. Steam issued from the spout of the plugged-in pot.

"What can I do you for, Chainey?" The old man clambered into his lounger. The chair's back was adjusted to a thirty-degree incline. His body seemed to meld with the Naugahyde; it was as if human and object had become one.

Chainey stood before his lordship. Her quest had taken her to him, and it was by his rules she had to abide—at least if she wanted to get straight answers. "I need a line on a couple, man and woman hired guns. One or both may have used the name Blanchard or some other names such as North or Harlow in the past. They may have operated around the Bay Area, too, Oakland especially."

Gilbarth wiggled his narrow butt in his chair. He reached a hand out and the dog lifted its head. The hand, with the consistency of a pterodactyl's hide, methodically scratched the underside of the dog's jaw. "Man and wife, you say?"

"Or just boyfriend and girlfriend."

"Could even be brother and sister." He ceased scratching the dog's head and the Methuselah of a canine drew back in on itself.

"I hadn't figured on that, Gilbarth. Sounds like you might know who I'm talking about. Or you're screwing with me."

"What kind of market value we talkin' 'bout on this service I may be able to provide?"

The younger man who'd been holding the water pump walked into view. "I'm going to run the stuff over to McNamara."

Gilbarth sat upright. "Make sure you get him to sign for it this time. I don't want to hear no shit about him sayin' we short-changed his green beer ass like he did last time. You got me?"

The young man looked chagrined. "Of course."

"Yeah, uh-huh, of course, just do it."

The other man had already turned and waved a hand in the air in either compliance or annoyance. He was soon swallowed up by the maze of after-market parts.

"Now, you were saying, Chainey, with your fine self?" Gilbarth had gotten up and produced a bone china cup and saucer from a shelf. He poured coffee for himself and returned to his position.

Chainey laid two one-hundred-dollar bills on the TV tray.

Gilbarth slurped noisily, not deigning to allow his eyes to linger too long on the bills. "News on the grapevine has it this might have something to do with a shipment of Frankie Degault's."

Chainey had to restrain herself from letting her voice rise. "Then sell it to the Degaults, Gilbarth. I'm not here to get on my knees or anything else to feed your fantasies. You want to deal with Baker, Frankie's Pretorian catamite, that's fine by me."

Gilbarth looked at her over the rim of the coffee cup. "No reason to get all touchy and everything." He set the cup on the TV tray and folded his arms. "This"—he indicated the money by jabbing an elbow at it—"is a little light for the exposure I might be, ah, exposing myself to."

"This couple bad as Bonnie and Clyde, is that it? You know they'll never hear it from me it was you that put me on to them."

"I know that," he said diffidently.

Chainey pointed at him. "You telling me Baker's already come to see you?"

"Got a call, some dude with an accent," Gilbarth answered. "Said he might be dropping by; didn't want me taking no two day trips in my catamaran anchored at the Oakland harbor, he said."

"Letting you understand you can't hide from him."

"Yeah," he said. "I may not be smart, but I got the clue alright."

"Then don't hold back from him, Gilbarth. Tell him all you know about them, but you tell me first. We go back; there are favors between you and me."

"Don't you think I know that?"

"Yes, you do." She put her hands on her hips. It would have been no good trying to convince Gilbarth not to talk to Baker, because he would anyway. And that would have only given him an excuse to blow her off.

Gilbarth picked up the money and folded the bills away in his breast pocket. "Here's what I know, and it ain't a truck full, Chainey. There was a gat job on a big-time drug middle man around here called Lace last year. Seems he was holding back on his partners. Now this Lace traveled with a squad of thugs, some of these guys had experience in the Gulf War, shit like that."

"The two," Chainey said impatiently.

"This man and woman team was like a fuckin' commando squad," Gilbarth went on as if not paying attention. "They managed to isolate most of the bodyguards from Lace. The couple got him bottled up one night in a Vietnamese restaurant he liked to eat at in East Oakland. Those two lit him up like a Fourth of July display."

"Names, Gilbarth, places these two like to hang when they aren't killing people."

"Damn, Chainey," an offended tone softened his voice, "I'm setting the stage for you, the big picture, right?"

"Sorry, impresario; it's your production." Realizing there'd be no invitation, Chainey pulled a decades-old tubular kitchen chair over and sat down.

"Thank you." He bowed slightly from where he sat. "I'm tellin' you this because you got to know this 'cause if you gonna run up on this couple, you can't be half-steppin'."

"Are they husband and wife?"

"That seems to be what people believe, yeah," Gilbarth confirmed. "They've been using all sorts of names, one of them what you said."

"What about other aliases?"

"All kinds of names, from what I hear."

"Any of them mean anything to you?" The old man liked to think of himself as a sage and derived a perverse delight in attempts of obliqueness.

"That Blanchard handle in particular."

"Why?"

"There's this widow, good-looker for her age, got a nice crib up in the Oakland Hills. She comes from money, and she's into helping the downtrodden and shit like that." He showed ferret's teeth and adjusted his cap with both hands, like he was trying to keep whatever bizarre image was inside his head from escaping.

"Anyway, I was at a party, some kind of cocktail thing to raise money for some such cause. Now this was after Lace got smoked, see what I'm saying?"

Chainey nodded. What she was dwelling on was how the hell this old grease monkey got himself invited to anything.

"Well, you have all sorts of people at these kinds of things."

"Evidently," she said, since he'd found his way there.

He didn't get or ignored the sarcasm. "Somebody was talking about the Lace killing, and this Blanchard broad is all ears. I'm telling you, Chainey, I can see it from where I was standing. This broad was asking questions and whatnot, very interested in the whys and whereofs about this hit."

Chainey leaned forward, elbows on her knees. "The hitters didn't go into the restaurant shouting their names, Gilbarth."

He snorted. "Of course they didn't. But this rich chick started describing the woman, or tried to be slick and ask a question, like did the woman have light hair, was she short, tall, that kind of thing. Now the guy telling the story about the killing didn't know any of that, so the subject got dropped."

"So what made you connect the rich woman and the killers?" Chainey had to admit she was getting interested in Gilbarth's tale.

He spread his arms wide, finally getting to his punchline. "About a month after that I get a visit from this guy I know in law enforcement in town here."

You're his snitch, she wisely didn't state. "And he asked you about the Lace killing?"

"Yeah. He tells me the cops got a tip that maybe the woman shooter used the name Blanchard from time to time. Now he don't know jack about the woman in Oakland and I don't hip him to her either. I figured this would be good to keep close to my heart." He patted the left side of his chest. Chainey didn't really believe such an organ could be found in Gilbarth.

Chainey stood up. "You have an address for the woman in the Hills? Her name is Zora Blanchard, isn't it?"

Gilbarth's crooked teeth split his parchment-covered face. "Named for the black writer from the twenties, she told me herself." There was a knock at the front door. "That might be your pal Baker."

Chainey shook her head in amazement. Gilbarth wasn't scared of Baker. He'd played that up to get Chainey to this point, the shakedown. "How much, Gilbarth? What's the price for the address and for not telling Baker I was here?"

Three upheld fingers were his succinct answer.

"I don't have that much on me," she lied. She needed to hold on to some traveling money. "I'll lay another hundred on you, and you know I'm good for the other two."

"This Baker won't come up short," he stressed. The knock sounded again.

"But he didn't make a run for you off the books that a certain party in Santa Cruz might find of interest should he find out about said trip."

Chainey expected him to go answer the knock and was surprised to hear the locks and the sliding bar being manipulated at the entrance. The door creaked open, and the din of voices wafted from the front.

"Yeah, but that was a personal matter, Chainey," he protested. "You let that get out, it's your ass, too."

"At that point that'll be the least of my troubles, Gilbarth. Gratitude isn't your strong point, but keeping your little semi-criminal enterprise going is what motivates you."

There were footsteps and Chainey braced herself; no sense trying to hide now. A tall young man, at least six-five, in a khaki shirt and oversized shorts, appeared. "The parts for the LaSalle are here," he said.

"Here," Gilbarth said, tossing keys to the man. "Let him around back."

The young man departed. Gilbarth gave Chainey a woeful smile, then said, "It's a deal, Chainey." The information man wrote down an address and handed it over. "But I better see the two by the end of this week." He added the new bill she'd handed him to the two others.

"Not a problem." She started to walk out. "Always a pleasure, Gilbarth," she called from the depths of the aisles.

"Oh, yeah," was his bitter reply as he trailed after her to lock up again.

Outside, two rooty-poot gangbangers were hanging around her car. One was taller than she, his partner shorter. They flexed. Chainey cooled whatever bunk they were about to unload with a look that made their grandma's spine tingle. She got in her car unmolested. And damned if a Jeep Cherokee didn't roll slowly past the passenger side of her car and the Apex building. Baker was at the wheel. He was looking for the address, and since she wasn't driving her T-Bird, he hadn't noticed her. At least she assumed he hadn't.

The Cherokee stopped, and the backup lights flared. Baker parallel parked and got out. Chainey watched as he crossed from the other side of the street, several car lengths ahead of where she was. Her engine was on, and she eased the nose of the vehicle out into the street. She made an illegal U-turn and could see Baker talking with someone inside the open Apex door.

Gilbarth would roll over on his own grandchildren if you made it worth his while. Any sense of comradeship wasn't a factor in their business relationship. But the old trader was certain if he told Baker about her visit, he couldn't be sure it wouldn't come back and bite him in the ass. Chainey reparked her car pointing toward the street's egress. It was a sure bet that once Baker left, he'd be heading back to the freeway.

Twenty minutes later the hatchet man's Cherokee was moving again. Chainey got the Activa going and fell in behind him two cars back. Rush hour had ebbed, and people could be seen walking into neighborhood taverns or markets along the thoroughfares. A block from the freeway entrance on the right-hand side, Baker got into the left-hand turn lane. The move was so quick, Chainey was stuck in the far right lane, having assumed he'd be taking the freeway. She went through the yellow light as Baker completed his turn.

There was a gas station right before the freeway entrance, and Chainey went through the establishment and out the other direction. She got on the street Baker had taken without much hope of picking up his trail. Had he made her? If he had, he'd be snaking down side streets to lose her for sure. She drove and spotted what she believed was his rented Cherokee in the parking lot of a bar called the Sledge Hammer. She doubled back and found an empty slot at the curb catercorner to the watering hole.

She got out and walked onto the lot. She didn't know the full license plate but had made a note of the first three letters and numeral. It was the right vehicle. Laughter and music reverberated from inside the place. Chainey was glad there was no side door for customers to the joint. That meant less hassle on her stakeout.

She peeked inside, but it was darker in there than a loan shark's heart. There was a 7-Eleven on the corner, and she got a cup of coffee and microwaved a bean and cheese burrito.

In her car, she ate half of the burrito and steadily drank the coffee. If Baker was dogging her, did it mean the Degaults hadn't engineered the hit? Clearly they wanted to find out who was behind it as much as she did. Or was Baker up north to chill her when the clock struck midnight? After all, if Gilbarth told him what he'd told her, why wasn't he looking for Zora Blanchard, as she would be?

Sipping the last of the brew, the answer to her silent query materialized. Baker exited the Sledge Hammer a happy sumabitch. He had his arm around a substantially built dark black woman with reddish-brown hair and stacked heels. The skirt she wore was just enough material to make a handkerchief out of it. The South African looked like he was in hog heaven.

The two got in his car, and it didn't take a Spenser to deduce where they'd be heading and what they'd be doing. Chainey tailed him.

Baker was on his knees, his hands tied behind his back. He looked up at the big black woman standing over him. She was dressed in flaming red panties and her high heels. Sweat collected between her mounds for breasts. His breath was ragged and tasted of the three Bushmills he'd had earlier in the Sledge Hammer bar.

"Get up, you white piece of shit," she demanded.

"Yes, Chainey," he said. He rose, his wrists straining against the cords. The slight inebriation of his senses accelerated the headiness of lust consuming him.

"Get my paddle, bitch." The woman sat down on the edge of the bed and crossed her legs.

"Yes, Chainey." A dog barked, and it took him a moment to orient himself. The damned motel was next to a goddamned dog and cat hospital. Good lord, these Americans. He started for the equipment bag at her feet.

"Did I tell you to walk, slave?" She put a cigarette between her orange lips and lit it.

"No, Mistress Chainey." Baker got down on his knees again and scuttled to the equipment bag. She opened her legs and put her hand down there, playing with herself.

"What are you looking at, dog shit? Get the bag open, you silly bitch."

He bent forward and after several tries got his teeth on the bag's zipper. But as he tugged, the zipper wouldn't give. He pulled harder, but the bag wouldn't stay still. It came off the floor as he tried to get it open.

"Can't you do one simple thing, slave?"

"I guess I can't," he said humbly. His face was sopping, and he turned his head to look sideways at the big woman. She was standing now, a haughty look on her face.

"Try again, fool." She played with one of her large nipples.

Baker was transfixed, knowing what would happen because he'd disobeyed.

"Shit, I said do it now." She spiked him in the chest with one of her heels. "Now, dammit."

Baker went back to his task. He found that if he inched the zipper along in quick jerks he could finally do what he was supposed to do.

"Move." She shoved him over onto his back. The woman straddled him as she poked through her bag of tricks. She seemed to pay no more attention to him than one might a chair one was sitting on. She got off him, holding an oarlike paddle drilled with holes at various intervals.

"Yes," he begged.

"Yes, what, shithead?" She tipped over the only chair in the room.

"Yes, please give it to me, Chainey." He started to sit up and she put her heel to his chest, halting him midway.

"Get the chair up." She smacked the paddle against her meaty palm. "And I order you to stay on your knees in a suitable position of groveling."

The sound of the whack sent a pleasurable shiver into his groin. "Yes, of course, right away, mistress."

"Right away is right." She lightly hit his bare shoulder with the paddle.

He was in hog heaven. Baker used the top of his head and inserted in it between the legs of the chair. As if he were a ram, he tried to butt the chair back upright, but of course that didn't work. The closest he got was getting the chair to teeter on two of its four legs, then come crashing down.

"Shit," the woman proclaimed. She gave him a stout spank with the paddle.

"I'll try better, Mistress Chainey," Baker promised. Next door, he could hear two cats going at each other, then they settled down. On his knees, Baker got to the chair and this time used his shoulder to push it back against the wall. Then he went over on his side and got one leg propped on the chair's seat. He used his other leg as a counterweight on the chair's two legs flush to the ground. He exerted the muscles in the leg across the chair's seat, and after three tries got it to an upright position.

"How's that, mistress?" He rose, huffing and puffing, a big boy waiting for his reward.

"You know what I want, worm food." She prodded him with the blunt end of the paddle. The woman sat in the chair, rubbing her butt in it, then got up.

In her heels she was his height, about how the real Chainey would come up to him in the same kind of shoes. Of course, the actual Martha Chainey wouldn't be game for this kind of recreation, he sadly realized. He bent and sniffed the seat. He remained that way so that his chin rested on the seat. With his hands tied behind him and therefore useless for support, a lot of his upper body weight rested on the point of his chin. He could feel the exquisite strain in his lower back and upper legs. As he concentrated to maintain the position, she began to spank him in earnest with the paddle. The pain charged him, and the fact that he could take the pain charged him more.

It had been a long journey for a lad whose only thoughts growing up in Messina were to make the rugby team sponsored by the local tire chain. He hadn't been to Jo'berg until he was sixteen. Make the team he had, but when his nation called him to duty, he did not shirk. Baker honorably reported to do his compulsory service in the army. And the toughness and reserve he had shown on the football field had translated to a ruthlessness he readily applied in his manifestation as a soldier.

"Don't look up, bitch." The paddle raised a welt across his buttocks and Baker grinned with delight. "Keep that head down."

He had been part of what stood against the radical Kafirs and the designs of their communist masters in Russia. And Soweto, bloody Soweto, had been his baptism of fear and death. His bravery there had come to the attention of the Security Branch. No sooner were the bodies of the students being hauled away

than he was called into a room to meet the Minister of Police,
Louis le Grange.

"How's that?" she asked, gulping in air.

"More, you beautiful coal-black whore."

"With pleasure, dog." She set to work on him again, sweat flying from the ends of her weave.

He didn't need to be convinced by le Grange that the Soweto
uprising was a product of Kremlin dreams and that brilliant but
misguided bastard, Steve Biko. He didn't have to read the re-
ports and view the surveillance tapes to know that this was a war
of them against the world. That even their strongest ally during
the Apartheid era, Israel, couldn't be counted on totally. The
Israelis also played up to some black African nations, all part of
the geopolitical chess match to block and counter Arab influence in parts of Africa.

Yet how odd it was that Afrikaaners, Baker mused as his butt
was swatted, the product of pro-Nazi ideology, could admire
Israel yet not abandon their strong strain of anti-Semitism? For
South Africans recognized that Israel, like South Africa, was a
product of tough colonialists fighting off the hostiles in a desert
land. Both countries were built on a tenet of one ethnic group's
superiority over the natives.

"What are you laughing about, bitch?" She lashed the paddle
against his broad back.

"About how funny the goddamn world is." He laughed again,
uproariously. After Soweto, Baker was transferred from the army
to the Security Branch of the national police. It was there that
he was taught to channel his enthusiasm into advanced planning. That brute force was necessary, but not always enough.
One had to observe and learn from what one observed. And
that was what he really found fascinating about Chainey. She
wasn't just a dumb fluff, though God knew she was the subject of
various sexual fantasies of his.

"You listening to me, ho?" The woman raised the paddle to
bring it down again on his backside. But Baker rose and the instrument bounced off his meaty biceps. "Thank you, my dear,
that was a rousing session."

She hunched her shoulders and put the paddle back in the bag with the other toys. "You paid for some Greek action; don't you want that?" She held her strap-on aloft.

"No, no, that's fine, you lovely stallion." Baker turned his back and she undid the knotted cord. "You did exceptional work tonight."

"Well, next time you're in town, you call me again, hear?"

"That I will." Naked, he leaned against the cheap dresser. He smoked a cigarette and watched her get her clothes back on. A lost look consumed his features while the woman quietly slipped from the room. The cigarette burned down to his mustache, breaking him out of his reminiscences.

He stubbed out the smoke and got back into his silk print boxers. Working for Frankie Degault had brought him around to the notion that different clothing set different moods. He ran a hand along the material, raising a static charge. Then he opened the half pint of vodka he'd bought earlier.

America, what a country, he toasted silently. He held the bottle aloft, then downed a considerable amount. Where you can buy liquor by the dram in ghetto corner stores with Korean countermen who sell incense called black pussy. He laughed out loud once more, plopping onto the bed with his vodka.

Baker sat against the headboard, drinking and thinking and smoking. That sly auto parts dealer he'd seen earlier reminded him of one of those Bantustan chiefs. He maintained his own little fiefdom amid the larger power structure. Yet he understood that he was merely a carp in a sea of pike. That any time the big fish decided they were hungry, or that the carp was getting in their way, they'd gobble up the lesser fish. And therefore he had to know who was in the lake of his existence, what were their capabilities and their liabilities.

Baker swallowed more vodka, its alcoholic warmth enwrapping him and making his bruised butt tingle. He laughed, scratching his balls, thinking more about Chainey and this goddamn assignment. Fucking Frankie Degault. How in the hell does someone like him get to be a boss? He was all surface and flash, not much better than some kind of rocker pretending to be a musician, as far as the South African was concerned.

He had another jolt of his booze, letting it glow in his stomach. He ran a hand over his flesh, regretting that his once concretelike lower body was now running to fat and gristle. The Vegas lifestyle had been too good to him. Sun City back home was but a pale comparison.

After all, Baker mused, sipping and scratching, that was what had initially drawn him to the place. He could see the ship of state under Prime Minister Botha turning to uncharted waters. Las Vegas was in the middle of the unforgiving desert. You could die of heat exposure less than a half hour's drive out of town if bad luck decided to make an example of you. And Baker knew about examples.

And his squad should have done more in the fucking redenamored African National Congress. But there were hordes of them, listening to that Oliver Tambo or Alan Boesak, that two-bit Lenin, Joe Slovo, his wife Ruth First, Nadine "middle-class traitor" Gordimer, and, of course, their king of the pride, Nelson Mandela. *My God, what has my country wrought?* He shook his head in wonder.

He finished the half pint and tossed the thick bottle at the trash can. It missed and bounced on the rug, raising dust motes.

As that crew of terrorists came to power, or rather had their battering rams banging against the palace doors, Baker knew the getting was good. Some of his mates went into the professional mercenary business. Some of these chaps did quite well for themselves, hiring out to emerging states in the region, or jumping in one side or the other in ongoing civil wars. Best yet, money and less personal risk were involved in parachuting in to provide security consultation to paranoid dictators like the late lord of the kleptocracy, Mobutu Sese Seko. Blokes like that you could tell anything to, as long as it involved bloodletting.

Baker stretched his big frame and fought the sleepiness creeping over him. The vodka had made the soreness of his ass tolerable. In the old days, there'd be no drinking on the job, let alone a rest stop to satisfy the mule, as he liked to refer to his sexual nature. In the old days it was go forty-eight hours if it took that to break down a recalcitrant prisoner. Some poor township bastard, his or her head full of rosy dreams sold to them by the ANC. Hell, occasionally the Security Forces allies, the Zulu Incatha members, would get out of hand and have to be dealt with, too.

His eyes fluttering, Baker imagined what it would have been like to get Chainey in Chamber 9, the room with no windows and only a grate in the floor to do your business. The room where he broke down African National Congress collaborators and the necklacers. Baker snorted at the images he conjured up in his mind. Those township blokes, troublemakers and beer hall bullies would whip up a crowd to surround some hapless kaffir who they suspected, often rightly, of being a Security Branch informant. The group would beat and pummel this poor suspect with their fists and rocks. Then, as the fool was dazed and out on his feet, the leader of the mob would put a burning tire around the beaten one's neck and shoulders . . . the necklace.

He laughed softly as the salacious picture in his mind crystalized. Chainey was tied to a chair, but in a standing position, bent forward across the seat. Naturally her dress was hiked up and her panties—what color, Baker? red, of course, and silk, too— were down around her ankles. He was behind her, his top off and sweat dappling his footballer-hard form as it had been some twenty years ago.

Baker was swatting Chainey with the special drilled paddle and she was begging him to do it faster and faster. For added pleasure, Victoria Degault was similarly roped in another chair. She still had that superior look on her face, but she too was wet with anticipation of him giving her the treatment.

His hand got busy between his legs. The next thing he knew, Baker suddenly came out of his fantasy with a start. It was if he could feel eyes on him. He knew the room wasn't bugged, but he'd learned long ago to trust the rumbles in his gut. Was it that whore? Had she come back in an attempt to rob him? The only illumination in the room was coming from outside, the lights diffused through the cheap, diaphanous curtains.

He moved quietly off the bed and got his gun. He remained still and soon relaxed. It must be that his fascination with all things sexual when it came to Chainey was starting to jangle his nerves. Yes, he realized as he got into his pants, he was going to have to relieve that pressure building in his mind about that copper-skinned titan. Just to be sure, he went outside and checked in and around his car.

Baker and bombs were no strangers. Those in his squad had been taught by the best, Craig Williams, the construction and delivery of exploding devices in many forms. He halted, sniffing more than examining the area around the hood. There was a fragrance that lingered there . . . a smell he'd committed to his memory. Chainey.

CHAPTER EIGHT

Earlier that evening, at the motel that sat next to a dog and cat hospital, Chainey disabled Baker's Cherokee. She'd used a screwdriver to pop the catch under the hood and gone to work. She knew something about cars and ripped a thick wire leading to the ignition unit. The electronic piece was in essence the coil in the modern, computer chip–dominated vehicle. Without the wire that sent a pulse from the unit to its receptor, the car's engine would crank but not turn over. She eased the hood back into place and left. This would give her a better chance at finding Blanchard before Baker did.

Traffic was flowing well by the time Chainey got back to her bed-and-breakfast in Berkeley, not far from the university. In her room she got busy on the phone, talking with a research firm Truxon often used. Providing them with an address cut down on time, and made for more efficient parameters they'd use to corroborate the information. This particular enterprise the average person would not find listed in the Yellow Pages nor encounter in an ad touting their services in a lawyer's magazine. Soon there were some faxed pages waiting for her at the Krishna Copy on Telegraph.

Chainey found a vacant chair and table at a coffee house and read the report on Zora Blanchard. The woman was the only

child of Harvey and Inelle Blanchard. The mother's maiden
name was Drury, and this was the side of the family with the
money—old, stolid, robber baron bucks. Seems Grandpa Arax
Ramsus Drury was a railroad magnate who had been a major
force in the expansion of the Santa Fe rail lines and attendant
towns along numerous spurs.

Reading through the matriculation stages of Zora Blanchard's
life, Chainey got to the part covering the period of The
Ascension. The report contained several paragraphs summariz-
ing the spa's history. In 1982 Blanchard and three other business associates had bought the property from the Bureau of
Indian Affairs and a year and a half later opened the spa. The
place was to be a combination retreat and health facility that
also allowed for "opening the doors in the mind," according to
an excerpt from a brochure.

Chainey read more about the entertainment and corporate
types the spa attracted as a base clientele. The write-up also
noted that Blanchard hired from the Agua Calientes to work in
the facility. Chainey wondered if she also provided scholarships
for some of the tribe to actually enjoy the accommodations. She
read more, including a few clips from various functions The
Ascension had. Apparently, until the late eighties, it was a happening venue in the Palm Springs area.

She tossed the papers down. That was all well and good, but
she needed a hook into Zora Blanchard. Chainey didn't have a
lot of time to follow up tangential aspects of the woman's life.
What was the connection between her and the hitters? Lacking
any other inspiration, she picked up the pages again and reread
them.

Prior to buying The Ascension, Blanchard had been married
and divorced. Her husband was named Gerry Zing. The para-
graph on him stated that he'd been involved in venture investments of several kinds, including restaurants and boat tours.
One of the locations listed for his operations was Atlantic City.
Maybe it was just his unusual name, but something tickled in a
compartment of her brain about this Zing. Chainey went back
to the Krishna Copy and used one of their rental computers to

send an e-mail to the research outfit. It would take an hour or so to get a reply, so she left and went through the next steps in her head, walking around the busy area near the campus.

Baker's presence could be interpreted in a number of ways. The strong arm could be on a long leash and merely shadow tracking her to see if her story was legit. He could also be around to clip her on or before her appointed hour of execution. She should have another day or so to find the thieves. And that was another question—would the Degaults settle for her identifying the crew and all would be forgiven? It seemed that way in the meeting. But she also realized that if she could take them down and retrieve the cash, her bones, as the boccie bowlers say, would be made.

She jaywalked across Bancroft. Coming from the other direction in the street were two Arctic blonde women in workout togs holding hands, fingers interlaced. One of them had a silver-gray Afghan hound on a pearl-encrusted leash marching proudly beside her. The dog barked once at Chaney as it went past. The one holding the animal managed a weak, apologetic smile for the courier's benefit. Then she and her companion resumed eyes front, noses up and destination certain. The dog, too, seemed to have forgotten about her.

She got to the other side of the street and wandered along, assessing her strategy. This was not the first shipment that had been ripped off from the wheels in Vegas. Nor was it the first shipment to be ripped off from Mooch, quiet as it was kept. But the ones who'd done that deed, back when Mooch was building the business and hadn't been as well-established as he was now, weren't around to say different. So Mooch Maltazar maintained a carefully crafted and honed image that Truxon Ltd. was the outsider concern that would get the job done—sometimes better than your own organization.

And since she'd been with him, Chaney had completed her assignments and worked steadily up to a position of responsibility. Initially she'd been the skirt, the dame who was part of the distraction element for the male couriers in the firm. Say a job required a certain amount of misdirection; then Chaney and a couple of other ex-showgirls or strippers had been used to fill those functions. They hadn't been required to do anything but look pretty and follow a plan that called for them to flirt with some cigar-sucking clown or make goo-goo eyes with a guy in a tux.

Chainey had determined that that was not going to be the role that Mooch, or anybody else, was going to prescribe for her. She'd asked Wilson McAndrews to show her how to shoot and clean a piece. By then, they'd ceased going around together but had remained close. "Never would have guessed I'd call some chick I used to roll in the sack with a friend," he'd said, his gruffness a feeble attempt at hiding the affection he had for her. McAndrews was not into that "Bruce Lee shit," he'd also said, but he got her together with a woman who taught a blend of martial arts styles from Brazilian jujitsu to the Israeli Karv Maga. It was not orthodox technique this woman was interested in imparting, but keeping women from being battered and bruised victims.

Yeah, she acknowledged fondly, Drew had been the real deal. Standing before the picture window of a rocking chair store, Chainey got herself centered. This was the first shipment she was riding solo on that had been taken. Because no matter how many times she got the work done, there was always that fleeting look some of them got behind their eyes when they saw her. That look that said, what in the hell was a woman, a black woman at that, doing in this gig?

So here it was; there was no choice, really. She'd have to hunt down the shooters. To turn it over to Baker, or worse, to ask his help, would be a sign that she couldn't cut it. When it came down to the nitty-gritty, she had to have a man bail her out. Fuck that. She turned from the store window and wound her way back to the copy place. After another twelve-minute wait, a fax for her came over the machine.

Sure enough, Gerry Zing, nee Gerry Zevonian, was a minor-league grifter who'd accomplished a string of cons and hustles from coast to coast. Reading through the brief output, it seemed that the wife had been the one to use her money and influence to save his tawdry ass from serious punishment administered by the law or cheated partners. The write-up didn't say how they met but did contain something else of interest: Zevonian had a sister named Molly, and she was a firecracker.

Whoever had answered her query at the research outlet had been thinking, and had sent over a sheet on the sister, too. Unlike her brother, she didn't go in for that white-collar finesse and preferred the more old-fashioned approach to getting what she wanted. A gun being so much more persuasive than words. She was linked to more than fifteen hits on individuals from biker leaders to Silicon Valley middle managers. Chainey made a mental note to get the names of those managers. There might be a connection to McLaughlin and Buchanan. The last five killings, including Lace, made mention of a man she was working with on the jobs. Not much was known about him, it seemed, other than that he went by the name of Stan. And that he might or might not be her husband. So far, no marriage certificate had been discovered.

Chainey completed her reading and folded the papers together with the previous ones. The bill was settled and she walked briskly back to her lodgings. Chainey called the Blanchard home and got an answering machine.

"This is about your bloodthirsty sister-in-law," she delivered in a clipped manner. "I'll be calling back." After that she packed and set out for the house. It was located in a section of the Oakland Hills where several of the hillsides bore scars from the fires that had scorched the area not too many years before.

Driving past the mansion, Chainey wondered what it was about this predicament of hers that kept bringing her back to upper-class houses and the secrets behind their expansive walls. Could be she was trapped in some post-Clinton era of "Peyton Place" crossed with "The Sopranos." Yeah, she considered, checking her gun, that must be it. A cosmic warp had taken place, and all that had happened to her since then were events being controlled by the spirit of Rod Serling.

She got out and studied the area. The house was large and filled a big lot. It was very modern in its design, all connecting curves and intersecting rooflines. There was a lot of glass fronting the street, and the houses up here were set with breathing room between each one. There was a driveway without a car, but that didn't equal an empty house. The garage was closed, and lights inside the house were on. Chainey went up the sloping walkway. In the flower bed a small sign was staked announcing that the house was protected by an alarm service. She rang the bell. It was 7:45; dinner time should be over and Blanchard might be curled up in front of the local news, maybe a snifter of brandy in her hand.

The chimes rang a tune Chainey tried to recognize as the sound came to her muffled by the thick door. A porch light came on. A dog's deep bark also sounded out.

"Yes?" a woman's voice said loudly from inside the house.

"I'm the one who called," Chainey said.

A strained silence followed; then the voice on the other said responded. "I can't help you, whatever your problem is. Whatever you have to do with Molly, you need to take that up with her. Now please go or I'll call the police."

"I need to get a line on your sister-in-law." Chainey leaned closer to the door. "Look, Zora, I'm sure Molly hasn't been the source of much joy for you. I know something of her history, that she's somehow latched on to you through her brother, Gerry Zing."

The dog repeated its bark, and the woman could be heard shushing the animal. "Who are you?"

Truth or consequences. "Someone your sister-in-law ripped off, looking to—"

"Ex," the woman corrected her. "I do my best not to have anything to do with her these days."

There was a quality to how she said those words that signaled an opening for Chainey. "That because you tried to help her back when, and she took advantage of your goodwill?"

Again no words were said on the other side of the door. Chainey assumed Zora Blanchard had gone back to her TV show, the dog standing sentry. Instead the door opened to reveal a petite woman in her fifties. Zora Blanchard had close-cropped black hair and silver-gray bangs. She wore a long, clingy skirt and a matching lightweight sweater, both powder blue. The sweater was open to a white shirt with a starched front. The dog heeling beside her was a Great Dane that panted profusely.

"What'd Molly take from you?" She patted the dog's massive head.

"Only money," the courier answered.

The other woman allowed a half-smile to light, then flit away from her features. "Okay, you sold me. You can come in, whatever your name is."

"Thanks. And it's Chainey; Martha is the first name."

"Your friends call you Chainey, do they?" Blanchard sized up her guest.

And my enemies, she kept off her lips. "True."

"Let's sit in here." She indicated a room through an archway. The dog followed.

Chainey sank into a plush leather-and-maple chair. The room was a den with a large built-in bookcase and several comfortable chairs. There was also a desk, where the screen-saver scene on a PC was the silent whirling of fiery pinwheels. Beside the computer was a leaded crystal ashtray, filled with butts, and a matching cigarette lighter. The smell of cigarettes was evident.

The woman of the house sat at an angle in a similar chair. She turned the volume down on a stereo unit next to her. The radio had been tuned to a classical station. The dog rested in the corner.

"I'm talking to you," she began, crossing her legs, "because the associates of Molly I've encountered before have tended to be of the tattoo-and-leather-vest variety." She fluttered a hand in the air. "Not that I'm denigrating anyone's lifestyle. I used to run a retreat center years ago."

Chainey had decided to avoid directly mentioning how she'd found her way to this house in the hills. She offered a card to establish her legitimacy. "This is the company I work for, Ms. Blanchard."

"I see," she said, reading the card carefully. "And Molly has absconded with"—she glanced at the card—"some sort of property belonging to this Truxon?"

"In a manner of speaking. It was some material we were employed to safeguard. We believe that Molly and two others, including her husband Stan, were the responsible parties."

Blanchard sighed audibly and looked toward the ceiling. "Yes, yes, I'm sure you're correct. But you must know that I have no way of knowing or caring where she might be." She looked at Chainey and grinned humorlessly. "She's tapped me dry, you see."

"She's used your name as one of her aliases."

"I'm aware that it's been more than once."

"You gave her money, even after you and her brother split up?"

Zora Blanchard shifted in the seat. Her head listed slightly to the side, as if she could hear a faraway sound. "I've been what you'd call an inveterate do-gooder. I married Gerry because he was witty and sexy, and not the kind of man I'd meet on the board of a stodgy foundation. Yes, he always had a scheme or two going, but they seemed like tilting at windmills, not the venal hustles I eventually learned they were."

"And Molly?"

Blanchard steepled her fingers, touching them to her lips. "I wanted to succeed with one member of that family."

Chainey didn't want to seem too abrupt, but she needed a lead, not this soap opera of personal history. "You must have some idea of her haunts."

"That I can provide." The woman got up and so did her dog. "Wait here; I'll be right back." She turned the stereo up and left with the dog at her heels. The melodic sound of a lute filled the room. Chainey rose and explored what the bookcase had to offer. When she worked the chorus, she used to read racy romance novels between shows. Projecting, she finally concluded, about some life and loves she'd never have or want. She was reaching for Ralph Ellison's *The Undiscovered Country* when she

saw a figure move quickly in a room on the other side of the
darkened foyer. The lute had given away to the strains of violins.

"Ms. Blanchard?" Chainey called out. The violins had been
joined by the sweet caresses of cellos and horns. There was no
answer, but there was the sound of unseen movement. "Ms.
Blanchard?" The music was soothing, inviting contemplation
and relaxation.

Chainey was diving as the first round of suppressed gunfire
tore into the airborne Ellison book. Another shot sunk into the
innards of the chair she'd been sitting in. Operating on pure
impulse, she shot out the den's overhead light. If she lived, she
vowed to stay out of fancy houses forever. Laying flat, she
cranked off return fire across the foyer. Then she crawled away
from the spot she knew Molly would be using her flash to pin-
point.

More shots rang out, rounds burying themselves in the floor-
ing and slicing into the stereo. The unit went quiet just as kettle
drums were building to a climax. Chainey belly-crawled to
where she recalled one of the other heavy chairs. She tipped it
sideways and shoved it into the arched doorway. If Molly rushed
the room, she'd stumble into the chair.

Focusing, she visualized the room as it had been. She crawled
in the dark. There was a scuffling sound and she shot at it. She
got to the table and found the lighter. She grabbed papers from
the printer on the floor below the computer and twisted them
into a makeshift torch. She moved forward cautiously, listening.
At the upended chair she hunkered down and lit the torch,
then threw it into the foyer.

A shadowed figure stood at the other end, her handgun
thrust forward. Chainey fired as the other woman scrambled
back into the dark. The torch burned on the stone, ashes floating around it in upward drafts.

Chainey pressed her attack. She used the club chair as a
shield, lowered down and sliding it on its side across the open
space of the foyer. She wasn't sure whether the chair's stuffing
would stop bullets, but she wasn't going to remain trapped in

the den. Two bullets thudded into the chair, causing Chainey to flinch. She deliberately placed the chair over the torch, which was still on fire. As the material heated up, smoke began to spread. Chainey stayed put, not daring to move from behind the chair's relative safety.

More smoke filled the foyer. The stuff had a chemical smell and made her eyes water. She peered around the column of smoke and clipped off a round at a form in the next room. There was a yell and the form dropped to the floor. Chainey waited. The smoke got worse. The arm of the chair had ignited. Her face was caked with sweat and she could barely breathe, but she waited. The chair was now going pretty good, only the patch near her hadn't gone up yet. The ex-showgirl shoved the now useless piece of furniture into the other room. It tumbled down short steps, the light from its flames thrown about like scattered confetti. Chainey leaped right behind it, her gun trained on the still form. It wasn't Molly; it was Zora Blanchard. And there was a gun near her still fingers. Chainey kicked the weapon away.

"Shit." Chainey barely got the word out of her mouth as the dog came at her from the shadows. The beast was snarling, its large, rending teeth bared. Chainey backed away, keeping the flaming chair between herself and the dog.

"No, Romulus, sit, boy, sit," Zora Blanchard said in a calming voice.

The dog went to his mistress, sniffing and licking at her face. Blanchard said, "I don't want to impose, but would you be so kind as to call an ambulance for me?"

"Why don't I just shoot you and your dog?" She couldn't, but Blanchard didn't know that. She hoped her gun hand wasn't shaking too much.

The rich woman angled her head, a grim smile having formed there. Her face had blanched, the redness of her lipstick more pronounced. "Because I'll tell them it was one of Molly's known associates and not you."

Chainey laughed nervously. "You're out of your fucking mind."

The dog reacted to Chainey's harsh tone, but Blanchard petted his side. "You may be right. Nonetheless, I love Molly and would do anything to protect her."

"I guess you're not talking about a platonic kind of affection, huh, Zora?"

Blanchard looked proud.

Chainey put the fire out and called the law, making sure the eccentric woman heard her do so. She wiped down her prints. The dog remained beside the woman of the house, who had managed to prop herself against the leg of a table. The onetime showgirl could only stare at the woman and think how close she'd come to killing another human in less than a week. Life during wartime. A forlorn expression had crossed the woman's face as Chainey left the house and its strange owner—not knowing what to make of some people.

CHAPTER NINE

That morning in Southern California, Victoria Degault had been thinking about Julian Bruan. He was reputed to have been an IBM computer geek who perfected the system of counting cards. That is, he kept track of how many small or large cards might be left in a deck. This determined whether the advantage had shifted to the casino or player, respectively. When the casinos got hip to this tactic, they defended themselves by introducing shoes to dispense cards for Blackjack, and then introduced multiple shoes to keep these counters off-balance. But everybody liked a challenge.

So these days you had groups of card counters and fronts for the card counters. Young men and women, mostly college types, were hired by outfits to hit Vegas, Atlantic City, the reservations, wherever, for one or two weekends. They cleaned up and cleaned out, never to be seen around for months as a new shift hit town the following weekend, and so on. There was always a guy or two wandering, the ones with the kitty. Their associates were at various tables, keeping track of where specific hands were at.

The one with the scratch got the signal and slid into the game to bet heavy by doubling down. Or he or she might lose big and thereby distract the pit boss and other floor management from seeing what was really going on at other tables. Constant shuffling of the cards helped defeat such tactics. And it didn't hurt that casinos could legally ban card counters from their establishments if they were discovered.

Victoria Degault shifted her mind back to the present as she powered her mountain bike over the last hill. Mercifully, this was a smaller rise than the previous one. At the bottom she slid to a stop and propped her foot against the side of the dirt rise. She took off her sleek, aerodynamic helmet. The pointed thing made her look like one of the metal insect guards from an old Flash Gordon movie—or so she imagined. She drank water from her sport bottle, put her helmet back on and completed her exercise.

She took her BMX mountain bike along the path leading back to the main track. The muscles in her upper thigh were tightening from her cycling, but the pain was good. Her calves—the gastrocnemius, she learned in an art anatomy class—were bunching and relaxing as she worked the pedals and gears. The tendons in the back of her legs strung taut like bowstrings that hummed as an archer plucked them. What an analogy, she mused to herself.

She reached the bottom. Degault had pushed it in her workout, and she felt it as she cooled down. The quadriceps behind her left knee ached, but she didn't think it was pulled. She did some extensions and leg lifts, the quad throbbing in the left leg as she worked through it. Tired but fulfilled, she walked the bike back to her Navigator, parked on one of the park's lots. She got the bike cinched and locked, laying it on the rack on its side on the roof.

Degault arched her body while she pressed against the rim of the door. She rolled the muscles in her upper body, breathing in and out, regularizing her pulse. She got in and drove off. At the wheel, she reviewed what she knew. As usual, her brother had sent Baker out on one of his "missions," as the South African liked to term them. The fact that her brother used that Boer schmuck still got under her skin and just fuckin' creeped her out.

Victoria Degault decided she deserved a reward for her hard work. If she was like her brother, that would involve something of a sexual nature. For though he enjoyed the milieu of the gaming world, he himself was not by any stretch a shark. His idea of a rush was to get a double header—a blow job from two women—and then walk around the Riverhead like the cock of the glitz walk. Turning onto Montana, she decided that was simply how men were, always guided by their baser selves. That when all was said and done, no matter how smart or ruthless, they were prisoners of their own testosterone.

Not that relationships, and/or a good fuck now and then, weren't important to her. It was, though, something she had come to guard against, more so now than in her days at Swarthmore. Experimentation with various controlled substances and the attention of young men was part of the initiation with the crowd she ran with.

A guy in a silver beamer zoomed in front of her from another lane to get a parking space she was heading toward. He was talking on a cell phone and wore the latest-style designer sunglasses. The jerk pretended she wasn't even there.

If that had happened to Frankie—and it wasn't within the confines of Vegas—he'd stop his car in a heartbeat. Then he'd be out and pounding on the hood of the other guy's car, reminding him in a loud voice that driving courtesy was a fucking skill to be practiced every fucking day. Then he'd dent the guy's door with his heel and dare him to do something about it.

She parked on a pay lot and walked to the coffee and juice bar. The place wasn't part of that ubiquitous and, some allege, sinister, chain of such emporia. This establishment was called Ferry's Bazaar, and offered house blends, a decent newsstand, and an open mic on Thursday nights. She walked past the asshole's beamer, hesitated, but kept strolling.

Inside, she got her coffee and sat at a corner table next to a window. The sun felt good on the side of her face and shoulder. Degault unfolded the *Wall Street Journal* she'd bought and perused the articles. Nibbling at her was the fact that this was just a holding action, a self-imposed lull that could only last as long as it took her to sip her brew.

In the *WSJ*, she did pay attention to a piece about changes in the tax credit law, and one on companies projected to be presenting their IPOs within the next month. But the more she tried to force the matter into its own box, the more it sought to take prominence in her consciousness. This business with the swiped seven million was not what it appeared, and that was what was working her nerve, as the woman who did her nails would say.

She put the paper aside and sampled more of her coffee. There was a sturdy-looking man in running shorts waiting in line. He had a pleasant if not overly handsome face. His legs and buttocks were well-proportioned. And those attributes combined with his broad back indicated someone who definitely worked out regularly. Degault crossed her legs and played with the idea of coming on to the man. He looked to be at least six years younger than she, and that could be exciting.

Alas, she resolved, a late-morning boinking was not going to alter the conundrum she had to handle. It couldn't hurt, she weighed, watching the man bend down and select his croissant in the glass case. And it wasn't as if she hadn't picked up a man for a lay and good-bye since her days in the dorms. But she was the COO of a multimillion dollar corporation and therefore had to be more constrained than her male counterparts. An unfair and sexist situation, but there you had it. Plus, she had to reluctantly admit, throwaway sex wasn't her bag anymore.

And there was the other problem—a two-pronged one. The money had to be retrieved. She didn't have much of an opinion one way or the other whether Chainey had a hand in the absconding of same. Outwardly, it would seem unlikely, as she certainly appeared sincere in her intention to get the money back. But her brother wasn't always full of shit. And he'd observed after their meeting that Chainey wasn't exactly shaking in her scuffed boots during the meet.

Conversely, should she play into her brother's typical male reactions to a woman who was composed and sure of herself?

Chainey knew how the deal worked and wasn't about to get all weepy-eyed because the Degaults were on her tit to deliver their goods. She grunted and stirred her latte. Degault observed to herself that she was starting to adopt too much of the quasi–wise guy lingo her brother and several other club-house gangsters had adopted.

Ha; maybe she should use more curse words and sexist slang in her speech. The younger man in his running shorts chanced a look at her. He was sitting on the other side of the coffee shop, leafing through the L.A. *Times*. Not bad, not bad, she discerned. Some reins had been loosened due to the reorder of affairs as Vegas had changed from a mob playground. To be sure, the Outfit was still around, but its bite was far less than the whole pie they gobbled up not too long ago. Though Lord knows you had to dicker with them on freight matters like produce and heavy equipment.

These days the new regime that ruled Vegas had MBAs and MAs behind their names more likely than not. Now you made your stones not by collecting debts with a bat or putting an ice pick in some guy's eye; you earned your thing by displaying another kind of coldness practiced in the suites since the time of the railroad barons. Pens had replaced gats. At least that was the story the creators of the never-ending show would have the world beyond the borders of Vegas believe.

Though the renaissance in many ways changed the character of the magnificent beast, its nature remained dormant but intact. The Mafia, too, had sent its sons and daughters on to higher education. Like the Kennedys and Rockefellers, the scions of coarsely acquired capitalism felt removed enough from how such lucre was accumulated to pretend they were something other than avaricious graspers. But when you fucked with their money, the fangs came out.

Victoria Degault enjoyed more of her drink, pleased with her overview and rationalizations. Unlike her brother, she knew she had a better understanding of the world they occupied. Oh, he tried to keep up, but he couldn't leave the tired methods alone. The post-millennium gangster had to understand that fear and intimidation had its place, but it was self-interest where you got them by their short and curlies, as the tough guys used to say in British crime pictures.

The hunk in the shorts had finished his refreshment. He was intently reading an article in the sports section, legs crossed at angles to each other. Victoria Degault nudged the impulse to get up and engage in small talk with the man to the side of her mind. Yes, a morning of slap and tickle wasn't a bad idea, but, goddammit, she hadn't quite gotten a handle on this situation. Though sex, or at least the anticipation of getting her adrenaline pumped, was a proven way to excite your neurons.

The man folded his paper and threw out his cup. All right, let's see if he can be clever, she decided. She worked a smile that went well with her face. She brushed at some hair on her forehead as he stepped past. He returned the smile, nodded and went on out into the daylight. She told herself, if the guy can't come up with a halfway decent opening line, then what fun would he be?

Her life, her personal situation, had spoiled her, she knew. Being a woman of power and means made many a man's penis go limp even before getting out of the starting gate. And it wasn't that she wanted some performing stud who could bang at the drop of her underwear. She liked walks and conversation about current events and holding hands after midnight. Then there were the others, who were of equal or more prominent stature. These men had their qualifications. Yet they, too, were into grabbing more from the world, so they weren't the types to want to sit quietly and snuggle.

Okay, Victoria, enough with these silly hot-sheet fantasies of mental distraction. You ain't getting none anytime soon, so you better take care of your business, girl. Which unfortunately meant she had to do a back-channel action on her brother. The bullshit story they gave Chainey was what she and Frankie had agreed to do if pressed. The truth was, the shipment was a surprise to her, too.

Brother and sister had intermixed and separate accounts derived from Riverhead Enterprises, Ltd. By and large, Frankie ran the casino since that fit with the public persona he worked hard to project. Her purview extended to the broader areas—possible expansion of gaming interests into Detroit, investments from such mundane opportunities as parking lots to more creative areas like music video production and distribution. And both of them answered to the same board. A board that by now must have heard the rumors about the rip-off, and would be calling an emergency board meeting demanding to hear what kind of answers she and Frankie had.

Money was exposure, and that meant careful planning and execution. The board hadn't known about the shipment, nor had she until the theft went down. Therefore, whatever her brother was actually up to, she had to know. She didn't think he was trying to freeze her out. They were competitive as siblings had a wont to be, but the two weren't out to cut each other's throat, were they? She stretched in her chair and rose.

She checked the time. By now, that rottweiler Baker would have Chainey's scent. And her source told her that two gentlemen from the Agua Caliente reservation had come into McCarran Airport yesterday, asking questions in the wake of Smith and Delacruz's murders. Time for some background info before getting her pieces in order for the frontal assault.

She got her cell phone out, then put it away. Better to be safe. She walked out of the coffee shop and dialed Vegas from a pay phone using a bunch of change. No sense leaving a trace by using her calling card. "Rena Solomon, please," she said as the line connected.

"Rena, Victoria. How're things?" She listened, then spoke. "I've got a few leads that might help you on the article you're doing on the murders," she said. "It has to do with another two who were murdered in Marin County." She heard her response. 'That's right, those two. I'm out in L.A. but will fly back to town by six or so. I came here to meet with a man who was doing business with those two.

"Exactly," she went on, "the same arrangement as in the past. I provide you with some deep background, and you tell me what you've discovered. Okay, talk soon."

She hung up and walked back to her car. Along the way she

CHAPTER TEN

It was a longshot and no oddsmaker would give you good book on it, but what other way was there? Baker was skulking around somewhere in all this, and he must be creaming himself, waiting to back her into a corner. She followed the ambulance that took Zora Blanchard to the hospital. It was a private facility on the border of Oakland and Berkeley. Chainey parked.

Now it could be that Blanchard was desperate because her love for Molly was so deep. And any threat to her former sister-in-law was to be dealt with permanently. But, Chainey hedged, it could be she'd reacted in such an extreme manner because Molly was close. That meant if Chainey was around, she might get onto her.

The unknown was whether Molly had reciprocal feelings. Even if she did, she was a pro, and pros didn't let emotions get in the way of their job. Chainey smiled at her own growing cynicism. The goal, then, was how to flush out the shooter.

She got out and took a walk around the small hospital. There was a main entrance that was also for emergency uses, and side exits that locked back in place. She briefly walked inside to catalog the personnel and walk out. As this was a private enterprise, the usual cacophony of public hospitals was at a minimum. Chainey watched nurses and orderlies use the side exits, but sneaking past them was not too likely. Off the building's loading dock she found several locked Dumpsters. She shot the lock off one, the echo of the blast way too loud. She dug through the bloody and contagious refuse of the physical reminders of how far, and at times how futile, attempts at healing were. She found some bloody scrubs and prayed she didn't have any cuts. She folded them up and tucked them under her arm.

She hung back across the street, waiting for her chance. Eventually another ambulance arrived, sirens blaring. As people rushed out to meet its passenger, an old women on oxygen, she strolled inside.

The traffic manager from the front desk was busy helping the paramedics get the woman situated. A guard sipping on an orange juice bottle glared at her, and she smiled back, but kept walking like she worked there. In a stairwell she put on the scrubs over her clothes. On the third try she found Zora Blanchard's effects in a closet around the corner from the nurse's station.

There were a few people in the hallway and she had to duck into the woman's bathroom so as not to call too much attention to herself. Eventually Chainey managed to get back to the closet and retrieve the woman's keys from her purse. She straightened up and closed the door.

"Can I help you?" a doctor in a splotched white coat asked impertinently.

"No. I was supposed to get something for one of the cops who was on the scene after the Blanchard shooting." From the reaction on her face, Chainey knew that answer threw her. No thief would know the particulars like she did.

"What cop?" she demanded querulously.

"In the lobby." Chainey pointed.

The doctor gestured with her hand like an impatient parent. "Come on. Let's see this officer."

"Okay." Chainey quickly stepped beside the doctor as a nurse walked past. Then she pressed the gun into the woman's side. "You know what this is and you know the effects of a bullet on the human body, Doctor."

The physician said calmly, "I do."

"Walk this way and talk to me as if you're explaining a procedure."

The doctor complied, and they walked away from the nurse's station. They came to an empty patient's room.

"Will you kill me?" The doctor couldn't take her eyes off the gun.

Chainey clucked her tongue and clubbed the doctor at the base of her neck, stunning her. Moving with speed, she tied the top of her scrubs around the woman's mouth. Using cord from the blinds, she tied her up and put her in the bed. She took off the scrub pants.

Chainey opened the door a crack and went out. Hurriedly, she left the facility and drove back to the Blanchard house. There was still police activity going on, so she drove past. Coming from the opposite direction was Baker in his repaired Cherokee. This time he saw her. Their cars slowed as they went past each other. Like the villain in an old movie serial, he used his index finger and thumb to brush the ends of his mustache.

Chainey knew she had to do something bold. She parked down the street and went back to the Blanchard residence.

"Can I help you?" a young slender Asian cop in a crisp uniform asked her curtly.

"I'm the nanny for the Raymonds"—she gave a vague jerk of her head that could have meant a house located on Jupiter. "I've seen that man in the Cherokee hanging around Ms. Blanchard's house." She pointed at Baker's vehicle, which was idling not too far up the street. As she'd calculated, he'd remained, curious to see what she was going to do.

"Is that right?" The cop looked in Baker's direction.

"Yes, sir. I saw him night before last as I returned with the twins in the stroller. He was parked right across the street and watching her house."

The cop looked at Chainey, gauging the information. "Okay, ah, you stay right here, got it?" The cop put his hands on either side of his mouth for a funnel effect and called out toward the house, "Lansing, hey, Lansing, I might have something here."

Detective Lansing was an overweight, middle-aged black man with salt-and-pepper hair wearing a fashionable double-breasted suit. He stuck part of his body out of the doorway. "What is it, Hu?"

Hu strode over to him, talking quietly to the plainclothes-man. Chainey glanced up the street. Baker had gotten hip and was driving away. Lansing and the younger cop raced to a patrol car and zoomed off after him. Chainey drove off and stayed away for more than an hour. When she returned, the last cop was leaving. She was a drab gray woman in a washed-out cloth coat putting up the customary yellow do-not-cross tape.

Chainey put on a pair of supple driving gloves and tried the keys she'd stolen. The cops had put their tape up and a padlock on the front door. But no one was going to justify the overtime and station someone to guard an empty house. Especially when they had a live suspect like Baker in custody. She got in through a set of back doors to a maid's quarters behind a thatch of chrysanthemums. And as she'd hoped, the officers hadn't set the alarm; Blanchard was recovering at the hospital, and hadn't been able to give them the code.

Fortunately too, there seemed to be no maid about. Evidently the cops had also carted the dog away. The best places to search were the den where she'd been attacked and the master bed-room. The desk in the den provided little save business corre-spondence. The bedroom, more specifically a locked chest in the voluminous closet, offered more savory fruit.

Zora had several amateur videos in which she and a rotating supporting cast were the stars. Watching a sample of the fare on a VCR in the bedroom, Chainey viewed moderate—or what she assumed to be moderate—S&M that included golden showers and leather whips. There was another of Blanchard being ser-viced by an especially large brother, and one of Blanchard and another woman frolicking. Chainey's excuse was that she had to look through the material in hopes of getting a lead, and not merely satisfying prurient interests. *How long has it been since being with a man there, Chainey?*

Fifteen minutes later she yawned and turned off the VCR. If

Molly was one of her partners, she didn't recognize her. She didn't get a good look at the woman at The Ascension, and the gunwoman hadn't exactly been sitting for a portrait then. Chainey went through more items in the trunk, letters and hard copies of e-mails in particular. Blanchard was heavy into the swinging scene, and not in the listening to Dean-O and driving a bomb '67 Coup DeVille sense, either.

Forty minutes later, she put Zora Blanchard's pleasure chest and its libidinous trove away. She checked the time. Baker would get himself out of his entanglement with the cops and come whizzing back here. She marched around, pulling open drawers and looking under the bed, anywhere she might find something to get her a line on Molly.

Pushing aside pillows and satin sheets in a linen closet of the bedroom, Chainey got a new idea. She went back downstairs. This time, she carefully and slowly read through the financial records in the desk in the den. The route to any pro is always the money road, baby, always, Drew had said over and over. And of course he was right.

There were several receipts for cashier's checks made out to a Jenny Harlow. That was one of the names Mooch told her Molly used. The checks were five to ten thousand, not the price of one of her hits, but tidy sums for going-around dough, pocket change in between her gigs. That might mean she either picked them up, or more likely Molly had them mailed.

But if the money was Blanchard's way of expressing her feelings, she'd send notes. She'd make a record of where she sent them so as to keep track of Molly. Even a mail drop would provide a demarcation point with which to backtrack. On the back of one of the receipts for the cashier's checks was a small notation in the corner. It was an address in San Francisco. Had Zora Blanchard made a personal delivery?

It made sense, Chainey assessed on the way to her car. Blanchard would want a chance to see her one true killer love any way she could. If she was a willing sap making the payoff, that was better than no chance at all.

Love ain't nothing but a one-legged mother that'll trip you

every time—so went another axiom of the late owner of the Rye Breaker.

The address across the bay was a spa. This one was appropriately in the Tenderloin, one of the last sections of the city to have its real estate inflated due to the steady influx of Silicon Valley moneys. The spa was named the Velvet Retreat and highlighted mineral baths, skin peels and mud dips. Chainey paid to park at a twenty-four-hour lot and watched the clientele enter and leave. From the yellow pages at a phone booth she located a local Rite Aid and bought a bathing suit and a combination lock. Stuffing the suit and lock in her jacket pocket, she walked up to the guarded door of the establishment.

Beside the door was a brunette in cut-off jeans and a leather vest. She had triceps the size of beach balls.

"Z'up?" she said in a surprising contralto.

"How much is membership?"

"Depends."

Chainey held up a C-note.

"Still depends," the guardian repeated. She let two regulars inside with a brief greeting.

"Jenny Harlow said this was a cool joint."

"Did she now?" the bouncer responded. "You and she pals?"

Chainey hedged her answer. "We've run into each other now and then."

The big woman scratched her biceps. "Thirty-five for the night, and that can be applied against your membership fee should you decide to join." Without waiting for an answer, she hit an intercom button and told whoever was on the other end that Chainey was coming in.

At a desk at the top of a set of purple carpeted stairs, Chainey had to show ID, sign in and pay. She was given a handout of the spa's dos and don'ts, a towel and a locker for the evening. She thanked them and mingled with women of various colors who were either tattooed, pierced, heavy or svelte, shaved or hairy or combinations thereof. Some had on sweats or towels around their bodies and others nothing at all.

Chainey got into her suit and walked up to the next level,

where the heated pool was. She cleaved into the water, its warmness bracing her, tingling her fully awake. She did several laps and pulled herself onto an edge, near a knot of women lounging and talking. This had to be careful going. Apparently Molly the switch-hitter frequented the club when she was in town. And she was bound to have friends here who wouldn't like an outsider—who they might tag as a cop—asking around about her. Or had Blanchard heard about this spot and enticed Molly into meeting her here in hopes of a little action?

Chainey listened to the women, who were talking about some other women not present. There was no smooth way for her into insert herself into the insular conversation so she jumped back into the pool. As she swam for several minutes, she noticed the arrival of a muscular white woman in a skimpy red suit. She was dark-haired and leaned on a wall. The woman had made a couple of furtive glances at Chainey, watching her form in the water. Chainey got out, grabbing her towel where she'd left it on a chair.

She stood drying herself and her hair, not hiding the fact that she was glancing at the woman in red. This woman had one arm done in a series of tattoos and her thighs were solid, defined, the result of many hours working the leg machines. She came over, chewing gum slowly.

"Why don't you let me do that?" She held out a hand.

Chainey gave her the towel. "Thanks."

The woman indicated the chair and Chainey sat. She got behind her, the woman's hard legs pressed up against the back of Chainey's head. She began drying her hair.

"Great texture," the woman said, stroking some of Chainey's strands. "And all yours."

Chainey angled her head up at the woman. "All those muscles yours?"

The woman in red grinned, showing white, wide teeth. "Yeah, baby. Feel." She stood so her leg was to the side of Chainey's face.

The courier latched a hand on one of the thighs and squeezed the firm leg. "Very nice," she whispered.

"I'm called Dejur."

"Well," Chainey managed, clearing her throat, "it could be my lucky day."

The woman tossed the towel onto another chair. "Let me buy you a smoothie at the juice bar."

"Sounds like a plan." Walking toward the juice bar, Chainey wondered what the hell she was hoping to get out of this. The idea of sex with a woman was tantalizing. And it wasn't as if she didn't know some showgirls who were lesbians. Hell, you get pawed and fanny-slapped and drooled on by enough slobs, who wouldn't want to cease having anything to do with the opposite sex?

Chainey reminded herself that this was not a mission to explore new realms. But Dejur seemed comfortable, like a regular. And therefore she had value of the sort Chainey needed now.

"This your first time here, isn't it, tall, dark and breathtaking?" Dejur asked, sipping her concoction from the juice bar. A Melissa Ethridge song played in the background. They sat opposite one another in canvas chairs, a small round coffee table before them. The juice bar itself was a designated section off the locker room.

"It is. I . . ."—she purposely hesitated—"I heard about this place from a chick who calls herself Jenny Harlow."

Dejur raised an eyebrow, her body stiffening. "Really?"

How to interpret that? *Tread gingerly here, Chainey.* "We're not exactly friends; more like business associates, you might say."

"And what else would I say about you?" Dejur's cheeks dented like craters as she took a pull on her drink. She kept her dark eyes on Chainey.

Nothing to lose. "I'm looking for her to settle accounts, if you catch my meaning."

Dejur put down her drink and crossed her legs. "I understand. That bitch chumped me, too."

"So she used to come here?"

"That's right, honey doll, 'used to' being the operative word. Harlow wore out her welcome here. She let that ultra-butch act of hers get out of hand with one-too-many women, always off the premises, mind you. But ours is a close-knit community in a small town like San Francisco, no matter how cosmopolitan we think we are.

"Anyway, word gets around, and one time this woman, Ivy League accent and all, throws all this drama with her here. She demanded that Harlow"—she snapped her fingers—"no, she called her by another name. Her real name, I'm sure, since none of us went for that Harlow bit."

Chainey didn't point out the irony of someone named Dejur saying that. "Did she call her Molly?" Two nude women rambled by, one giving a piggy-back ride to the other. They went into the showers.

"That's it," Dejur confirmed. "Molly started slapping this woman around, getting off, you know what I'm saying? You could tell this other woman had it bad for our roughneck, though." She shook her head, commiserating. "Me and Riley had to pull Molly off this poor chick."

She assumed Riley was the built sister on the door. "You and Molly ever get together?"

Her slight nod was affirmative. "That's how I know a couple of her haunts."

"Then we're in business," Chainey brightened.

They both stood. Dejur's breath was hot on Chainey's face. "And afterward? What then?"

"I could be mean and lead you on, Dejur, but—"

"Yeah," she reasoned, "I had a feeling you weren't really one of the tribe." She twitched her packed shoulders. "I'll help you. Whatever you're up to that trips up Molly can't be all bad, can it?"

Chainey made a noncommittal face. The women got dressed in their street clothes and left the Velvet Retreat. Dejur offered to drive and they rode away in her tricked-out '43 Dodge pickup.

"The best place to run down her whereabouts is this bar over in Albany. She likes to strut her new finds there," she relayed bitterly.

The bar, the Black Onyx, was a bust, and they tried another

hangout back in the city, which also proved fruitless. "Sorry. I guess this detective shit ain't like it seems on A & E," Dejur lamented.

"Come on, third roll is always lucky," Chainey said. What else could she do? She felt loose, unhurried, though the big clock was ticking. She was charged because she was ahead of the game. Baker and his Afrikaaner ass would never have gotten into the lesbian spa and found Dejur.

"Okay," Dejur concurred. "At the spa I heard there's a queer rave happening in San Leandro. The ones giving it are known in the community, and it's a place we might at least find someone who's seen Jenny recently."

"Then let's hoo-bang, girl."

Chainey paid to gas up the truck and they arrived in San Leandro a few strokes past midnight. The function was in a stone building in an industrial area behind a uniform cleaning plant. The music pulsed through the thick walls.

"It's bumpin'," Dejur yelled into Chainey's ear as they entered. Dejur had been recognized at the door and both women had been waved on through.

Partyers were gyrating and bopping from metal stairs, makeshift platforms and a catwalk. The DJ was a thin woman in a hooded sweat top who spun her wheels of steel inside a translucent green plastic pyramid. Someone handed Chainey a drink and she sniffed at it.

"This isn't like some joint where you have to worry about a man spiking your shit with roofies," Dejur advised.

Chainey handed the drink off to a young women in a striped tube top and a sarong. "Not while I'm working."

"Girlfriend," a voice hollered at Dejur. The person was a tall Ru Paul sort with platinum dreadlocks. She/he hugged Dejur tight.

"Mazey, hey, what's up?" Dejur enthused.

"Girl, I got to give you the Four-one-one on that ho Sally."

Chainey tapped Dejur on the back. "I'm going to look around."

"Okay. Meet me back here in"—she looked at her watch—
"half hour?"

Snaking her way through the crowd, Chainey heard the trans-
vestite ask in a huffy tone who she was. Dejur's answer was lost
due to a Chemical Brothers' bumping beat. She wedged her way
to one of the bars, a door set horizontally on two sawhorses.

"What'll you have?" the bartender with green hair asked.

"Beer," Chainey said, pointing at a keg in a tub of ice. There
was bottled beer in another. She stood less chance of the stuff
being tampered with from the keg, she'd determined.

The bartender poured her brew and Chainey paid her two
dollars. She turned, looking over the happening, wondering
how the hell she'd gotten herself into this mess. By now Baker
was driving around with a hard-on to catch up to her. He might
already have the sanction from the Degaults to pop her, and
here she was sippin' and chillin' at an after-hours set.

People started whooping and hollering and she glanced in
the direction of the noise. Three women were on a raised platform of thick stacked plywood, dancing and entertaining the
crowd. One was hiking up her miniskirt to wild applause.
Another one went on her knees, miniskirt stepping over her,
bumping and grinding. The third one worked her top off, revealing healthy breasts that she flaunted to even more acclaim.
The act was a genuine crowd pleaser.

Even Chainey had to admit she was enthralled. If this was her
last night on earth, why not enjoy herself? Voyeuristically, she
pushed closer, getting into the spirit of the bacchanalia. Like
the others, she ogled the women and their show, and found herself getting high on the excitement. There was a palpable energy the gathering gave off. One of the women jumped into the
waiting hands of the crowd. She had stripped down to her
panties and was carried along to the periphery and then passed
back toward the platform.

At some point Chainey dropped her beer, but of course no
one had noticed. She helped hold the woman aloft and bumped
into another person in the process.

"Sorry about that," she shouted.

"Whatever," the other woman said, also lifting the seminaked woman along.

More people pressed forward. Chainey pivoted to get out of the crush. Then she happened to glance at the woman she'd just spoken to. The woman was doing the same. From this one's shocked expression, it was clear she knew who the courier was.

"Molly," Chainey mouthed.

A wary look replaced the surprise on the thief's face. She was of medium height, in tight cords and a loose flannel shirt. She might have a gun under that shirt, Chainey speculated. Her own piece was back in her car in San Francisco, but Molly couldn't be sure—yet.

Chainey tried to move forward. Her way was suddenly blocked as a new set of people had barged forward to enjoy the sexcapade. Molly took off in the other direction. No time for pleasantries as Chainey surged after her quarry with renewed vigor.

"Hey, watch it, bitch."

"Yo, slow your roll, girl."

"Be cool, fool."

The last speaker was a hefty number in a biker outfit. She got in Chainey's face and pushed her. "Apologize," she snarled.

"I'm sorry," Chainey said, decking her with a left hook. The biker stumbled into a knot of people, and some got the bright idea of transporting her aloft. Chainey continued eddying through the currents of bodies and got to the other side. There was an opening and she plunged through it as the happy biker was now having a good time working out on the platform.

Finding herself in a darkened recess, she proceeded cautiously. Molly had bolted to get to better ground. She was no more going to let Chainey go than she her. But she needed a weapon. There were several cardboard boxes with trash spilling out of them. She grabbed a bottle and went forward.

A body hurtled at her from the gloom and she almost brained a very drunk young woman.

"Hi," the drunkard said, holding herself up by spreading her fingers along the wall like Spiderwoman. She'd come from the restroom.

Chainey moved past and could now see a fire door propped partially open. She stepped to the cool metal and listened. The revelry mere yards away seemed like distant thunder. Her radar was tuned to what lay beyond that door. *Let's do it,* she decided, and kicked it open. The door slammed back against the outer wall, two rounds suddenly ricocheting off its surface.

Chainey had wisely hung back, pressed against the wall of the passageway. It probably didn't matter to Molly if it was her or someone else stepping through the exit when she'd fired. She was a cold-blooded predator who'd do anything to survive.

The tall woman looked out and could see the silhouettes of rectangular shapes among tall weeds and grass. It was a grave-yard of appliances, she guessed. She crept forward, keeping low. There was a crescent moon in the sky and its weak light bathed the field. Molly would have moved from where she'd been fir-ing. Playing the percentages, she'd bet her money the gun-woman was also seeking the most cover she could. Off at a right angle from the doorway was an angular array of what she sur-mised to be a clump of refrigerators. Would she hide there if she were Molly?

Chainey got another bottle and readied herself. She threw one at the refrigerators and another to the side of them. That got a few shots in the direction of the shattered glass, allowing the break for Chainey to scamper to the left across the field. Molly readjusted and correctly compensated, letting her shots loose toward where she estimated Chainey to be heading.

The absence of light and the discarded goods of con-sumerism provided enough barriers so the running woman wouldn't be cut down. She found shelter beside an indistinct form she hoped was solid enough to withstand bullets. Always ducking and dodging, she chastised herself.

Chainey sucked in air, blinking sweat from her eyes. She heard the unmistakable scurrying of rat claws moving over the objects all around her. She moved off, finally identifying the

thing she'd been crouched behind. It was an industrial air conditioner unit, squarish and squat. The red eyes of rats, pinholes
against a yellow background, stared at her from atop the dead
machinery.

Chainey knocked the rodent away. A wind had kicked up and
the smell of rusting metal cut the air. This was getting old; she
wasn't going to be a target for Molly again. With the conditions
as they were, she figured she had more of a chance to get the
drop on the woman. Chainey moved off, wondering how she
was going to compensate for a lack of fire power.

She halted beside another hulk, listening for the rustle of feet
in the tall weeds. Of course Molly must also be listening, but that
couldn't be helped. Groping the thing she was hiding behind,
Chainey locked on a rodlike piece. She tugged on it and felt it
lose its moorings. She pulled, but it wouldn't give. She got a foot
against the apparatus and pulled harder. Chainey fell to the
ground as the shaft came loose. The tall woman scrambled to a
kneeling position.

Holding the pole closer, she concluded that it was part of the
handle of a walk-in freezer locker. It had weight and made for
excellent head bashing. Now to get close enough to use it without getting drilled. Something crashed near her, and Chainey
instinctively went flat as a shot boomed. The flash came from
above. Molly must have climbed on one of the appliances in an
effort to try to locate Chainey. Her shot was way off the mark,
probably intended to see if she could make her opponent make
a sound.

Chainey crept forward in a straight line from the locker.
Molly would climb down, also moving around. Who was the cat
and who the mouse? she mused. Gun versus club, woman
against woman. She stopped, trying to separate out what little
sounds there were. A creak; what the hell was that? What was
Molly doing? *Move, Chainey, don't keep still.*

She went to the right, the outlines of the discards now easier
to distinguish against the marginally lighter night. There. Not
far. Some dry grass cracked. In that direction were various forms
of machinery, some upright and others listing. It was as if she

was viewing a city scape after a massive quake. And somewhere in that mass the way out of her predicament lay.

Chainey swung the handle at a refrigerator, causing a loud hollow bang to ring out. Molly wasn't going for it. No shot, no scuffling in the foxtails. Chainey went low and crawled toward the mass on all fours to make less of a target. A shot erupted from the mass, closer to where she was this time. But the flash told Chainey what she needed to know. She crawled some more, willing herself to be as silent as possible. Don't hurry; glide through the grass like a stalking animal, belly low to the ground, teeth bared for attack. Burs on the ground dug into her palms, and the aroma of rotting gear oil made her retch. A disturbance near her, rats? Molly also creeping around? Operating counter to her instincts, she kept in motion.

Again the disturbance and then the crackle of gunfire. The round whizzed by close this time. Chainey was already on her feet, chopping with the club at a rounded shape among the angular masses. Two more shots heated the space between Chainey and her quarry. Had she been standing in the same spot, Chainey would be dead. But she was already on the other woman, her makeshift weapon striking Molly solidly.

Molly grunted and Chainey, using the handle as if it was an ax, brought it down in a short stroke. The club smacked hard against the thief, and Molly's body went loose. Chainey brought up a knee and landed it in the woman's groin. *The gun, get the gun away from her,* Chainey screamed to herself. She dropped the club to free her other hand and leaped on Molly.

The two women crashed against hard, bulky objects, knocking some of the junk over. Chainey lost her balance but held on to Molly as she went over some goddamn piece of something. Molly punched Chainey, stunning her. A corner of whatever it was she'd fallen over was poking her in the back, making her wince in pain. She rolled to get free. That maneuver also allowed Molly to get free and she was up and running. Her gun must have been knocked from her hand as they tussled, Chainey hypothesized—correctly, she hoped.

She was also up and dashing after the fleeing figure. There

was only one place to run and that was toward the dim light spilling from the rear of the rave. Molly was easy to see now, and she could hear her even better. *Use those long legs of yours, Chainey. You don't smoke, you work out and you drink moderately; you can catch this decadent bitch. Move your ass, Chainey. What did Drew used to say? Effort is fine, but winning is better. Knees up, girl.*

They were almost to the door and Chainey left her feet, tackling the woman. Their bodies slammed to the ground, and Chainey had the upper hand. She socked Molly with as much force as she could deliver, causing a satisfying "ugh." Then she jumped up, preparing to kick her in the ribs.

"Yo, y'all need to take this 'round-the-way ruckus somewhere else, hothead," a woman in a baritone voice yelled. The owner with the bass had two meat-and-gristle mitts to match and put them roughly on Chainey.

"Get the fuck out of this." She tried futilely to slap the hands away.

"I'll get the fuck in what I feel like." Baritone was a good-size black woman in overalls, a lit cigar in a corner of her mouth. The newcomer stepped through the doorway. She smelled of whiskey and smoke, and she didn't seem like the type to back down.

"She, she attacked me," Molly whined, having got to her feet. Her eyes were wide with pretend fear.

"Oh, please," Chainey began, grabbing for the killer.

The bruiser in overalls interceded. "Naw," she exclaimed, huffing in front of Chainey. "It's bitches like you that give the cops an excuse to roust us. You probably got kids and an old man in Daly City and think you can get all ghetto when you want to muff dive."

Molly was making for the passageway, a smirk on her face.

"This is a private matter," Chainey retorted.

"Then take y'all's beef somewhere else, way the fuck from here." The big woman rolled the cigar around in her mouth like a drill sergeant.

Chainey tried to force her way past Baritone, but she was quick and not as fat as she appeared.

She put a bear hug on Chainey and Molly bolted, giving her the finger as she did so. "I said be cool," Baritone repeated.

"You're really getting on my nerves, you know that?" Chainey delivered twin chops with the flats of her hands on the woman's sides. She winced, her hold loosening. Chainey flexed and got free. She backed up as the big woman came forward. Chainey went low, and using a modified judo move, flipped her temporary opponent on her back. She was already through the door, the woman squawking as she rose from the ground.

Chainey dashed on into the club, only to run into Dejur. "Hey, I was wondering if you left me for another prospect." The pupils of her eyes were small.

"Did you see Molly?" Chainey asked, not stopping for her answer.

"Damn," she exclaimed, "somebody ran through here causing a commotion, but I was on the other side of the room. Shit, I'm sorry, Chainey."

Chainey was already bulldozing through the crowd but was pretty sure it was a useless effort. She got outside, where people were milling about, smoking and talking.

"You see a woman rush out of here, short blond hair, in cords?"

"Cute ass?" a woman asked, dragging on a clove cigarette.

Chainey nodded. Baritone showed up, too, out of breath.

"She climbed into a car and split." She glanced from Chainey to the big woman, then back to Chainey. "Girlfriend?"

"Bosom buddies," the courier said.

Dejur also arrived, an eager expression mixing with her high state. "Well?"

Baritone was unsure of what her role was now. She chewed on her cheroot, eyeballing Chainey.

Chainey asked the woman smoking a cigarette, "Can you tell me what kind of car?"

"One with four wheels, baby. I don't know jack about cars. Sorry."

Chainey put a hand on Dejur's shoulder. "I'll drive you home," she said to an obviously drunk Dejur.

CHAPTER ELEVEN

Chainey dropped Dejur off at her place on Larkin, near the St. Francis Hospital complex. Her new friend mumbled that she could use the truck, and the courier went back to the hospital where Zora Blanchard was recuperating. This was as quiet a locale to retrace her steps as any. Baker would have gotten to the house by now and searched it thoroughly. One of the factors in her favor was that he underestimated her, but she didn't slight his abilities. She knew he was a cunning and resourceful bastard, though it was unlikely that he'd discover where Blanchard had been taken for several more hours.

What wasn't clear was the Molly Zevonian question. Would she show up once she found out her sponsor was wounded? From all indications, theirs was a one-way love affair, but maybe that was part of the deal, too. Maybe Blanchard got hot on the butchness of her ex-sister-in-law and put up with so much because she wanted it so bad.

Sex, like gambling, was a hellified habit, her old friend Wilson McAndrews had pontificated more than once. "Weaning yourself off one or the other is a back-breaking job 'cause sure as shit that urge is bone deep," he'd gone on. "And if you have both addictions . . . well, then, son, just blow your brains out now to save yourself all the grief and hand-wringin'."

He'd laugh that way-back-from-the-country laugh of his and
pull her close—her on his lap and oft times a tumbler of C & C
in his hand. She filed the memory away, the present demanding
her full attention. Checking her watch, she assumed the place
was shut down save for a skeleton crew this time of the early
morning. The doctor she'd jacked would have been discovered
and a police report taken. Her description would be floating
around for a few days, so maintaining a low profile as far as the
law was concerned was paramount.

Using a pay phone across the street from the clinic, a
recorded number informed her that the facility, barring emergencies, would be open again at eight that A.M. Holding back a
yawn, she returned to the truck and drove off. She went back to
Blanchard's house and let herself in. She looked around and
was surprised. It didn't seem that Baker had been inside. Maybe
he never got free of the cops; Degault could have been so mad
he didn't get him a mouthpiece.

She used the shower's cold water to wake herself up.
Afterward she smeared her prints on the tile with the washcloth.
Chainey then slipped from the house, careful not to be seen.
Driving fast, she took the truck back to Dejur's place, even
though the partygoer had said Chainey could use it till morning. She slipped into the woman's apartment. It was sparsely
decorated in what might be called Turkish prison sublime. A
few seventies-era Fillmore posters broke up the plainness. A
nude Dejur was sprawled across her bed, snoring, the clothes
she'd kicked off leading a trial to her.

Chainey left the truck keys on the dresser. From there she
called a cab and was driven back to her rental. Despite herself,
fatigue was beginning to overtake her and she had to rest. No
sense getting so worn out she'd be no good to herself when she
needed to be sharp.

Back to Blanchard's house again. It was now past three in the
morning. A light fog had materialized and Chainey's feet were
heavy as she got to the door. The alarm was off, as it had been
left, and the door locked. But she heard a bump behind the
door. Baker?

Alert, she went back to her car and fetched her gun. She went around the house, looking into the windows. There. She saw a flashlight beam. She could confront Baker, but to what end? She was as much an intruder as he was, and why try to interfere with him anyway? If he turned up a lead to Molly, that was all to the good. If he got Zevonian, the Degaults still had their culprit and she was off the hook.

She watched, crouching low in a set of plants beneath one of the side windows. Waiting there, Chainey worked a kink out of her neck. As she looked up, she saw the flash of a beam on an upstairs window. She looked through the bottom window where she was and got a brief glimpse of a beam as its owner swept it over a room. There were two people in the house. Baker and a partner seemed unlikely. The Afrikaaner worked alone.

She went back to her car and repositioned it around the side, off the study where the French windows were. Given that this was the spot you could leave without being seen from the street, she guessed the sneaks would use it for their exit. Could be your regular antisocial neighborhood burglars in there, she mused.

Sitting in the seat felt too relaxing. Even with the window down and the cold night coming in, she was yawning and blinking her eyes rapidly. But she perked up when she saw Vern Sixkiller and his factotum, Leopold, emerge through the French windows. They proceeded to creep across the tended lawn of the house.

The two got in a dull-colored Buick and scooted away. Chainey took off after them. There was a better chance of her being spotted this time of the early day, with little traffic around, but that couldn't be helped. The two men followed a route to the freeway. Soon Chainey had a notion where they might be going. Sure enough, the car wound its way into Richmond.

Chainey took a different exit than the one she'd taken earlier. She got to Gilbarth's ahead of the two. Anxiety made her head hurt. She might have guessed wrong. Five minutes later, the Buick showed up on the dead-end street. Chainey was parked the wrong way, the nose of her car pointing out toward the street on the same side as Apex. Their vehicle slowed to a stop. The two got out.

Out on the street were four men who probably weren't contemplating civic improvement schemes. The quartet were lingering in front of the recycling place, as if such was a natural thing to do past four in the morning. Two of them drifted toward Sixkiller and Leopold. There were words; the two American Indians had their back to Chainey's position. The two men floated back to their comrades, no doubt being convinced easier pickings could be had with patience.

Sixkiller and Leopold looked around, seeking some egress into the Apex building. They disappeared down a narrow passageway. Chainey stretched. Sitting in a car or getting shot at were both habits she'd be glad to break. Sixkiller and Leopold rushed from the passageway as an alarm louder than the Tower of Babel scorched the air.

The duo split, Chainey right behind them. Back on the freeway, she thought Sixkiller, who was driving, had spotted her. He'd sped up, and she'd had to match him. Fortunately there were trucks and some commuters out now. Her car didn't stick out so much as she kept pace. Eventually they arrived at a roadside motel back in Oakland. Chainey rolled up as the two entered separate rooms off the open courtyard.

She parked and analyzed the situation. Baker was sent by the Degaults to track her and, presumably, find out who nabbed the swag. Vern was on the case because his tribe assumed the Vegas association had done their boys in. Then why was he up north when it made sense for him to be in the Capital of Sin?

The woman at the gift shop had told him Blanchard had the half-track towed to The Ascension. Could be she knew Sixkiller from way back. Did that mean that Sixkiller was in on the robbery? Had he been double-crossed by his partners Magic Molly and her tolerant husband?

If she was real tough, Chainey told herself jokingly, she'd break into Sixkiller's room and beat it out of him. Well, that wasn't going to happen. And waiting around for S and L to get moving again would consume a large amount on time. Plus, it was more likely they'd spot her the more she drove around after the two.

Still, she needed a line on Zevonian. She might already be in transit, but where to? The only possible help was Dejur. She had to talk to her again, Molly might have inadvertently dropped a name or made a reference to where she went when she wasn't in town. It was getting close to dawn; maybe girlfriend had slept off some of what she'd imbibed.

Chainey got back to the woman's place, a baronial Victorian that had been segmented into smaller apartments. "Shit," she cursed arriving on the doorstep.

She'd returned the keys and couldn't let herself back in. There was a wire mesh screen door built cagelike over an older vestibule that contained a wooden door with a large glass pane. White linen curtains were behind the pane. She leaned on the buzzer to Dejur's apartment but got no response. Pressing it again, she could see shadows moving behind the curtain. An early riser on the way to work, she reasoned.

The door opened, and it was Dejur. Next to her was a man with a cap on, head down, mumbling words to her. He jerked her arm with force, like a teacher who's lost patience with an obstreperous student. Dejur's eyes got wide upon seeing Chainey. The courier quickly stepped to the side, turning her body as the wire mesh door was thrown open by the man.

From the angle she was at, Chainey was beside Dejur, the man on her other side. "Yo, Dejur, what's going on, lady?"

The man looked at her, recognition setting his mouth in a scowl. It was Molly's husband, the one called Stan. Dejur elbowed him in the face, causing him to let her go. He staggered back, the knife he'd been pressing against Dejur still in his hand.

Chainey brought up her gun and fired at him. She refused to second guess herself; she had to be hard-hearted and take this fool down.

Stan threw the blade. It bounced off stone as Chainey got out of the way. The man was already jumping into the vestibule's cage, going low.

"Gun," Chainey yelled as Stan produced a piece.

She and Dejur ran around the nearby corner of the building as he returned fire. Visibility was good thanks to street lamps and the burgeoning sunrise.

"I'm sure glad you showed up." Another bullet sent particles of concrete dust into the air as it sunk into the building.

Chainey was trying to get a glimpse of his arm or body. He was using the cage effectively to peek around and get off a shot or two. "I'm getting awfully tired of this family trying to kill me," she muttered.

The idea that they couldn't blast each other all day without a cop showing up must have occurred to both of the shooters at the same time. Molly's husband let off three more rounds in rapid succession, keeping Chainey pressed back. She heard footfalls going away. She peeped around the corner to see him jetting away downhill.

"Not the third time," Chainey declared, already putting her body in motion.

"I'll help," Dejur said, running up to and passing Chainey.

The man had rounded the far corner and Chainey yelled to the swifter Dejur, "Stop, he might be waiting."

As if he'd been in the wings anticipating his signal, the man appeared from around the building, shooting stance crouch, gun rigidly extended. Dejur dove for cover behind a parked car. But she wasn't his target. You always go for the bigger threat first if you can. He fired at Chainey as she fired at him. As she'd warned the other woman, she'd gone flat, rolling into the recessed doorway of another apartment building.

The man had ducked back and the gunfire ceased. Chainey strained to hear sirens but couldn't detect any. That didn't mean cop cars weren't on their way, though. Nothing happened for several moments, Dejur and Chainey alternately staring at each other or the corner.

Chainey left the doorway, hugging the side of the building with her back as she wormed her way toward the corner. She motioned for Dejur to stay put. *Make a sound you bastard,* she pleaded to no particular deity. She stopped, expecting him to pop up any second. She went along haltingly again, the grip of her gun clammy in her hand.

About two feet from the corner she came to a dead stop. She held her breath, willing the man to show himself. *Wait, wait . . . come on, do something.* Chainey raced around the corner and almost fired at a fire hydrant, thinking that was him squatting. Involuntarily she grimaced, expecting to be rocked by a shot to her abdomen. The street was quiet, cars parked at the curbs but no taxis, no buses going by. He didn't leave; he couldn't. Molly Zevonian had sent him to find Dejur because she knew something.

Dejur started to walk over.

"Stay back," Chainey said without looking around. "He's not gone." There was an alleyway midway down the other side of the street. There were homes he might have barged his way into, but that was too risky, too complicated. *Where are you, asshole?* He wanted her to search for him because he was sure she couldn't let him get away again either.

"Chainey—"

She held up a hand for Dejur to keep quiet. And then wouldn't you know it, two police cars arrived down the block from where she stood. Their reds and blues swirled atop the vehicles, sans sirens. Chainey had her gun at her side. She wiped it against her pants and simply released the gun from her fingers, letting it drop to the sidewalk. If she'd have tried to throw it or hide the gat, the motion would have been noticed.

"Cops," she yelled to Dejur. She ran into the middle of the street, waving her arms—the ideal target. The man could easily cut her down from wherever he was hiding. But he'd give himself away and then be chased by the SFPD.

"Oh, thank God you came." Chainey kept waving her arms to let them know she wasn't packing.

"Stand still," the officer in the passenger seat demanded over the car's loudspeaker. "What happened?" His car and the other were now stopped in the street, each angling in on her form.

"Me and my girlfriend were coming back from a club and this guy jumped us." She turned and gestured for Dejur to join her.

The other woman had already been standing up, looking at what Chainey was doing. Tentatively she came forward. "The fuck took my purse, all my cards and everything in it."

Chainey didn't dare whisper anything to her, and she hoped she'd follow her lead. "Isn't that right, honey?" She put an arm around her shoulders.

"Yes, yes, that's so," Dejur stammered. Her expression was so classic, Chainey had to hold back a laugh.

The cops were out of the cruisers. One handled a shotgun, the other three handguns. All four of the items of firepower were pointed in their general direction. And eight weary cop eyes regarded them suspiciously.

If the two were separated and grilled, Molly's husband would get away for sure. "He's still around here," Chainey blurted. "He dropped his gun right there." She pointed at the hydrant.

One of the cops walked over to the spot and looked around. He spotted the gun and called back in the affirmative.

Two of the others started surveying the area with interest. The fourth, a sergeant whose nametag read REESE, said, "What's this clown look like?" He had a bushy mustache he stroked as he talked.

Chainey gave an accurate description of the hiding man.

"If you don't mind, for your own safety, can I have you two wait in the squad cars?" Reese asked too nicely.

It was a move to separate them to make sure they couldn't co-ordinate their story. She laced the fingers on her hand with Dejur's. Together she led the way to one of the squad cars. "Tell the same thing over and over," she whispered, leaning in close to Dejur, as if she was comforting her.

"If you would, each in a different car, please," Reese elaborated.

Silently the two got in their respective vehicles while three of the cops fanned out. Reese called for backup. Straightening up, he glanced in at Chainey. "You seem to have calmed down considerably."

"Must be shock," she ad-libbed.

He stroked his mustache and got busy.

Chainey clenched and unclenched her fists. She could feel Dejur's stare boring into her and she turned her head, giving her the high sign. The other woman started to pantomime something. Chainey frowned and made a cut gesture with her hand across her throat. She tried to settle back but was too anxious, too close to getting a hook on the scratch not to be walking the razors.

Of course there was the small problem of whether, if the law should find and arrest the husband, how could she sweat him? The guy would go dumb and not cop to anything, anyway. There might be a computer trail linking him to some suspected hits, and the feds might even get in on the act. If that happened, he'd be totally inaccessible to her. And with her play pals Baker, Vern and Leopold sniffing around, things would really get unpleasant.

"Halt, goddammit, stop," one of the cops yelled.

Chainey jerked around, trying to locate the source of the sound. Reese came running from around the near corner. Two other police cars screeched into view from down the hill. There was a shot, and the man bolted from the alleyway midway down the block. Two uniforms were on him like a cheap suit.

He vaulted and rolled over the hood of one of the newly arrived cop cars. The driver was out, and as the man landed on that side of the car, he shot the cop. He yanked the officer out of the way and jumped into the driver's seat.

Chainey could hotwire the cop car she was in, but that would only convince them she was an accomplice. The man now commanded the stolen vehicle and was bearing down hard on the corner, past her. Reese was firing at the car but hadn't stopped the man's flight. The man saw Chainey and fired his gun at her, destroying the driver's side window.

Having anticipated this, Chainey had gotten herself out of the car, ducking and moving. One of the bullets went through the car's rear door, whizzing just above her head. It buried itself in the backseat's upholstery. The cruiser careened past, almost cornering on two wheels. The man skillfully negotiated the turn and was straightening out when his windshield disintegrated in a fulmination of brain and glass particles.

Unguided, the cop car slammed into a passing Muni bus. The larger vehicle's antenna connecting it to its overhead powerline slipped its track as the bus went sideways. The car's radiator was ruined, and steam rose from the front end as sparks showered down from above. The effect of the twinkling lights in the mist lent an eerie atmosphere as the police officers descended on the driver, their guns locked and on target.

"Goddamn," Dejur summed up, standing next to the police car she'd been sitting in.

Chainey was tempted to walk over, too, but knew that would at minimum get her cuffed and at maximum get her shot by a nervous officer. The cop with the shotgun—the one who had shot at the car as it completed its turn—peeked into the passenger-side window. He straightened and gave a thumbs-up sign. Chainey had just rolled craps.

The shaken but uninjured Muni bus driver was taken away in a supervisor's car. She had been in the process of starting her route and was the sole occupant of the conveyance. And so the SFPD faced one less lawsuit from irate and possibly injured citizenry.

The would-be escapee was bagged and tagged and carted away by the ME's office a little after 9:30 A.M. The live morning broadcast crews had arrived at some point in the blur of events and were still around as Chainey and Dejur, separately, recounted their stories several times in the field. One of the interrogating inspectors, Sorenson, was a beer-bellied individual with a gas problem. He made constant grumblings about taking the women in and "getting to the fuckin' bottom of this mess."

But Chainey's one, never-varied account apparently played well with Dejur's more flighty version. Had both been the same, there would have been more than grumbling. The basics, though, were consistent.

The two had a few minutes to go over a rough version of the tale as the cops had been busy with the dead shooter, the car and the bus. And Chainey gave her a fake name to tell the cops. It was a false name with a background that would show up once the cops ran it through their R & I. She'd also told them her purse had been taken by the assailant, and who knew what he'd done with it?

"We'll be back to talk with you once we have an ID on the fella," Sorenson announced to the two women.

"We'll be around," Chainey said cheerfully.

There was another eruption in Sorenson's gut that he talked over. "You make sure about that, Stretch." He ambled away and got into his unmarked car. He tossed an empty coffee cup out of the window and took off.

"I need to take a nap," Dejur said.

"Sorry about all this." Chainey walked with her back to her apartment.

At the mesh door Dejur paused. "Am I gonna get another visitor?"

Molly had probably seen the morning news. They didn't have a name to go with what little remained of his head. But the news had given the area of the shooting, and she'd make the connection.

"No," Chainey said, "she'll want to settle accounts with me."

"You didn't kill her husband."

"I don't think that distinction matters to Molly." They were walking up to her apartment. Several cops were still lingering about, and she couldn't break her cover now.

Dejur didn't misinterpret Chainey's intentions. "You can do whatever you like until they leave." She unlocked the door. Sorenson had asked in the way that cops do, which is actually a demand, to "look the place over." He was hoping to find a meth lab in the kitchen, or cash in a plastic bag in the closet; anything to account for the gunman singling them out. Chainey had firmly declined and Dejur had backed her up.

She knew the purported missing purse with "all her ID" stuck in his craw, but what could Sorenson counter with? The guy threw the purse away; it wasn't her fault that only the knife turned up when the officers fine-toothed the landscape. And the cop with the rumbling gut had complained aloud about how the shooter had missed the two women, what with them being unarmed and all. He got a hunch of shoulders for his curiosity. And it would take a day or so for ballistics to confirm that the spent shell casings and bullets were from two different guns.

Dejur took off her shirt, holding it over her shoulder à lá a Frank Sinatra pose with his suit coat. She stood there, in jeans and nothing else. "You sure you want to get on the road? Something about getting your life threatened makes a girl tingly all over."

Chainey touched the other woman's face. "I'm flattered."

Dejur kissed her palm. "Thanks for saving my life, Chainey."

"You can return the favor. What the hell did he say to you?"

A piquancy clouded her features but the emotion passed. "He used your name, said he was supposed to deliver a packet from you. What did I know, you're one action-packed gal, man."

"And did he take anything with him when he was up here?"

She shook her head in the negative. "He was only interested in hustling me out of here like pronto."

Chainey wondered if Molly had been close by. No, she hadn't rushed to his aid, and it did seem that the only person she was loyal to was him. "She'd spotted you at the rave, but why send him after you afterward?"

"Revenge, or to make sure I didn't tell anyone else about her?" Dejur had walked into her bedroom and was slipping out of her clothes—the door open.

Chainey looked out the window as the heavy-duty tow truck hoisted the crippled bus. "No, what's the percentage in that, Dejur? What's done is done. Molly knows about me, knows I'm not turning anything I know over to the cops."

Dejur leaned on the door, yawning. Her muscular, coppery legs protruded below a short pink T-shirt. "One of these days, you'll have to tell me who you really are and what you really do."

Chainey put the window to her back, folding her arms. "Somebody else I know said that to me recently. There must be another reason she wanted you, ah—"

"Dead," Dejur added. "Or maybe she wanted to beat me up to find out what I knew about you."

"That might be part of the answer." Otherwise the man would have simply killed Dejur in her apartment rather than kidnap her. But it nagged at Chainey that Zevonian wasn't operating totally in the dark concerning her. And what with Vern Sixkiller, Leopold and Baker out and about, there were too many players in orbit for there not to be hidden connections. "Come on, you'll sleep better if you can think of anything else."

She stamped her foot like a kid and said, "I'm tired, dammit."

Chainey held her arms wide, a big grin on her face. "Please."

"Agghhh. Look, Molly and me got it on a few times and it ain't like she sent me a postcard or love letter. . . ." She pointed at the tall woman, shaking a finger. "Hold on." She went into the bedroom and drawers could be heard sliding open and closed. She returned, leafing through a leatherette address book thick with papers. "Here it is," she said victoriously. She handed Chainey a scrap of paper.

It was a piece of a check deposit slip. On the torn section was the name of a company, APB Enterprises, and a POB. The city was Henderson. Over it a phone number had been hand-printed. Blanchard's number, Chainey noted.

"She gave me that the night, well, after the night we spent together here." Dejur blushed. "She said I was terrific and we'd have to get back together. Jenny, Molly, whoever, told me to call her."

"Why wouldn't she just call you?"

Dejur made a funny face. "I was having a little cash flow problem then. My phone had been cut off." She said seductively, "I told you, Chainey, once I put my good thing on my lovers, they can't get enough."

"Thanks, Dejur." She kissed her on the cheek and they hugged.

"You ever coming back this way, Good-looking?"

"Who can say?" She left, made a call and got lunch at a diner in China Basin. Matters had come full circle, and the trial apparently was taking her back to her old stomping grounds. She'd called Mooch and he would run down this APB Enterprises. No doubt one of the front identities Molly maintained. But if that was so, why go to all the bother of attempting to snatch Dejur? Could be that APB was one of Molly's drops, a place she received her money and assignments. What would be the chance that leaving her local number on the slip would ever come back to bite her in the ass?

Chainey had her head propped in her hand, her elbow on the table in the diner. She dozed and snapped awake, realizing she'd been going strong for more than twenty-four hours. Though time was slipping away, she had to rest. She rose, placing bills on the Formica, and headed to her car. Her intention was to get a room, rest up and then probably head back to Vegas. By then Mooch would have whatever information there was to have.

Once she was driving it occurred to her that she wanted to know about Blanchard. That is, had Baker or Vern and his second skin been by? She didn't think Molly would show at the clinic, but no sense letting it go without trying to find out. She called from a pay phone, but whoever answered didn't know much of what was going on. Hanging up, she decided to go for broke. The doctor she accosted would have gone home by now, having been rattled, and given the less hectic demands of the private facility. What were the chances there'd be a sketch of her plastered all over the place? At least the cops this morning hadn't been looking for her.

She bought flowers and drove to the hospital. The facility was a smoothly functioning organic machine as Chainey walked inside. The guard on duty wasn't the same man as last night, and there was a different traffic manager, too. He was a medium-built man in an open-collared checked shirt. Several thin silver and gold bracelets were on one of his wrists, and the sleeves of his shirt were rolled back to his forearms.

"Excuse me," she said, gliding up to the front desk. "I just got word that my dear friend Zora Blanchard was involved in some sort of incident."

The man looked toward a computer screen, rapidly moving several fingers over a keyboard. "Yes," he drawled, "Mrs. Blanchard had successful surgery but is in the I.C.U. under heavy sedation." A well-practiced concerned look set his fair features as he looked up at her. "Unless you're immediate family, I'm afraid I can't let you see her right now."

"That's okay," she said. "Is it possible to leave my flowers?"

"Yes, I can take those," he said without the slightest sound of being put-upon in his voice. He rose and accepted the bouquet. He wrote on a Post-it and put it on them. "I'll see that these are placed in her room within the next hour."

"Thanks a lot." She turned and began to walk out. Then she suddenly stopped, as if remembering something else. "I was just wondering," she called from the doorway, "has another visitor come by, a big man with a mustache and a thick accent?"

"Yes, he was here not more than an hour ago," the receptionist confirmed. "Do you know him?"

"An acquaintance," she fudged. "I was hoping to run into him." She moved back toward the desk, an expectant look on her face.

"I'm afraid he didn't say what time he'd be back, ma'am. I told him the same as I told you. He left."

"I appreciate your time."

"Not a problem."

Chainey got back into her rental and, after checking, found a flight out of Oakland that was available. So much for sleep. On the plane to Vegas, she used the onboard phone and called Mooch.

"*Chica,*" he rushed out as soon as he came on the line, "where you calling from?"

She told him. "Why?"

"Because this phone is secure, and I wanted to make sure yours was safe, too."

"What's up, Mooch?" The plane hit an air pocket and Chainey got a sinking feeling in her stomach. It was Mooch's tone that was getting to her.

"I already knew what APB was when I got your fax. And you shouldn't be surprised to learn that the Degaults know about it, too."

"Shit." The man in the seat beside her turned his head, then turned back to face the front. "I can't say that's too big of a surprise."

"It doesn't mean what we think it might mean," Mooch went on.

"Yeah, I realize that," she added, taking care to speak in a lower tone. "It might mean she and her dead partner had some inside information and made use of it. Or the right hand doesn't know what the left hand is doing inside the Degault offices."

"Don't forget, Baker could be working his own brand of South African voodoo in this stew."

"You have a point. Sixkiller was crawling around the Bay Area."

"Give me your arrival time. I'll pick you up."

It was serious if Mooch through his own volition was going to give her a lift. She gave him the information and replaced the phone. The sun was getting low on the horizon, but there were more than three hours of daylight left. Plenty of time to stir up more trouble. And more than enough time to get herself buried head first in the desert floor.

CHAPTER TWELVE

It was only after getting into Maltazar's sleek new Jaguar S-Type that it occurred to her this could be the proverbial "taken for a ride" bit. That was how it happened, right? Wasn't that the way they whacked Joe Pesci's character in *Goodfellas?* All this time he's lusting after being a made man, and lo and behold, that day arrives. Only what it really winds up being is a trip to a cornfield where he's beaten to death with baseball bats, stripped and dumped into a ditch. Damn. Good thing she showered earlier.

"You with me, Martha?" Ibrahim Ferrer, the rediscovered Cubano ballad singer, was crooning "Nuestra Ultima Cita" over the car's stereo.

"Been a long day, Mooch." She snuck a glance at the backseat to alleviate her anxiety. "What do you think I've stumbled onto?" The car worked itself into the flow of other vehicles along Tropicana Avenue.

"Frankly, that's what's got my left eye twitching, *chica.*"

"You're the one who says not knowing how the players are playing is not the game you should stay in," Chainey said.

He turned down Ferrer. "I guess the curse of living until your hands are dotted with liver spots is having your words haunt you." He maneuvered the car into the center lane to get out of the slower right lanes as people headed toward the MGM Grand.

"We got to find this crazy broad who likes to shoot up people."

Chainey pointed at her chest. "You mean *I* have to."

A large flat-bed truck wheeled past. Laid out in the back was part of a massive neon sign that depicted a pig humping a lightning bolt. The pig was smiling.

"I can assure you," Mooch replied, "you don't want to rely on my shaky hand for accuracy."

"Don't kid me, *jefe maximo,* I know you're plotting the moves on the chessboards yet to be set up."

"Is that it, Martha? You think I'd feed you to the great whites if I thought it would untangle the business from this mess?"

"Honestly, yes."

Maltazar shook his head as if were on a swivel bearing. "I can't believe how cynical you've become."

Was this part of the pitch? Was she supposed to be suckered into seeing him as the big daddy who'd take care of everything? Maybe Mooch was feeling out whether she and Molly had been in on this together and had now fallen out. Then he could be in a position to get a taste of the loot and still turn her over to the Degaults.

"Has Baker returned?" she asked.

"I haven't heard, and I do have a few of my ears to the ground." He glared at her through his large-framed glasses. "Open the glove compartment."

She imagined an Austin Powers–like booby trap where a mechanical hand came out and shot her with a poisoned dart. Instead, she removed a nine-by-twelve gray envelope.

"Particulars on our Molly Zevonian."

Chainey turned on the dome light and looked through the material. Some of the information she'd reviewed in the Bay Area, and the rest was new to her. Stan was an alias. His real name was Elwood Porter.

"Why is Porter's name familiar?" she asked, rereading his

physical description next to an old booking photo. It was the man who'd attempted to kidnap Dejur.

"The Porter brothers," Mooch illuminated. "They were newly minted legends when you got to town, Martha. Those two were hellions from Texas City, Texas, and did bone-breaking for the Gambinos out this way."

"And he was, what, the son of one of them?"

"Yeah, Elwood was Bryce's boy, taking up where his father left off."

Mooch drove the car on into north Vegas. Away from the constant pulse of the Strip's lights and sound, this part of town looked like any other city on the fast road of mass tract housing development. Every day it seemed as if well-heeled town house enclaves with precious names like Shadow Pines or Diamond Spur were sprouting whole from the desert. But what was Vegas if not a paean to dreams on the half shell? And in the new century, Vegas had also become the fabled city at the end of the technicolor rainbow.

"We headed to APB?" Chainey found it ironic that she could rhapsodize about all the new development when her own subdivision wasn't yet a decade old. But here in the capital of gambling, ten years was a long, long time.

"APB is run by a friend of mine, Ethel. I've known her from the old days." The Jag had crossed into Henderson.

"You must," Chainey remarked. "Nobody names their children that anymore."

"They did when 'I Love Lucy' was all the rage, am I right?"

"*Sí*, Señor Maltazar."

APB was a drop. It was inside a private club off a side road on the outskirts leading to Boulder City. The club, the Blue Parrot, was known to Chainey.

"I'll be damned, it figures," she said as they got near the place. "They've done some remodeling since I was here last," she noted.

"Ethel Franz was friends with McAndrews, by the way." Mooch pulled to a stop beside a Highway Patrol car. Several other cars, pickups and a few limos, were also parked around the three-story building. The structure was a mixture of Beaux Arts, Roman, Renaissance and Medieval—the usual mishmash of architecture à la Vegas.

Mooch and Chainey walked toward the entrance. "It makes sense the Blue Parrot would be where you'd find APB Enterprises," she said. "This place has been around since the seventies, and I bet it was used as a drop by the Porters."

"Among others," he answered with a twinkle in his bird-of-prey eyes. He tugged on one of the double giant maple wood doors and the portal swung outward on hydraulic hinges.

"Mooch." A woman with large biceps dressed in a vest and black slit mini greeted him. "This the wife?"

"Martha Chainey, one of my best freight handlers."

"Pleased. I'm Steelo." She extended a hand with a weight lifter's glove on it.

"A pleasure back," Chainey replied, taking in the surroundings. On the opposite side of the doorway was a male bouncer clad in a business suit. He was svelte to her chunky. What he lacked in brawn he apparently compensated for with the gun she could tell was tucked inside his coat.

"Come on. Madame Franz is expecting us." Mooch led the way to a staircase.

Through an open doorway Chainey spied a small group crowded around a craps table. A Highway Patrolman was rolling the dice. The decor of the room was Edwardian. The waitresses wore silk top hats and the briefest of outfits. The two went up to the second floor. On the landing was another bouncer duo who also greeted Maltazar.

"So this is where you do your gambling," Chainey surmised.

Mooch nodded slightly as they moved past another room open to the hallway. In this one, the decorating was retro sixties bachelor pad. There were several poker tables going. The women serving in here wore form-fitting dresses with plunging necklines. Their hair was a mix of beehive and page boy.

"One more." Mooch pointed to yet another stairway.

The third floor contained four bouncers sitting around. All

the doors on this floor along both hallways were closed. "Naturally," Chainey said, wearing a crooked smile.

"Shh, people are working." Mooch winked.

The bouncers acknowledged the two and let them pass. At the end of the longer hallway was another set of double doors. These were painted in glossy black with oversize golden knobs. On each side of the doorway were modern columns done as twisted metal slabs. And what appeared to be water flowed in continuous thin sheets across their respective polished surfaces, disappearing into slots in the floor.

They entered the office to find the boss talking on the phone. She waved for the duo to take a seat. The pair sat in chairs that looked as if they'd been removed from the Luxor's lobby. The room was done up in Egyptian decor, at least by way of a DreamWorks production. Purple-and-gold-trimmed curtains hung over the windows and there was a cockatiel in an ornate birdcage in the corner.

"Yes, I'll have Herman deliver it tomorrow before ten." Ethel Franz was in her sixties and still a handsome woman. She wore a dark blue pantsuit and her dark hair was pulled back in a pony-tail. She replaced the handset.

"Mooch, what say you?" She settled back in her chair, her arms held wide open.

"We need a line on this wild chick."

"*Puro?*" she said, using the Cuban slang for cigar. She stood and slid a teak humidor toward the older man. "And you're Chainey, right? Want anything to drink?"

"I'm fine."

"Ethel, if we could . . ." Mooch indicated for her to take her seat again. He did take out a Padron cigar and roll it around unlit in his fingers. "We need a line on Zevonian."

Franz swiveled back and forth in her chair. "As I said, you gotta convince me that breaking my word is in my greater inter-est. You know those from the old school use my drop 'cause they're guaranteed confidentiality."

"Molly Zevonian isn't honoring anything, and she will come gunning for you," Chainey told the older woman.

She aimed a silvery pink nail at the younger woman. "What makes you Kreskin?"

"I'm the reason her old man got killed, and she's going to shut down any link leading back to her."

Franz tucked in her bottom lip, and ran the tip of her tongue over the flesh. "That kinda gives the old man a new wrinkle, now don't it? Of course you're making the argument it's you she's going to take off this earth, not me."

"There's no argument there," Chainey fatalistically agreed. "The question is, which will she see as an easier task to accomplish, and in what order."

"I've bunkered down here before, young lady," Ethel Franz said archly. "I've weathered *hombres* and *muchachas* much tougher and more cunning than Molly. Though I will admit she is the headstrong sort when she puts her mind to it." Her eyes got a faraway look, then refocused on the two before her.

"You know her, you have some sense of how she thinks, how she operates," Chainey retorted. "She's already tried to kidnap someone else who she thought would be a connection to her."

Franz looked at Maltazar for his input.

"Martha's on the level," he said. "Nobody's going to see you as a rat on this, Ethel. This Molly is a problem who's not going to go away. She's not a team player."

Franz snorted. "That's cute, Mooch. But from what I understand, this is a business matter between you two and the Degaults." She raised a plucked eyebrow. "It's all over town, Mooch, you know how it is. Rumors and whispered words, this one says it's this, that one says it's that. But anytime you got that lummox Baker prowling around, then the Indians, then I get your call . . . well, you see my meaning."

Chainey was going to say something, but Maltazar made signals for her to be quiet. He rolled the cigar between his long finger and thumb, studying the movement. "What you say is correct. This is a matter between us and them. Yet what remains is that Molly and her crew ripped off a shipment she should have had no knowledge of whatsoever."

"These things happen," Franz remarked.

"They do, they do," Mooch acknowledged.

Maltazar leaned forward, biting off the end of the cigar and putting the discard in a heavy glass ashtray. "But here it is." He finally put the cigar in his mouth and Franz lit it with a lighter designed as a miniature Louis XIV coach. "Let's say Molly is partnered with one of the—oh, how shall I call them?" Maltazar made a circular motion with his hand.

"One of the intimates, so to speak." Franz smiled sweetly.

"Good word," Maltazar said. "Yes, she might well be involved with one of the intimates in this unfortunate business. It might even be the Indians."

"It might. So what if it is, Mooch?"

Chainey was getting impatient and was irritated that the woman hadn't talked to her as an equal. She chalked it up to the age thing and held her tongue.

"Then you don't owe Molly squat," he said. "She's working against all our interests, isn't she?" He blew smoke toward the ceiling.

"Only if that was the case, and you don't know that for sure."

"Give us a chance to find out, Ethel. Because even if she's just a freelancer, your reputation for confidentiality won't mean anything to her. Like it or lump it, Martha's not going away either, and as she brings things to a head, there're bound to be casualties."

"You sound like a man backing one horse there, Mooch. And a filly at that. That don't sound like the guy I know who always hedges his bets." Franz sat back, absorbing the information.

Maltazar puffed contentedly. "As we get more around the bend, the look ahead is scarier than the look back."

This was getting far too existential for Chainey's tastes.

"I'll see, Mooch. I'll see after I've made a few inquiries, okay?"

"That's all I ask, is a fair shake, right?"

"Not in this town, buttercup." She stood and came around the desk. The two kissed each other on both cheeks and then she extended a hand to Chainey. "Be well."

"Sure."

They left and were silent until the got back into Maltazar's car.

"Did we accomplish anything in there?"

"The fact that she talked to us for more than a minute, yeah." He backed up and straightened out, still puffing away.

"Maybe it's slipped your mind, boss man, but the deadline is *mañana.* I've got to come up with a solid lead to go with the name."

"Half of the answer is damn good work, Martha."

"You say it like I should be grateful for that. I'd better be delivering a head on a plate."

He patted her knee in a fatherly fashion. "We're going to make sure it's not the other way around, *qué no?*"

"Damn skippy."

Maltazar cracked the window and let blueish-white cigar smoke trail behind them as the Jaguar prowled the thoroughfares of the brightly lit night. Ferrer was signing "Aquellos Ojos Verdes," and Chainey felt herself slipping into a mellow mood despite the crushing nature of events. As the car rounded the corner of an upscale strip club—which you could tell by the kind of cars in the lot—she suddenly sat forward in her seat. In her head was the image of her plopping her tired butt down on her couch and going right through the roof like in an old Monty Python sketch.

"The bomb, Mooch—did you take care of the bomb?"

He plucked the cigar out of his mouth. "I figured you knew I took care of that. Why even sweat that nuisance?"

"It's not like a leaky faucet, Mooch."

"I know, I know. It was taken care of," he said placatingly.

"The bomb man have any ideas on who might have planted the thing?"

"It's a bomb." Maltazar bunched his boney shoulders.

"But when he called to say the job was done did he say anything, you know, a fuckin' clue here, Mooch?"

"What are you, Ivan Monk, PI, all of a sudden?"

"Well, it might help to have some idea who planted it since we don't exactly know our friends from our enemies."

"Allies, not friends; there's a big difference, *mi chica.*" He grinned at her, the reflected light obscuring the eyes behind his lenses. "I'm just having fun with you, kid."

"You got a bad sense of humor, anyone ever tell you that?"

"They have," he acknowledged sadly. "Anyway, our boy did mention that whoever put it together knew what they were doing, but it was nothing fancy. He said the electronic parts could be gotten from any one of those commercial supply places. You know, like that one near our office."

"What about the explosive material?"

Again Mooch elevated his shoulders and let them fall. "You can thank all that Internet anarchist, white-supremacist bullshit for that," he professed passionately. "He said the bomb itself was a metal box taped up and filled with a mixture of gunpowder and, you know, that soaked fertilizer that crazy McVeigh used in Oklahoma. The damn recipe is easy to obtain, he told me."

"So you did ask him questions," Chainey noted.

Again the oblique look from the crafty rascal. "Of course."

Chainey patted his shoulder and settled back and enjoyed the crooner's singing on the CD unit. For sure as the odds always favored the house, her relaxation wasn't going to last.

CHAPTER THIRTEEN

Chainey showered after using a flashlight to check under the couch. Not that she didn't trust Mooch, but one needs to have peace of mind. Of course that didn't mean there wasn't another one rigged up somewhere else in her pad, but being overly paranoid would give her no rest. Once out of the shower, she napped for about two hours, then got up. She was still fatigued, but a nightmare had made her so edgy, there was no sense lying in bed awake.

She made coffee and finally checked her answering machine. She was surprised and pleased that Rena Solomon had left two messages. Knowing her friend kept odd hours like she did, she called her.

"Martha, glad you rang, girl."

"I'm sorry we had a falling-out, Rena." Reflexively she stirred a spoon in her cup.

"Makes me no never mind; I know you're in a delicate business, you might say."

Chainey chuckled. "Hear anything new and exciting about our red brothers who are recently departed?"

"I heard you were on someone's trail."

"Oh, who?" Chainey asked too innocently.

"Ah"—Rena cleared her throat—"I hear rumors. I do have

sources in this town, you know. I might even have something else, but we got to trade, Martha. I got an editor to satisfy."

Suspicious, Chainey said, "Yeah?"

"I tag along when you go get her."

Batman liked sidekicks, but she was annoyed at the prospect. First Dejur, now this. But Rena, despite her command of the English language in print, was a 'round-the-way girl and had had more than one gun put in her face when she was on the pipe. She could swing when it mattered, but there might be events happening she'd never want on the public record. Nor to be put in the position of compromising Solomon.

"How about I promise to give you, well, most of the details? First thing when it's over."

"That supposed to satisfy me?"

She wasn't in the mood to bargain. "Rena, almost full disclosure, you hear me?"

"Almost?"

"Enough to get you a cover story."

"Sold, baby. I'll talk to you soon." Rena hung up and cursed loudly. What was she doing? She'd all but blurted out Zevonian's name, and of course her friend would want to know how she knew it. And those were questions she wasn't going to answer. Panicking, she'd diverted the conversation but was trapped by her own lie. She had to do something or Chainey might be killed because of what she knew but couldn't tell her directly.

Not too long afterward, Solomon scoped out the scene in the casino/bar. There was no main room for gambling per se, but one quadrant of the big room was devoted to video poker, slots and a few tables for live action. In particular, a heavyset woman in an outfit that included a pillbox hat and feathers was on a roll throwing dice.

"Eights my point, now don't disappoint." She bit the middle knuckle of the hand holding the dice and let them fly. Damn if she didn't cover the fade. Jubilation poured from her newfound friends even as they calculated how long this chick's streak would last.

Solomon turned from the craps maven and searched the bar

area. The bar itself was a stylish Art Deco affair with portholes and studded leather. Coy and small turtles could be seen swimming behind the portholes. It had been a while since she'd seen Gina. She supposed she could have simply prowled the streets and got some hooker to make the call. Or better yet, utilized one of the massage ads in the back of her own paper. But that seemed tawdry, beneath the seriousness of this situation. At least this would be someone she had a connection to.

"Nancy around?" She leaned over the bar, talking to a brunette in a tight top. She filled it out admirably.

"Nancy who?" A half-smile parted her red mouth.

"Nancy Hilliard—Nancy?"

"Yeah, it's me, Rena. Long time since we kicked up our heels at the dinner show at Caesar's."

They shook hands. "Damn, you're looking good."

"I'm trying. Been off the pipe for three years and four months." She rapped the bottom of a glass against the bar.

"Five and five for me," Solomon said. "I'd like to pretend this was nostalgia week, but I've got a problem and I need you to do me a favor."

Nancy Hilliard got the look anybody who's been in Vegas any amount of time gets when someone asks for a favor. They'd rather have bridgework done without anesthesia. "Yeah?"

"A phone call, that's it." Solomon crossed the flat of one hand over the other. "I can pay you for your time."

"This connected to your reporting job? I heard you were some kind of investigative journalist for that rag—sorry, that radical weekly."

"It's only radical by Nevada standards. Anyway, the truth, part of it, is this is connected to a story I'm working on."

"That Indian thing?"

"Correct."

The feathered woman signaled for drinks and as the other servers were busy, Hilliard left the bar to fill her order. Solomon waited on her stool until the woman had finished her run.

"One call, no repercussions?"

"Yes." Solomon hoped she was right about that.

"Okay." She produced an old-fashioned dial phone from underneath the bar. "What do you want me to say?"

Rena told her and she made the call. In a terse voice once the line connected, she gave her message and hung up. "Two goombahs wearing droop collars and stickpins aren't going to come waltzing in here to break my legs, are they?"

"No." She slid a folded fifty over to her.

Hilliard looked at the money, a wistful expression on her face. "It would be cool to say it was on the house, but I don't exactly pull down the ducats from this gig, dig?"

"I do." She tapped the bill with a fingernail. "For old times and the in-between times."

"Ain't that the truth." She put the Grant in her pocket. "I guess if you get back this way, say howdy."

"Thanks, Nancy. I owe you a solid."

"Take it slow."

Solomon left, mulling over the choices we all make in our pasts and where they take us. And Nancy, a woman from that past, was a convenience she needed to escape her own responsibility. No, that wasn't quite right, was it? As she unlocked her car, a drunk man smacked his lips at her as he wove past her. She did the right thing; she provided her friend with another lead. Of course, she had to do it in such a way as to hide her involvement with Victoria Degault.

She got behind the wheel and got the car going on the fifth crank. Tomorrow, tomorrow for sure, it goes into the shop. Driving through the night, Solomon realized everyone has his secrets in Las Vegas.

CHAPTER FOURTEEN

Chainey clicked off her cell phone. She was puzzled as to what to make of the call. Was it a trap set by Molly Z? Would she be that direct when she'd been playing cagey all this time? The woman on the other end sounded detached, unemotional. "You lookin' for this broad, right?" she'd asked rhetorically. "I understand she sometimes deals with a swingers' club called the Summit. It changes location but recently has been operatin' out of the Glass Anvil."

Chainey had been anxious, needing to be moving out and about as the minutes clicked off in her head. Not everybody had her cell phone number, but she supposed it wasn't too hard to get if you tried. It just didn't seem like a setup, and frankly, she wasn't in any position to snub any gift horses. She called Maltazar at home and ran down what had just happened.

"Or is somebody else interested in feeding you information?" he asked.

"Why?"

"More than one player means more than one agenda."

"You mean sister against brother? Are they not one big happy family?" She made a turn off of Russell Road as she headed past the Liberace Museum.

"It wouldn't be the first time siblings hadn't seen eye-to-eye on the running of a business."

"And might be willing to do dirt to the other one. What do you know, Mooch?"

"Just speculating."

"My ass."

"Martha, I hear a lot of stuff about the people we come in contact with, and a lot of it isn't worth repeating. Hang tight and let me make a call to Madame Franz."

"You going to try to get her to confirm or deny?"

"Something like that."

They broke off and Chainey continued heading toward the Glass Anvil. The restaurant and bar was one of the newer places in Vegas, meaning that it had been built within the last two years. Unlike the normal big production venues, the Glass Anvil was designed for the middle-class, middle-aged Vegas partici- pant. The influx of more people of means who bought condos in town as second homes had necessitated the development of nightspots with their tastes in mind.

They liked a restaurant with a trendy menu where they could entertain clients or guests without all the hoopla of roller coast- ers, flashing lasers and video slots clanging as some pensioner won a measly fifty in silver dollars.

Not that the owners of the Anvil were thick-headed. They un- derstood what was the life's blood of the town. The gaming room was upstairs from the main dining area and you had to be able to plop down five hundred minimum at the baccarat table to play. And the talk that was the other part of the equation that kept the city running 24/7 was also available in a more discreet way at the venue.

The cell phone rang. "Mooch?"

"Ethel confirms that Molly Zevonian has some contacts who frequent the Glass Anvil's extracurricular offerings. And I've learned separately that at least one of Molly's clients may be con- nected through this Summit swingers' operation."

She pulled to a stop across from the club and lined up to park her car on a commercial lot. She continued to talk on the phone. "It occurs to me that I can't skip in there and ingratiate myself with this crowd. And I am damned sure getting tired of staking out these joints waiting for our girl to come sauntering along."

"Then what do you propose?"

"That's the golden question for the night, Mooch. Look, Molly is hunting for me like I'm chasing after her."

"Which is all the more reason why you should at least show yourself at her haunts, let her know you're closing in. She's bound to have her ears to the ground, too."

"Yeah, but she doesn't have a sword hanging over her and I do. For all I know, she's hip to this and will wait for me to get iced by the Degaults, which would make everything swell again." Her frustration was becoming corrosive, eating into her self-confidence.

Maltazar asked cagily, "Where you going with this, Martha?"

"Where am I going, period?" She had finally gotten to one of the attendants but suddenly backed up, almost banging into an Impala's bumper. She straightened the car and got off the lot. *Fuck the Glass Anvil and fuck Molly Z. while you're at it.*

"Martha," Maltazar repeated.

"I'll call you, Mooch." She tossed the cell phone onto the passenger seat and put both her hands on the wheel. Who'd she'd been kidding? Vegas was built on a foundation of deals and counter-deals. The town was a mirage hiding quicksand that sucked the chumps in day after day, and still they came. She'd come, hadn't she?

What choice had she, but what did that matter? Yeah, the tool-and-die guys had pawed after her; after all, what was the difference between a chorus girl, a stripper and a hooker? Price, so the joke went. You used your tits and ass to keep a roof over your head, you had to expect men not to understand that a show was just that, a goddamn fantasy. It was a barker's come-on to get you to stay in the casino longer and lose a little more at the craps tables. 'Cause you knew you were going to hit that hard eight on the next roll. You just knew it.

And that chick, the third from the left with the great smile and the okay rack buried in all those bangles and feathers, was vibing on you, right? The old lady was up in the room or out shopping, and she couldn't help but be swayed by your manliness. Goddamn men. Vegas was built so they could have an excuse to drool and grope and play out movies starring themselves.

Well, goddammit, Chainey was going to get herself out of this fucked-up production. She headed back to her place. The phone rang; it would have to be Mooch. Later for that. She had money stashed, wisely, in other places than in town. And she'd been clever not to have the dough in the obvious cities like L.A. or Palm Springs. She had the scratch in the unhip parts of America, the rest of the country the sharpies who came to Vegas flew over on their way to the next high-stakes game.

How far could she get? Would she always have to be on the run? Change her face? Gain weight so as not to be so recognizable? Then there was the matter of her fingerprints. But it seemed she'd read about expensive procedures where lasers could burn and alter their whirls and such. Was that possible? Would it be necessary? The Degaults would have a reputation to protect, so the price on her head would remain. And then there was Molly Zevonian.

Chainey had the top down on the T-Bird, the air stifling and clammy as it blew against her skin. Yet she felt cold, as if detached from the actions her mind was committing her body to doing. She drove past the new Gelson's supermarket near her Lakes development. A stab of regret consumed her momentarily and she almost burst out laughing. She was going to miss buying Starbucks coffee and Haagen-Dazs ice cream as a month-end treat for maintaining her diet. Yeah, but this stuff must be available in Des Moines or wherever she wound up.

Pulling into her driveway, she considered escaping to London. She went there once on a summer review of the stage version of *The Hunchback of Notre Dame*. She'd actually got to play Esmeralda in several of the matinees. That performance garnered the attention of a Nigerian-born barrister, and he'd shown her the parts of the city not on the tours—from the after-hours spots in Brixton to an authentic Mexican restaurant in Piccadilly.

Get real, Chainey, she advised herself, getting out of her car. London wasn't on the program. She was going to have to live below the radar for the rest of her life. Or maybe she'd hide out for a year or two, then strike. Molly would take some contract and Chainey'd been on the watch for her. Chainey knew people; she could have feelers out. Of course that also necessitated a certain amount of exposure, so she'd have to be careful.

She was absorbed in working out her scenarios as she punched the combination to deactivate her alarm. She closed the front door and simultaneously reached for the light switch. Something disturbed the air in front of her, and instinctively she reached for the piece strapped underneath her oversize shirt. A hand latched onto her arm, preventing her from freeing the gun. Whatever was over her face was giving off a sweet smell that was causing her knees to wobble. It couldn't be Molly; the attacker was taller than she was, and clearly had it over her in upper-body strength.

"Baker," she rasped into the cloth held over her mouth. What the hell was he doing? She let herself go limp and could feel him dragging her backward, his arm around her waist. He was muttering something but she couldn't make out the words. It wasn't even English, it occurred to her. Crazy bastard was going on in Afrikaans.

He was dragging her toward the short hallway that led to the attached garage. As in all modern sub-developments, the garage was accessible through the house, and that must have been how he got in. The garage door wasn't wired to her alarm. Mr. Fuckin' Security Branch.

Chainey made her move the second he let her sag against the wall while he opened the door. She spun with a vicious kick at his leg, making it buckle. She fell back against the wall, the stuff in her system hampering her reflexes. She reached for her piece, a .380 Smith & Wesson tucked to the rear of her Gap capri pants. Baker was lunging and the two of them fell over, he on top of her.

"Ah, Chainey, you're tougher than most men. You should be out."

She hadn't learned to pace herself through the second, the dinner show and sometimes a third by not knowing something about breathing. But she could feel herself slipping along a greased tunnel, dropping down to a cushion of dark cushiony material. Baker's hot breath was in her face and if she wasn't hallucinating, the fuck was hard, too. Gawd.

"Argh," he yelped as she kneed him in the balls. He struck her face and Chainey felt the folds of velvet open to receive her like one of those plants that ate insects. Her arms were unresponsive and she could feel her eyelids begin to flutter uncontrollably. *Come on, girl, you can't let this happen.* She had the impression she'd hit him somewhere on his body but consciousness was rapidly escaping her. Her final sensation was that goddamn cloth with its sweet smell closing over her nose and eye. All became nothing, and she fitfully dived into that dark, sparkling velvet, swallowed up while sinking to the bottom.

CHAPTER FIFTEEN

Chainey came to and retched, making her mouth wet. Then she dry heaved two times and tried to get her hand to her face to wipe at her mouth. She couldn't get her arms to function and she thought they'd been broken in her fall. She was trying to remember how it was that she'd fallen, and where. Had she tumbled from the hallway of her house into the garage? But that was only one step. Had she been drunk? Unlikely, as she never drank to excess. More than three drinks of any kind of alcohol made her queasy—the way she felt now.

She tried to get up, but that too seemed like an impossible task. What the hell was going on? She got her eyes open with an effort as a hacking cough gripped her momentarily. Her throat cleared and she looked around. She was in a room, a cabin, really. The walls were exposed wood slats and there was an American Indian rug tacked over a stone fireplace. Assorted bric-a-brac was on the mantel. One of the items was a framed photograph of two figures that were familiar to her.

As she stared at the photograph, her mind assembled what had happened. "Baker," she hollered. "Baker," she repeated, screaming his name with venom. "Get your P.W. Botha-lovin' ass in here and untie me, you pop-eyed motherfuckah." Chainey was roped to a straight-backed chair atop a throw rug of some

African design. She hopped up and down, making the legs thump against the rug and the floor beneath. She grunted, more angry than scared. But she was also aware that Baker had stripped off her top, though he'd left her bra and capri pants on. And he'd taken off her shoes, the punk. She looked around for a video camera and there wasn't one. At least not one that was evident; but what with fiber optics and micro circuits, she wasn't comforted. It almost bothered her as much to be a prisoner as to think that if her torture and rape were to be preserved on tape, Baker would be able to relive the incident over and over when she was cold and gone.

The room was stifling hot and she guessed it was still night. There was a window, but Baker had put heavy parcel paper over it to block out prying eyes. That meant the cabin wasn't totally isolated and probably was somewhere in Red Rock Canyon or the Lake Meade area. She assumed she hadn't been out too long. Though getting to Laughlin, about ninety-two miles from Vegas, wasn't improbable either.

Yet where was her Boer version of *Henry, Portrait of a Serial Killer?* Great, the only reference she had for this kind of bullshit was that disturbing movie she and Rena dared each other to sit through. They had, and both were upset about that film for weeks afterward. Was this part of the drill? Make the victim get all worked up by her own imagination to make the real torture that much sweeter? If so, she wouldn't let that fuck have his fun. Maybe he was watching her squirm through a peephole or monitor. There were several stuffed big game fish and African masks on the walls, and Chainey looked hard to see if eyeballs were moving behind any of their slits. This was too much. She couldn't believe this was on orders from the Degaults. They'd at least have the decency to take her out with a slug at the base of her skull. This scene was all Baker, she concluded.

If he was watching on the sly, time to find out. Chainey rocked her body and let the chair fall over on its side. The bonds were good and didn't loosen. The chair was also solidly built and hadn't cracked. It wasn't going to be easy, goddammit.

"Ah, Chainey, always up to the mark, aren't you." Baker stood in the doorway, carrying a grocery bag with paper handles.

"Asshole, what do you think you're doing?" *Don't give an inch,* she told herself. She wasn't going to play to his fantasy any more than she had to.

"Let me help you up." The big man put down the bag and righted the woman and the chair. "That's better." He copped a feel of her breast, smiling.

Chainey made her face immobile. "How long are you going to drag this out, Baker? What the hell would Frankie say if he knew you were doing this?"

"He might applaud my initiative." Baker stood back, taking in her and the room. He was staging his erotic tableau and everything had to be just so for this bent Martin Scorcese. He went to the mantel and rearranged the stuff on it. Then he went to a desk in the corner with an old-fashioned Underwood typewriter on it. Baker as Hemingway, she thought glumly. That was why there was no video recorder going. Baker was going to immortalize this incident in text, part of his twisted memories.

"But how does it play in the book, Baker?" She tried to sound nonconfrontational in her tone. Maybe a little understanding would go far, like she saw on some damn documentary about reasoning with nut cases. Or maybe it was another movie and the clown got more upset and hacked the woman to pieces.

"A certain artistic license will be applied when I relate our rendezvous." He extracted a paddle, a studded dildo and other S&M goodies from the bag. "I want you to know, I really respect you, Chainey." Baker averted his eyes, as if he were a blushing schoolboy.

Was that genuine? Was that something she could play to and maybe get out of this predicament? No matter how lovestruck and lustful he was, Baker still wasn't a chump. But he was a man, and he was acting out the limits of his libido. "You going to do it to me, is that it, Baker? But why take me alive now when you wanted to kill me earlier with that bomb of yours?"

Baker was hunched down and looked up from his tender inspection of his tools. "I did no such thing, girl. My orders were clear: backtrack you and make sure you didn't . . ." He stopped himself. "Oh, you do get me to gossip so," he chuckled. He didn't go on about how he didn't exercise the option to kill Gilbarth. He'd already talked to Chainey, so what was the point? He took no joy in killing for killing's sake.

"You mean make sure I didn't tumble to the truth," she finished for him. "And now?"

Baker straightened up, inclining his head. "I've purposely been incommunicado for the past several hours, Chainey. Frankie knows you're back, though."

"Knows I'm chasing Zevonian?"

Baker didn't let anything show on his face, which itself was a giveaway.

"Did he hire her, Baker? She and her husband Elwood were brought in to take down the shipment. Kill me and the two Silicon Valley guys."

Baker brushed at his mustache with his blunt fingers. "Sounds like a lot of imagination, Chainey-girl."

Make this good. "Could be I'm trying to keep up with yours, Baker." Did she sound slutty enough?

The South African looked perplexed. "What are you saying?"

"I'm saying you don't want this to be a one-way thing, do you, Baker? You want me to get into this, don't you, darling? Or is that how you get your kicks, working over helpless women?" *Careful, don't push him too far, just far enough.*

"No, that's not it, Chainey. I—" he stuttered, the paddle in his hand. He gazed at the object as if seeing it after it had been put away for a long time. "It's just that this presented such an opportunity."

"You mean my death warrant from the Degaults? But you said you'd purposely been out of touch these last few hours. Or are you saying it doesn't matter, Baker? That you know I have to go since they have to make sure I don't run down Molly Zevonian? So this was a golden time for you to make your wishes come true."

Baker pushed the edge of the paddle between her breasts,

rubbing it back and forth on the material of her bra. "Chainey, you are a clever woman, aren't you?" His breathing was jagged, and the glare in his eyes didn't inspire confidence in her. She had to get him on her side.

"There's another way, Baker." *You sick bastard.* "You and me. We take out Molly and expose what the Degaults have done to their board. After all, it's their money they've ripped off."

He was unbuttoning his shirt, revealing his hairy stomach and chest. "There's always another way, my good girl." He rubbed his belly and stepped close to her, his eyes wide with anticipation. He turned the chair around and tipped it over, thus leaving her rear end up to him. His hands grabbed at the material of her pants, pulling them down.

So much for the empathetic approach. "You goddamn faggot," she screamed. "I always knew you were weak, Baker. That how it was back home, killing Bantustan kids in their sleep and running over old ladies from the back in your Land Rover?"

"Shut up." He swatted her exposed bottom. "I was a patriot." He took another swat, enjoying her squirming.

"You're nothing but a punk, Baker. A small-timer who got out when it got too hot and they wouldn't let you bugger fifteen-year-old boys in the new regime."

"I'm a man, you black bitch." He kicked at her and she and the chair fell to the side. Baker was heaving as he took off his belt. "You can't talk to me like that."

Go for broke. "I'll talk to you anyway I like, you bloated fuck. You can't get a woman any other way, that's why you tied me up. You're scared of experiencing what a real woman can do when you're not paying for it, aren't you, Baker? Did you think about me in that motel room in Oakland?"

He whipped her with the belt, rasing welts across her face and torso.

"That the best you can do, bitch? Maybe you'd like to knock me out so you can really feel brave and bad."

Baker leapt on her, his hand alternately feeling her up and working on the bonds. "You're all talk, aren't you, Chainey-girl?"

"I'm still more man than you, Baker."

"Is that right?" He struck her across the jaw, making fireworks go off behind her eyes.

She had to hold on, had to stay alert. The rope was looser, and he hauled her body and chair off the floor.

"Now I'm going to show you what a real man can do."

He laughed, spittle flying in her face. Baker had her by the upper arms, his strong hands squeezing her. *Time to do it.* She used the top of her head to butt him under the chin. She caught him good as he reflexively let go of her. Chainey dropped to the floor, her pants down around her ankles. She got one leg free, pulling it through the end of the pant leg. The impact had loosened the bonds some more. The anger at being humiliated overcame the fear gnawing at her brain.

Baker was grabbing at her and she rolled out of the way. The large man crashed into the floor, but she knew that wouldn't slow him down. His blood was boiling, powered by the lust and madness wracking him. He reached out a hand and snatched her by the ankle as she attempted to get up.

"Come here," he bellowed.

Chainey used her other foot to stomp at his head. He let go of her and she turned, heading for the desk. Baker was quick and tackled her from behind. Both went down, with him on top.

"This is how you wanted it, isn't it, Baker?" She gave him a toothy, humorless smile.

He gulped, and for several moments he didn't seem to know what to do with his hands—caress or throttle her. He made up his mind and got his beefy paws heading for her throat. But Chainey was scooting back, using her strong legs to move out from under his heavy body.

"Don't you want to feel me, girl?" He all but cackled, his hands latching on to her lower body to keep her from moving.

"Feel you go limp, yeah." She did the unexpected. Rather than knee him, which he'd be ready for, she did a knuckle strike against his temple. Her hand was formed so the middle knuckles of her fingers were prominent. The move was a modified Krav Maga blow and got the big man rocking. She followed with the flat of her hand, chopping into his windpipe.

That got him gasping, and Chainey was up and grabbing the ancient Underwood. She clubbed him on the head as he rose up, flailing for her. He sunk to a knee, dazed. She battered him on the shoulder blades; as she wanted him awake to talk. Baker staggered to his feet like an alkie on Sterno. "Now, why be unfriendly?" He chuckled, his head lolling to one side.

She clipped him on the jaw with the typewriter and he went over on his back, his hands holding the bottom of his face. She found a gun in the desk drawer. It felt natural in her hand.

"Good God, you're a right Willie Mays, ain't you?" He made a sound through his hands, and it seemed he was laughing and sobbing all at once.

"Question-and-answer time, Baker." She wanted to pistol-whip him. She got her pants up.

The enforcer rolled back and forth on the floor, his hands still on his face. He moaned, and it seemed as if he'd suddenly become aware of how demented he'd been acting and was embarrassed to face her. He started to rise.

"Stay down on your knees." She gestured with the gun.

Baker complied. "That's how I like it." He winked. "Can you do it, Chainey?" He smiled at her, looking like a strange dwarf, what with his large chest and his knees to the ground. His jaw was swelling and purple from the blows. "Torture is an exquisite endeavor, my girl. It takes a steady hand and a focused mind to make it go right." He started to laugh, then coughed, holding his stomach. "You can't get carried away, you see? Like a pie, all the ingredients have to be balanced to create the result you want."

"I'm not interested in your theories developed in windowless prison cells in Pretoria, Baker. I'm not interested in how all that pain and shit you dispensed has fucked up your mind." She got closer with the gun for dramatic effect. "This ain't a therapy session we're having, you sick mother."

"I could stand a session with you." He waggled his tongue lasciviously.

She resisted the urge to backhand him with the gun. "Did the Degaults hire Molly and her husband to rip off the shipment?"

Baker began moving his upper body, as if he were moving to a tune in his head. "What do I know?"

What he wanted was a beating from her. He'd like nothing better than for her, still without her shirt on, to work him over so he could come. She had to convince him that she was willing and able to take it to a very deadly level. "I need an answer, Baker."

"Don't we all?" he taunted.

She shot past his ear—very close past his ear. She wasn't an expert with firearms, and frankly wasn't sure where her bullet would travel. But try as she might to run away from it, she was in this goddamn snare and had to claw her way out.

"You do have my attention," he said. The fright had snapped him back to a semblance of reality. His normal caginess seem to overtake him again.

"This is my life, so I'm not gambling here, Baker."

"You know I can't tell you anything. I'd be finished."

"So you're willing to bet your own life, is that it?" She leveled the gun at his head.

"You can't do it, Chainey. I can, and have. But killing unprovoked, in cold blood, as you Yanks say . . ." He shook his head dismissively. "I believe we're at an impasse."

Chainey couldn't show it on her face, couldn't show him that he was right. But she had to do something, had to up the ante.

Baker had a smug expression below his mustache. It looked almost comical, given the protrusion of his jaw line. "Tick-tock, Chainey-girl."

She put a round in his upper leg. There was a look of surprise on both their faces.

"Good God." Baker put a hand on the wound as crimson stained his pants.

"Tell me, Baker. You're through anyway for pulling this rape shit. Not that the Degaults are prudes, but they can only use you if you can keep your mind on business."

"They'd never believe you." He stole a glance at his bag and the toys lying around it.

"It's all over, Baker. Even without the goodies, you'd have to explain how I got the drop on you and how it is that I know what your little hideaway looks like."

"I'll tell them we were lovers."

Now it was Chainey's turn to laugh. "Even if by some bizarre notion they went for that, how would that sound, Baker? You were supposed to be shadowing me, and we've been knockin' boots all this time. Well, shit, maybe this was a double double-cross, and you two were lookin' to make off with our money."

Baker's tenuous position made his body seize up. He realized it was his own lack of self-control that had brought him to this point. But it had seemed so right. She was a dead woman any-way; why not take advantage? "You heartless shrew," he uttered through clenched teeth. His wound flowed eagerly.

"Yeah, imagine that," she snorted. "I should just be a good girl and let you bang me any which way you want, then plant my body in the desert 'cause men just want to have their fun." She paused, her last words forming a picture in her head. "Like you put Smith and Delacruz in the desert, huh, Baker? I bet if a forensics crew took a good look around this place they might find something, huh, Baker? Maybe some matching fibers or blood you only scrubbed off the floor. But how about in be-tween the floorboards, on the sides of the wood—what about that, Baker?" She stamped on the floor; the boards were rough hewn, with various irregular gaps between the planks.

"Did you supervise them, Baker, as they did the dirty work? Frankie get the two men up here on the ruse of a new deal?"

He tried to look together, but she could see the anxiety creep-ing into the corners of his eyes. "Then what's our deal, Chainey?"

"I let you get to a hospital, you twisted bastard. What you do after that is your lookout."

"You're a hell of a negotiator."

Some of the color was leaving his face. He'd fold, she knew.

"The answer is yes, Chainey. Frankie had his own shipment ripped off."

"Victoria part of this?"

"She didn't know about what went down until Maltazar's call

about the rip-off. It was just bad luck she was there when the call came in."

"Then Molly hadn't told Frankie I was still alive after their ambush in Marin?"

"Yeah." Baker winced in pain, straightening his wounded leg. "But what could he do? He had to pretend he was as surprised as anybody else."

"Here." She tossed him a flannel shirt that had been draped across the back of a chair. She put on her shirt, which had been tossed on a cot. Baker made a tourniquet from the shirt. "Give me the big answer, Baker, then I let you go."

"I don't know why, Chainey. I had to know about Molly because it was my job to backtrack to make sure nothing you did led his sister to that woman and her husband. Victoria had given you three days, and Frankie knew it had to be those two to get you. It couldn't be me doing you in." He was about to go on but censored himself.

"But you had to deal with Vern Sixkiller when he came to town."

"That's right. Those redskins showed up, and Frankie wanted me to find out what they found out. Sixkiller and his factotum asked around but didn't find out shit." He seemed pleased with the knowledge.

She assumed Sixkiller and Leopold had followed her to the Bay Area but said, "I guess you have a phone around here?"

"A portable, over there." He gestured with his head.

Chainey found it on the desk and powered it up. "Keys," she said.

Baker got them out of his pants and slid them across the floor to her. In return she let him have the phone. "I suggest you make yourself scarce, Baker. Take whatever money you have salted away and split. I guess you can always get work in Zimbabwe, a man of your talents," she mimicked in a South African accent.

"You aren't out of the tall grass yet, lassie. Frankie isn't going to let you walk around scot-fuckin'-free."

"We'll see what Victoria has to say, champ." She made to leave. As she did, she passed near the mantel and the photograph upon it. The shot was a younger, leaner Baker, smiling broadly in his rugby shirt and shorts, a ball tucked under one arm. He had his arm around a stouter, older man who favored him around the eyes and nose. Both men looked as if they didn't have a care in the world.

"Chainey, does this work change us, or is it what we're suited for to begin with?"

She looked at the rugby player today. His face was lined and his middle was going soft. *Our deeds are going to catch up to all of us.* "I'm just trying to cover my house note, Baker."

"So you say."

She walked out of the room, shutting the door on the wounded man. Baker's cabin was in a flat area set back from some rock formations that speared the black night sky. There was a gravel path leading down, and she could see light from other cabins. The stone had a rust-red appearance, so that meant Red Rock Canyon. But the Canyon was large, encompassing areas such as Ice Box Canyon and Calico Hills. Chainey didn't exactly know where she was, but down was usually a way out, so that was good enough. She climbed into Baker's Dodge Ram truck and started down the incline.

As she bumped along, she tried out several scenarios in her head. There was always the direct approach, calling up ol' Vic and laying the story on her. Of course, she wouldn't buy it. But she'd have to tell her brother, and he would send Zevonian after her. That could work. It was a way to smoke the wild woman out and take care of her once and for all. If Baker booked like she figured, then what she knew would have credence. Let the Degaults handle their power struggle internally.

Of course, such matters usually resulted in others eating slugs, too, but what other hand did she have to play?

She crested to a paved road and could see twinkling lights to her right, down below on a flattened plain. Vegas looked like millions of phosphorescent pearls strewn on a black rug, just waiting for the suckers to come along to trip and fall.

"Curtain call," Chainey said to herself as she aimed the truck for the lights.

CHAPTER SIXTEEN

Chainey called Rena Solomon from her cell phone but reached a recording. She tried her at home and left a message on that machine, too. Still heading back to the city, she punched in another home number and got yet another answering machine.

"I haven't got time for you romancing any of your old girl-friends from your Alpha 66 days," she kidded over the phone. "This is *muy importante,* Mooch; call me back on my cell." She hung up and sure enough he rang back in less than a minute.

"In the wake of the Elian mess, you should be careful about making fun of those crazy anti-Castroites and their covert organizations. And anyway, I only tolerated those zealots because the sister of the local commander had a great pair of legs."

"Now that we've established that, listen up." She described the events of the last few hours.

"Incredible," was his immediate response. He'd been silent during her recounting of her kidnap and subsequent bizarre encounter with Baker. "Are you sure he won't go crying to Frankie? If he knows the real score, it would make sense to keep close to Frankie, even if he has to admit his, ah, predilection, for you."

"But that means they've got one more secret to keep from

Victoria. And he's got to go under the knife to get that bullet out; he's not going to be using a phone at least until morning."

"So the countdown has begun," Mooch remarked.

"You got that right. But I think there's a more basic reason Baker can't call Frankie."

"Which is?" he said on the other end of the line.

"Our girl Molly. If Baker cops to what he's done, essentially jeopardizing this scam of Frankie's while trying to get his rocks off, what do you think he would do?"

"Send her to take care of the horny Mr. Baker," Maltazar commented.

"Exactly."

"So now what?"

"I think you're the only one Victoria is going to listen to, Mooch."

There was a pause of several moments on the line. "I don't know, Martha," he said hesitantly. "What have we got in the way of hard evidence?"

She considered his words. Mooch was not one to put his neck too far out. From his perspective he had to do business in Vegas, and if that meant when the push was on, it was her or Frankie, he'd come down on the side with the power. On the other hand, Frankie had to be sweating with Zevonian around, and he'd probably called Baker and got no answer. "You can't be neutral in this, Mooch," she cautioned, choosing her words carefully. "At some point Frankie is going to correctly assume you know what I know."

"You're letting this town get you too jaded, Martha," he said with the proper amount of indignation in his voice. "I told you, I don't let anyone who works for me down."

"I know, Mooch, I know," she responded, also with the right amount of diffidence. "But I also know you've got a reputation to uphold." *Not to mention looking out for number one, you old sharpie.*

"I'm just saying, *mi chica,*" he went on in his best friendly uncle manner, "we have to walk carefully here. There're scorpions with stingers among the sugar cane, no? It's understood

Frankie and Victoria handle the business differently. But that doesn't mean that if we go to her and she hears that her brother has done something behind her back, maybe to shaft her, she'll thank us for the information. Or that she will even believe us."

She had to concede to the logic of his argument. "On that we agree. But we have to force the matter now, Mooch. Molly is out there most certainly gunning for me."

"Yes . . ." he said, trailing off.

She stopped at a red light. "Are you thinking what I'm thinking?"

"I'm afraid we've both been corrupted by this wicked city." He almost sounded sincere.

"We let it get on the street that Baker has been wounded, and that he's been talking." Chainey was surprised that she barely felt a tug of guilt inwardly. The job was changing her, she acknowledged, as she put the car in gear as the light turned green.

"That might flush Molly out," Maltazar concurred. "And that would give you an opportunity to get a drop on her. The problem is, can it happen in time?"

"I don't know, Mooch. Plus saying it aloud shows how many *ifs* are in that plan. And how do we know Baker doesn't know some doctor who doesn't exactly keep a shingle out over his porch? I certainly heard of a few back-alley types. Been to one or two of them to help a friend." She'd obtained painkillers for Solomon when she was kicking the habit without a prescription from such an individual. Of course, like Baker, this guy had a thing for showgirls. And certainly there were chorus girls who'd gotten kitchen-table abortions.

"But you have to figure that Zevonian would know of some of these types. I certainly do, too," Maltazar added.

Having no particular destination in mind, Chainey had steered a course toward the Riverhead casino. Less than three blocks away, she could make out its distinctive outline among a raft of distinctive outlines. "For this to work, I need to know where Baker is." She chastised herself for not anticipating this development. Had she staked out the cabin, she could have followed him to where he would be taken.

"From what you told me, he probably called an ambulance. There's plenty of private ones in the two counties."

She eased the truck into a self-park pay lot. "Why not call a buddy to help him?" She didn't want to be too conspicuous going into the casino. She might have a better chance of blending in if she didn't use the valet.

"I would think too risky at this point," Maltazar countered. "He's had as much exposure, to use the pun, as he can stand. As it is, if he goes to a legit hospital, he's going to have to have a convincing lie for the cops to explain the gunshot wound. You know, he was cleaning his gun and it went off, something like that."

Chainey disagreed. "That only adds to the idea that he's going to have to use an underground doctor to treat his wound. Can you get a line on him?" She parked and shut off the engine.

"Yes," he said, "I know of one that is, shall we say, discreet. But this individual and I go back some. Where will you be?"

She was going to lie but told the truth. "At the Riverhead."

"Is that wise?"

"All roads lead back there."

"That doesn't necessarily mean you have to cross that particular Rubicon, Miss Chainey."

She was walking. "Hey, I only had a year and a half of community college, so don't get all literate on me. I'll just be laying in the cut, Mooch."

"I'll call as soon as I know something."

"Right on." She clicked off and put the cell in the back pocket of her pants. The gun was tucked in the back of her waistband, underneath a loose-fitting shirt. What a day. There was no packing and running; she had to see it through. And if that meant being more ruthless than the ones she was going up against, it seemed she had no recourse. They'd backed her into this corner and it was up to her to fight her way out.

Until she'd put that bullet in Baker, she hadn't known if she was capable of shooting someone . . . well, unarmed. The third gunman at the Marin house had been the first time she'd killed anyone. Not the first time she'd had to defend herself, but actually canceling someone's ticket was different. Much different. And then so quickly after that she'd had the shootout with Zora Blanchard, again almost killing someone.

She stopped suddenly, propping herself against a light post. It was as if she'd just been dealt a body blow by an invisible fist. Her head felt light, and her stomach rolled over. Possibly her nausea was a vestige of being knocked out earlier. Could even be a mild concussion. But she suddenly felt the psychic weight of shooting human beings.

People walked past her, their faces blank or showing toss-off contempt. No doubt they'd concluded she was either drunk or high. She touched her forehead and her hand came away clammy. She retched, as she'd done upon waking. Then dry heaved again. People now took wide arcs around her. She tried to push off the pole, and her body seemed to be the prisoner of some other gravitational laws, not those of earth.

The screech of car tires sounded, and a big vehicle pulled into the driveway to the all-night cleaners where Chainey had stopped.

"You look like hell, woman. You been walking around in the sun all day or somethin'?"

The face in the passenger window of the El Dorado was impassive, the lips compressed into a bemused expression. The man was awfully familiar, but who the hell was he? She finally was able to stand; the sidewalk had stopped having seizures.

"Just getting my second wind, Vernon."

Sixkiller smiled broadly, leaning past Leopold's calmly composed face at the passenger window. "Come on. I'll give you a lift."

"I don't think so, Vernon."

"We're going to the same place, see the same people."

"How about I meet you in there, then." She started walking again, trying not to show how watery her knees were.

Sixkiller leaned out the driver's side as she went past. "We're on the same side in this, sister."

"We are, are we, my red brother?" she called back, heading toward the Riverhead.

He nearly whispered. "I know why Smith and Delacruz were popped."

The girl with green-streaked hair waving in the wind was yelling at the top of her lungs. Victoria Degault watched her and the other riders on the roller coaster as they silently looped past her outside the glazed window to her brother's office. It said something about his personality that he always wanted to see the action happening. She, on the other hand, preferred an office that was a sanctuary. There was no reason to always be on.

"The Vic." He beamed, entering the office from the side door. He was freshly shaven, though it was getting on to be eleven at night.

She leaned her backside on the front of his desk, folding her arms. Her brother made himself a drink at the marble-and-chrome wet bar. It was a stall tactic designed to make it seem as if he was relaxed, that everything was cool. Everything was going to shit.

"Who the fuck is Molly Zevonian, Frank?" Her trip to L.A. had been fruitful. The woman's name and a few other details had surfaced upon her asking the right people the right questions. She'd passed the name to Rena Solomon to get a brush fire going in her brother's backyard.

He sipped, then rubbed the side of his face with his palm.

"Your shave is fine," his sister said. "But unless *Details* magazine is sending somebody around now to take your picture, can we get to the subject?"

"Have you been getting rumblings from the board?" He crossed the room and at first was going to take his seat of power. He was going to demonstrate that he was in control, that all was under his purview. But he knew his sister wouldn't be snowed, so why make the effort? Instead, he watched the roller coaster and the big neon of the Strip.

"You mean do they know for certain? I don't know. But an emergency session has been called for the morning, early." She went to the bar and poured a neat Glenn Fiddich sans ice. How many calories was that? She took a pull. It felt real good, warming her throat. That's why they called it a bracer.

"It's a little complicated, Victoria. I wasn't doing anything to jeopardize your position, I assure you." He wiped his fingers at the area under his nose.

"That's not how the board sees these things and you know it, Frank." She finished the scotch, enjoying the burn. "On the one hand you're the man and therefore they, including our two women directors, defer to you. It isn't PC, but that's the way it is. Conversely, when their money's fucked with, both of us have to ride that beef, as daddy used to say." She stepped closer to him, placing her hands on her hips. "And what I'm getting a picture of means whatever boneheaded play you've made is about to get both our respective tender appendages in a ringer."

Frankie Degault put his drink down and rapidly rubbed his hands together. "Okay, this is going to work out, Vic. Zevonian or Baker will shut down Chainey. She was supposed to be taken care of in the Bay Area." His elbows were tucked to his sides, his hands held out and palms up. "Who knew this second-rate Rockette would be so goddamn savvy?"

"Let's not go into your penchant for underestimating women. Although you did hire Molly." She snapped her fingers. "No, you hired Elwood, her old man. The crew Daddy ran with had used the Porter brothers a few times back in the free-fire days, so you figured the apple hadn't fallen too far from the tree."

It always irritated him when his sister could get inside his head and understand his motivations. It was particularly bothersome because he couldn't do it to her. "The plan was to make it seem the shipment had been ripped off and the money gone missing."

"How'd you hook up with Buchanan and McLaughlin?"

"Remember that new technologies convention last year over at the Convention Center?"

"So you were putting this in motion then?" She didn't bother to keep the edge out of her voice.

"They came to see me," he said defensively. "Well, actually, several of us on the Strip. It was that time when you were in Detroit seeing about our expansion possibilities. They wanted to do this synergistic thing." He gestured in the air. "All about making online games, souped-up graphics for video poker, tie-in with a TV show; it was actually a pretty good marketing idea. And these guys had the track record to make it happen." He reached for his drink, then decided not to imbibe. This was a time when he needed to be on his mark.

"And you did all this to do what, Frank? If you weren't going to invest in their company, why all this bullshit? Particularly now that you've set off ripple effects like a goddamn seven point one." Absently, Victoria Degault buffed at her cheek with the front side of her deep purple nails. "This has to do with Smith and Delacruz." She pointed a rigid index finger at him as he bowed slightly. "Goddammit, Frank, what were you thinking?"

"What everybody in Vegas does, li'l sis." He stuck his hands in his pockets and watched the roller coaster go around one more time. "I was thinking about money, and how to make more of it."

"And whatever means we use are justified by the bottom line?"

He grinned even teeth at her. "Don't go getting all socialist on me, Victoria. You like money as much as I do."

She had her arms folded, one foot at an angle to the other. "I also like straightforwardness and not having knives at my back. Especially not those poised by my own family." She put emphasis in her voice. "What did you do, Frankie?"

He took his hands out of his pockets and pushed his palms toward the ceiling. The picture of a kid caught cheating on his math test. "Just a few murders, Victoria. That's all."

CHAPTER SEVENTEEN

Some woman with a bouffant in a sweater unraveling at the sleeve was bouncing up and down on the stool. A red light was swirling on top of her, and a claxon was whooping from the video poker machine where she'd just hit the jackpot. She was frantically hollering for a woman named Linda to get there quick.

Chainey, Sixkiller and Leopold calmly strolled past the winner into the confines of the Riverhead casino. The tall woman pointed toward a set of stairs, and they began ascending to the second level of the place. A shift supervisor she knew was descending the stairs, and the two exchanged brief nods.

Upstairs, the area was less traveled this time of the early morning hours. The mezzanine level contained an elaborate rain forest construction that included a stage and chairs for the children's show of puppets and mechanical birds. There were closed gift shops, the buffet section, and a few-fast food outlets still open. A smattering of men could be heard yelling and slapping each other's hands as they racked up points blasting aliens and zombies to hell in the video arcade. Beyond the arcade was an enclosed walkway with more shops leading to the Bellagio.

The three got coffee and seats at the Carl's. There was something wrong with the establishment's flourescent lights as the people and objects in the outlet were bathed in greenish hues. Chainey idly fantasized that the color of the lights was deliberate to trigger a need for a burger—after, of course, you came away from losing the rent money at the craps table.

"So how come we're all buddy, buddy now, Vern?" She sipped her tepid coffee. "Last time we were together, you really showed me what a stud you are."

Sixkiller managed a self-effacing expression. "You know how it gets, Chainey. You get too wrapped up in your work and you can't see things for what they really are."

Leopold shook his head in ascent.

"And how are you seeing things now, Vern?"

A man and woman in their early twenties listed into the burger joint leaning onto each other. The drunk couple both wore bell bottom jeans and were cracking each other up with their goofy jokes. Incoherently, they attempted to convey their order to the woman working the counter.

"Like I said," Sixkiller answered, "we're working toward the same interests. As you probably know, me and Leopold have been doing our share of nosing around since you showed up on the res. Particularly, we discovered some interesting correspondence between Smith and Degault."

Chainey leaned forward, her hands guarding her coffee cup like an inmate. "You find these letters in Smith's house?"

The drunk couple ambled away, unable to communicate their food preferences. The two giggled and pushed each other as they left.

"That's right," Sixkiller confirmed. "But these weren't physical letters actually. Even us po' redskins have gotten on the cyber tip, homegirl." He tipped his head at his partner. "Leopold is a master at excavating this kind of stuff off of hard drives."

Chainey looked at Leopold for a response and got a wan smile. Did this dude ever say anything?

Sixkiller was talking. "Seems the holiday pushing incident Frankie Degault had with Smith was a put-up job. Degault, from what Leopold was able to reconstruct, wanted to make it seem he was down with his fellow Strip players in opposing expansion by the tribe into Vegas."

"And no better way to do that than a public fight," Chainey reflected aloud.

"But in reality, Degault wanted to lay off some investments in Indian casinos on the sly."

Chainey held the cup to her mouth, but she couldn't abide any more of the rank stuff. "The money I was transporting wasn't enough to make that happen, unless this was some kind of installment-plan arrangement."

Sixkiller glanced at something he'd seen out of the corner of his eye, then looked back at Chainey. "On that point it's still a little vague. From what we can tell by the e-mails back and forth, Smith and Delacruz were going to be silent partners with Degault. As you might be aware, just like in any business, various tribes have found themselves competing with each other for patrons, and of course any high rollers and whales we can get."

"But you guys do come together around matters such as Propositions 5 and 1A," Chainey noted, "and the gaming pact worked out with the governor of California."

"That's business," Sixkiller allowed. "People of color might squabble and fight among themselves, but when the whites threaten our shit, we got to show a united front, don't we, my sister?"

Chainey laughed. "Sure, you're right. Still," she mulled over, "there's something wrong with the whole deal, Vern. And it's been nagging me since I stumbled onto this so-called scam Frankie was supposed to be putting over on the two Silicon Valley dudes."

"Which is . . . ?" Sixkiller asked. As if by hidden signal, he and Leopold simultaneously drained their cups.

"Seven million barely covers the cost of wallpaper in a casino unless you're going to have one in a trailer, you know that."

"Could be like you said, it was a down payment sort of thing." Sixkiller glanced at Leopold, who remained noncommittal.

"I've learned a few things being a courier," Chainey said.

"And I know that's not how and why you move cash around. And if he was going to secretly invest with them, why have them killed?"

"Frankie is a greedy motherfucker," Sixkiller reasoned. "Say he did the math and figured he could make more on his return by being a solo investor. The rumor going around the res now is that the three had intended to go into a casino to be built on the other side of Palm Springs, a white-Indian partnership. Essentially some of our tribe who ain't happy with the way the elders' council runs the show and were going to strike out on their own."

Chainey shook her head. "If anything, Degault would have to be worried if Smith or Delacruz caught a cold. How the hell could he be involved in a casino with other partners and not have the murders a constant point of contention? That don't float, Vern."

Leopold shook his head in agreement with her point.

"What then?" Sixkiller made a gesture with one of his hands.

Her face got a determined look. Then she said, "I guess we ask him."

"Right," he said sarcastically.

"Right," she repeated, pointing at them. She took out her cell phone. She thumbed the device on and brought up stored numbers on the screen. Finding the inner office number for Frankie Degault, she entered the digits.

"Are you kidding?" Sixkiller asked.

She winked. Chainey felt loose, ready to rumble. The line was picked up. "Victoria," she said, after the woman on the other end gave a greeting. "You know who this is, right? Okay, I'm glad it's you who picked up. I bet at this moment your brother is standing there in front of you, isn't he?" She listened to her response.

She'd tried to ride the oaks, as the hoopsters say. She'd tried to run and they wouldn't let her. She'd been ready to throw it all away, but that was before that punk Baker had her panties down around her ankles getting his swerve on by spanking her booty like the freak he was. But at least his sexual obsession was understandable in a distorted, fun-house mirror sort of way.

"I know that, Victoria," she interjected, then listened some more. Frankie thought everybody was expendable as long as he got what he wanted. He was a spoiled child with the demeanor of a sociopath. Fuck him and his sister, too, if she was going to defend him.

"Listen to me, Victoria," she said as the woman wound down on the other end. "I'm not going to meet about shit until Molly Zevonian is taken care of. In fact," she continued in an assured manner, "I plan to recite chapter and verse to your board on how your brother—and for all I know you, too—schemed to rip them off for seven large in profits. I know that ain't much compared to the monthly haul the Riverhead brings in, but how much you want to see if this doesn't get their attention?" Victoria Degault started to speak, but Chainey cut her off. "I don't care about all that. What I care about is staying alive and getting out from under this rock. You tell your brother I've already taken care of Baker and I plan to do the same to Molly. I'll see you, Victoria."

Chainey hung up, hoping that Sixkiller and Leopold didn't notice the tremble in her hand.

"Goddamn," Leopold commented.

"You do talk." Chainey got up.

The two men also rose. "When he has something to say," Sixkiller commented. The trio went back downstairs. Chainey led the way to an area near the kitchen doors where the bathrooms and pay phones were located.

"Now that you've got their attention, what do you plan for an encore?" Sixkiller watched one of the scantily clad cocktail waitress in her rainforest leathers drift by.

"Force his hand," Chainey said. "He's got to send Molly out to get me now."

"And you get her first."

"Hopefully." All of a sudden she felt trapped standing in a casino owned by the man out to get her. She wanted to be on

the offense, doing something rather than standing around gab-
bing. "Look, Vern, as you've pointed out, we both want Frankie.
Now we can't get that until we get Zevonian out of the way."

Sixkiller demanded, "How'd you take care of Baker?"

"I put a bullet in him. He won't be around till he heals up."

"Goddamn," Leopold said appreciatively again.

"You guys have a cell?" Chainey asked.

"No," Sixkiller responded.

Chainey kept rolling. "Then I need you to go rent one so we
can stay in touch. If you can't find a place off the Strip, there's
an all-night pager/phone/escort place in the Fourteen-hundred
block of Jackson not far from here in what the folks over there
lovingly call 'Lost Fuckin' Vegas.' "

"The black side of town," Sixkiller stated. "The area not
found in the guidebooks, I suppose."

"You suppose right. After y'all get hooked up"—she handed
him her cell number, whicht she'd scribbled on a napkin—"hit
the bricks and see what you can turn. The main thing is to be
seen, so that Molly Z comes out of hiding."

"You're her number-one concern." Sixkiller folded the napkin and put it in his pocket.

"I know. But her in-laws are the Porter family, and there
might be one or two cousins or uncles around, looking to settle
the score with whoever they think is working with me."

"We'll be careful." He checked his watch. "It's half past midnight; why don't we check with each other in an hour or so and
see where we're at?"

"Good." She started to go, then stopped, speaking quietly to
the men. "You two are strapped, right?"

"Of course," Sixkiller exclaimed, chuckling. "Although you
don't seem too concerned about the prospect of us getting
jammed up by the cops, Chainey."

"I'm not allergic to jail, just death," she countered. "An hour,
then." She went back out into the warm evening, a certain fatal-
ism having overtaken her emotionally and psychologically.
Maybe the feeling was what consumed soldiers when they were
on patrol, knowing a sniper or another patrol could open up on

them at any second. Maybe it was what went through the minds of sky divers as they prepared to jump from the plane. They were as prepared as they could be, but anything could happen. At some point you had to say the hell with it and just get it over with.

A car suddenly tore down the street and Chainey put her hand under her shirt, thinking her pal Molly was about to do a drive-by. But the vehicle proved to be a load of twentysomething men whooping and hollering and passing a bottle around. The car was swallowed up in the general constant maelstrom of the Vegas night. She went parallel to Flamingo Road and headed east past the Bellagio and its massive fountains. She crossed Las Vegas Boulevard and continued on past Bally's and got near the Paris casino.

The outdoor/indoor restaurant, the Mon Ami Gabi, was still feeding diners. A pastry chef she knew waved to her as she went inside. Chainey knew several former employees of the Riverhead now worked at the Paris casino. Some might have quit legitimately and others might be doing a little-light duty industrial espionage. This kind of thing had gone on since the days of Moe Dalitz and Gus Greenbaum.

You "fire" an employee and they take a job at a newer, flashier casino. Of course, what they're really there to do is report now and then on what kind of floor show was going to be added for the Christmas crush, what fight they were angling to host, and so on. To a certain extent it was low-level stuff in the big scheme of things, but a Tom Jones here or a Whitney Houston there could be a couple mil per week in terms of customers coming to your venue. And after a fashion, you were talking about real money in Vegas terms.

Making her rounds in the 85,000-square-foot casino, Chainey was sure somebody would report to Degault that she was out and about. In turn, Zevonian would get the word, too. After half an hour, she started to head off the main floor and was making a right at a bank of slot machines when she ran into Shirley Bassey.

"Martha, isn't it?" The famous singer was flanked on either

side by two men in tasteful suits. Several yards of material must have gone into making their clothes, it occurred to Chainey, staring at their size twenty-four necks.

"That's right. We met last Fourth of July at that party Krekorian International had at the MGM Grand." They shook hands.

"Of course," she said in that throaty voice of hers.

"You just finished a set?"

"No, darling, I'm going to try my hand at the baccarat table. That's why I brought my good-luck charms."

One of the behemoths twitched a smile.

"Well, I'd wish you luck, but you know what they say."

"What?" Bassey asked, her teeth absolutely sparkling in her handsome face.

"The good ones don't need it. Ciao." Chainey waved and walked out into the night and a press of people. No one tried to shank her and no bullets came whizzing at her. She was gripped with the need to clear her head, get her bearings straight to sharp and on guard. Running into the singer had been the kind of unreal moment repeated often in Vegas. Like the time she'd managed to climb back out of the hole playing a hand of high/low poker and walked away from the table five thousand up.

High from her good fortune, she'd gotten to talking to a woman loading change into a slot machine, and it turned out she was Mary Ann Vecchio. Years ago she had been made immortal at fourteen as the young woman crying on her knees next to one of the students slain by the National Guard at Kent State. That was the weird dichotomy of Vegas. A capital of sin was surrounded by cowboys, red necks, Mormons, X-Files nuts and survivalists. No wonder that strangeness leaked into town.

Wanting to get her head back into the proper frame—psyched up, as it were—she took the elevator in the Eiffel Tower of the Paris. Looking out of the glass-walled conveyance as she rose in the eleven-story structure, she saw the Arc de Triomphe and what she knew to be a reproduction of the River Seine. She had no way of knowing if these faux constructs were true to their famous Parisian originals, but considering the joint and its environs cost some $800 million to build, you figure they could afford accurate blueprints.

She came out on the observation deck, the sweltering air blowing against her face and through her hair. There were two couples kissing and nuzzling each other in the semidark of the deck. Indirect lighting was supplied by bulbs underneath the railing. She walked along as she looked out on the bright lights below. At one end of the deck was an old man with a white beard wafting in the breeze. Incongruously, he was dressed in a long black alpaca coat and a black Stetson. He looked like a character out of a John Ford western she'd seen on AMC. The old man had one of his booted feet pressed against the wall below the railing and he had a deck of cards in one gnarled hand. Using his other hand, the man in black methodically removed a card from the deck, then flicked the card over the rail. His face was as solemn as a temperance advocate.

Each of the cards was briefly caught on the warm wind, the sparkle below coruscating across their coated surfaces. Then the cards would either flutter away across the spires and rooftops or drop down into the canyon of artificial light. A guard who was nearly invisible tucked in another corner did not interfere with the old man and his work.

Chainey stayed there, willing herself not to project too far into the future. She simply intended to be alive when the sun came up. Her cell phone rang and she answered it.

"Vern?"

"None other. I think we got a line on Miss Molly."

"Yeah?"

Sixkiller said, "There's several members of our tribe who work in the various casinos. Through some contacts in the hotel and culinary unions, we've talked to a few of them and given them a description of her."

It occurred to Chainey that she hadn't told him what Zevonian looked like but would ask him how he found out later. And how it was they'd been nosing around in the Oakland Hills. "So they got a line on her?"

"She's been spotted around the—what do you call it?" His voice trailed away from the phone and she assumed he was asking Leopold a question. "Glitter Gulch, that's it," he said, coming back on.

"You close to there?"

"Less than fifteen minutes on foot."

"All right." Her mind assembled a plan. "You two come in from the north off of Main near the railroad tracks. I'll come up the Strip and enter off of Fourth Street. Now remember, she might have some help, so be alert."

"Will do."

"See you there." She clicked off and pocketed her phone. She stepped to the elevator and got on, the old man also joining her. They rode in silence to the street and the door hushed open.

The old man leaned against the wall of the car, his arms before him, as if he was praying. One of his hands was clasping the wrist of his other arm. A red ruby ring was prominent on his finger. He didn't move from his repose as Chainey stepped across the threshold of the elevator when it stopped.

"You got the touch, ma'am." The old man touched the brim of his hat as she exited the car.

Chainey was standing in the area underneath the Eiffel Tower and she turned back to say something to the old fellow. The elevator doors closed on an empty car. She looked each way along the open air concourse but did not see him. There were people about, but no one in that distinctive coat. No one holding such a coat over their arm either. She smiled ruefully and continued on her journey.

Wanting to get to Glitter Gulch on time, she hailed a cab on Las Vegas Boulevard. The car that pulled to the curb was a Yellow Cab, a Crown Victoria dripping coolant from behind the front bumper. Getting in the back, the woman cabbie turned to glance at Chainey.

"Where to, leggy?" She was a broad-shouldered young and pretty Filipina with sienna-tinged lips lined in black and large hoop earrings dangling from her small ears.

"Up to Fourth and Carson."

"Sure thing, heart-stopper."

Not that she didn't find it flattering, but what was it about her and women cab drivers? she wondered. The woman piloted her hack expertly as she went east over to Paradise, then went north, effectively cutting time off the meter though it was geographically a longer way around. The traffic along the Strip, even at this time of the morning, was heavily compacted. Who'd figure a city in the middle of the desert would not have enough room?

"Five-thirty-five, honey lamb." The driver had pulled to the curb and turned around in her seat, giving Chainey the up and down. "You used to be a showgirl, right?"

"I did my time on the chorus line." She handed across a five and two ones.

She retrieved a card tucked between the visor and headliner. "Don't be a stranger." She gave Chainey the card. "Call me when you want to ride, all right?"

"Sure, Prossy," she said, reading the handwritten name above the printed company logo. She'd also written in her pager number. How many of these cards did this chick whip out in a week? "I'll see you."

"I should hope so." She saluted and took off.

Absently, Chainey touched the area of her shirt where the gun was holstered underneath. She walked toward her destination. Glitter Gulch was the slang term for the Fremont Street Experience. It was a converted four blocks closed off to vehicular traffic. This was downtown Vegas, home of older casinos such as the Golden Nugget and the Horseshoe. Greeting you at the entrance of the area now landscaped with a park was that famous smoking neon cowboy. The dude had a cigarette that bobbed up and down in his mouth and was seen all the time in films and TV shows shot in Vegas.

In late 1995, the downtown casinos had been fed up taking it in the shorts as more and more potential patrons gravitated like moths to the incandescence of the Strip's casinos. Who could resist the pirate battle at Treasure Island or the multicolored lasers and stories high projected on pharaoh's face at the Luxor? And so they put their heads and pocketbooks together and created a fourteen-hundred-foot-long, 90-foot high canopy over the entire area.

This hard-shell canopy had some two million tiny lights in it, Chainey recalled reading. She walked past the neon sitting cowgirl showing some thigh, who rode up and down on a shower of sparkles blowing out of her ass. The underside of the canopy, which you looked up at, was then a constantly changing computer generated show of dancing girls, swirls, rocket ships, exploding amoebas and so on and so on. Certainly given this Blade Runneresque optical input and impact of the population boom in and around the city, the Gulch never hurt for pedestrian traffic. But this was still the old side of gambling Vegas.

Not too far away was the El Cortez, the last original casino in town. She pushed history, or being part of it, from her mind.

A prickliness moved its way along Chainey's spine. *Be cool, girl, be cool.* Drew always said you got taken out not 'cause the other guy was a better shot or fighter than you, but because you thought they were. When your life was on the line, that was the time for confidence. You can take anybody if you're set, he'd warned.

If she was Molly, where the hell would she be? Up on a rooftop, taking aim with a sniper's rifle? There were a lot of people out, but Chainey wasn't a sharp shooter, so she wasn't sure that meant she was safe from that kind of attack. She did know that getting up high wasn't as easy as all that. Like the Eiffel Tower, the casinos routinely posted guards toward the heights because you did indeed get a fair share of jumpers in Vegas, what with folks being depressed after that winning hand they knew they had didn't mean shit.

She was scanning the upper reaches, but what with the glare, she couldn't distinguish much. Or would it be like in an old movie, Zevonian at one end of the promenade and Chainey marching toward her from the other. Her reverie ended when she heard her name being called.

"Chainey, over here." Sixkiller gestured vociferously in front of the Fitzgeralds' casino.

"You got here quick," she said, ambling over. Her internal alarms were amping up.

"Figured time was of the essence, right?"

"Where's Leopold?"

"That's why I was looking for you," the security chief replied. "He's over near the courthouse. Your girl Molly, or at least we think it's her, is parked in a car there."

"What, just waiting?"

"For backup, probably." Sixkiller was in motion. "We can get a jump on her."

"Right on." Chainey was behind Sixkiller and slipped the gun from underneath her shirt. She kept it pressed against her side. If anybody saw it, what would they do? The precariousness of the modern world said the odds were in her favor no cop would be called. If someone did notice the piece, they'd rationalize that it was a cell phone or electronic date book. Who the hell would walk around in a crowd with a gun in plain sight?

The section he led them to was a dim area with only a couple of lampposts behind the Four Queens casino. The courthouse being to their left was set back from an expanse of lawn facing Third Street. There was a row of adult newspapers racked along the sidewalk. One hooker strolled by, making sure Sixkiller saw the swing of her hips. It was nice and quiet and unhurried in this part. The din of the nearby crowd seemed like a recording. All around Chainey were dark shapes containing who knew what.

"What's the deal, Vern?" He stopped walking, his back stiffening.

"You want to get Molly, don't you?" His voice was flat, without inflection.

He began to turn and Chainey told him, "I'll put one in you, Vern, dead in the goddamn heart. Maybe Leopold or your girl's got a night scope trained on me from the courthouse, but I'll get you before I drop." The shadows were deep where they stood, caused by the spill over of light from Glitter Gulch. But Sixkiller was right in front of her; there was nowhere for him to go.

"You're all worked up there, Martha." He stopped pivoting, and now he was in profile to her. "We're working on the same team, remember?"

"What I remember is you and Leopold sneaking around Zora Blanchard's pad in the Oakland Hills. And how is it you know what Molly looks like when you never asked me for a description of her?"

The big security chief ratcheted his head around to glare at Chainey. A perplexed expression screwed up his features. "Leopold said he found another e-mail from Smith when we came here to Vegas trying to dig up more information."

She snorted. "What, he have a psychic vision?"

"His laptop."

Sixkiller was turned around all the way now. In the diffused lighting, she couldn't be sure if he had his piece out or not. Her palms felt sweaty, but she wasn't going to be suckered. *Be quiet, let Sixkiller talk, let him make the move.*

"He always takes it with him," Sixkiller went on. "He'd already tapped into Smith's hard drive, and he told me he'd could access it at any time."

"And how did Molly come up?"

"Some people think we're joined at the hip, but—"

The retort of the shot was louder than Chainey thought it would be. That was probably because she was so primed for something to happen. Both of them were in motion by the time the second shot sounded.

"Courthouse?" Sixkiller was crouched behind a concrete trash receptacle. His gun was pointing across the street and not at her.

"Pretty sure," Chainey responded. She was flat on the ground using the racks and the gloom for whatever cover they afforded. "But this ain't no war movie, sarge. I'm not about to have my pretty black ass shot up rushing that place."

"You don't expect me to go, do you?"

"Then we back off and reconnoiter."

"You sure you haven't been watching old Jeff Chandler flicks on the tube?"

"Come on." Chainey pointed to the side of the Four Queens casino and ran with all her might for it. Sixkiller was right on her heels. Two more shots sounded. The bullets were close but didn't strike them. And they'd been shot from a pistol, not a rifle. Chainey purposely chose that part of the casino because it was dark. They put their backs against the wall and a service door opened. A cook was stepping out to smoke in the night air, and the two rushed past him.

"Hey, you can't come in this way," he shouted. Then he stopped talking as he noticed their guns.

"I suggest you hold off on that nicotine break, my man," Sixkiller said as they dashed out of the kitchen. Hitting the main room, they wisely tucked their pistols away.

"Come on," Chainey urged.

"Where?" Sixkiller asked, following her.

"It was either Leopold or Molly shooting at us." They headed toward the front, snaking through the crowd.

"Are you sure it wasn't both?"

"They would have set up a cross fire. It was the same gun shooting at us."

"Damn, Chainey, you do have balls big as grapefruits, don't you?"

She wasn't working on a witty come back. "Which hotel are you guys at?" She scooted through the front doors, nearly toppling a woman with a cane.

"Watch it," the woman grossed.

Sixkiller was beside her on the sidewalk. Overhead, the canopy displayed what looked like red meteors colliding with tumbling silver refrigerators. "You think it was just Leopold who was shooting at us?"

"Yeah, Frankie got to him somehow. Or maybe he was always the inside man. Who better to set Smith and Delacruz up?"

"Shit," he mused aloud.

"Shit is right. You said he doesn't travel anywhere without his laptop. I'm wagering he's got to go back and get it now that he knows we're on to him. If he left it, we might find another computer whiz to find something in his hard drive."

"I'll go for that." They hailed a cab and got back to their hotel, the Woo Inn off Valley View Boulevard.

"Who's got the keys to the car?" Chainey asked as Sixkiller paid the bill.

"We both do; it's a rental."

"Is that it?" A new Lexus was tearing away from behind the motel.

Sixkiller running after the car answered the question. Chainey joined him. The big man was shooting, which Chainey did not think was the best of all ideas. Conversely, she didn't have an alternative to propose. The Lexus fishtailed into a left and leapt into the night.

The cab, of course, had hightailed it out of there at the sound of gunfire.

"We better make ourselves scarce," Chainey hissed.

Sixkiller seemed to suddenly realize he was standing in the night, a warm gun in his hand. "Oh, yeah." He tucked the piece away and they walked, calmly, away from the motel. There weren't many pedestrians out in this part of town, and the two made it unmolested to a coffee shop. The place was called the Silver Dunes and the design looked as if it had been transplanted there from 1957.

"When did you first hear about Molly?" Chainey sipped water, too keyed up to handle coffee.

Sixkiller tapped at the table with an index finger, "Here, in town. Leopold is the one who came up with her name in all this."

"But if he's bought, why tell you about her?"

Sixkiller pursed his lips. "Maybe they're figuring with you running around I've got to talk to you, which is what me and him decided. That way they get us both together. Leopold goes back home and tells everyone it was this chick Molly who did me in."

"And he'd have your job," Chainey added.

Sixkiller frowned. "But that would leave unanswered Smith and Delacruz's murders." His order of meat loaf and mashed potatoes arrived. He forked some down.

Chainey observed, "No, he'd tell the tribe the truth. He'd confirm that it was Frankie Degault behind it. But it wouldn't matter then."

"Because Frankie was going to be gone, leaving his sister to catch the heat." Sixkiller chased his food with gulps from his glass of Pepsi.

Sixkiller pointed with his fork. "The seven large was running money."

"And for starting over," Chainey remarked. "What I think is ol' Frankie has either been skimming from his partners, including his sister, or he's done something that's about to blow up big time." Three handsome middle-aged women in business attire went past them, in lockstep, each with an arm in the crook of the other. The trio were laughing and talking as if the world was theirs. They looked like they'd stepped out of a commercial as they sauntered down the aisle.

"So now what?"

"Obviously we've got Frankie's panties in a bunch. And he's not going to be sitting still."

"Well, " Sixkiller said, adding another forkful of food to his mouth, talking around his chewing, "we can spend more time trying to flush out Molly or we go for the big dog."

Chainey concurred. Out of the picture window they sat next to she saw two black-and-white patrol cars go past, moving toward the motel. She said, "That's what I was thinking. No more fucking around, we get this over one way or the other. But what about Leopold?"

"He's got to run. He knows I'm going to call Lieutenant Lizardo and have him on the lookout. So going home ain't in the program. Eventually we'll catch up to him." He ate some more.

"Glad to see the situation hasn't affected your nerves."

"I eat when I'm tense." He patted his stomach. "Been getting too upset lately." He pushed the plate away. "So, you gonna call them back and taunt Frankie?"

"He's got to do something. It's after three now. That leaves him a little less than six hours to get rid of me and you if he doesn't want his board to know what we know." She drank some water that tasted soapy. "Unless . . ." she began.

"He's already running," Sixkiller finished, this time pointing with the blunt end of his empty fork.

"The question then," Chainey said, scooting out of the booth, "is, would his sister simply let him do it?"

"Call her back," the big man suggested.

"Good idea." She dialed the number and it rang several times with no pick up. Absently, she put a tip on the table and walked toward Sixkiller, who was paying the bill. "No answer, but I have the feeling nobody in the Degault family is sleeping this morning."

As he got his change back, he offered her a toothpick, which she declined. He inserted one in his mouth and took several more to place in his jacket pocket. They walked outside and Chainey dialed another number.

"Who're you calling?" he asked.

"Mooch."

Sixkiller made a face at a name he didn't know, but waited.

"Shit," Chainey swore. "He's got his machine on." She clicked off and fumed.

Sixkiller folded his arms and leaned against a pillar on the coffee shop. He knew she'd come up with something else.

She did. Chainey dialed another number and got lucky. "Rena, sorry to wake you, but this is drop-dead time, homegirl."

"I understand, Martha." Solomon didn't sound too groggy, but if she had a man there, more power to her.

"Listen, do you know of anyplace Frankie Degault keeps around town? Maybe it's in Reno or Laughlin, whatever. You know, someplace he uses to bring working girls to entertain some whale or shark he's trying to impress."

"I don't offhand, but there's a couple of my contacts I can check with," her friend answered.

"This is no time for politeness, Rena. I need you to call these people, pound on their doors, offer 'em money and get back to me. I'm going to his board, but everything falls my way if I give 'em Frankie too."

"I'm on it," she said eagerly. "I'll get a hold of you on your cell phone."

"Good." She clicked off and explained to Sixkiller who she'd been talking to.

Rena Solomon had been lying awake on her back on the couch in her clothes. She'd been worried about her friend; what if the Glass Anvil lead was useless? Or what if this Molly Zevonian got the drop on Martha, that it had been a setup that Victoria had suckered her into? And she'd be implicated in the murder of her friend, the woman who had helped get her clean. What kind of scumbag would that make her? And what would she do if that happened—how would she expose the truth? Then her phone rang.

After getting off the phone with Chainey, she knew there was only one way to get the information she needed. She got Victoria Degault on the phone. "It's Rena. What the hell have you gotten me into?" she said angrily.

"I'm busy right now, Rena," the other woman said sharply.

"Don't you hang up on me," Solomon warned. "You owe me some answers."

"I don't owe you shit, Rena. We have a barter kind of situation, and that's it."

"We got more than that and you'd do well to start getting on the memory tip, Victoria. I'm not the only one who's been served by Mr. Boo." She didn't wait for a response and rushed to her next question. "Where the hell is your brother?"

"This for Chainey?"

No sense lying. "Yes."

"I honestly don't know." Her voice had softened. "We had a big blowup."

Solomon plowed ahead. "We'll get to that later. You must have some idea where he is now. Where he'd hole up."

There was just the line buzz on the other end; then Victoria Degault spoke. "There is. But I'm only telling you for my own reasons."

"You're only telling me 'cause your dear brother has screwed you and you need him put in check. But I'm sure we'll get to that later too, Victoria."

"Yes, I guess we will," she said with finality.

Solomon also adjusted her tone, putting more understanding into her voice. "Let's be real here. I'm guessing you need Chainey more than you need your brother, at least at this moment. You need her to run interference. You have to have been thinking about this."

Guilelessly, Victoria replied, "Your talents are wasted on that pinko rag you work at, Rena."

"So people tell me. Now where's the place, Victoria? It's your ass or his once the board finds out."

"This I know. But you're asking me to go against family."

"I'm not your therapist, Victoria. We both know we're talking about self-preservation here. I'm not trying to convince you of anything you aren't already wrestling with."

"Fuck," the other woman swore.

"Now you're talking," Solomon said.

CHAPTER EIGHTEEN

The house was a two-story number on a butte overlooking the north shore of Lake Mead. The road they'd come in on was a tributary off Highway 167. The house was an older model, built in sixties flair along rectangular lines, with flagstone and glass as the detail ingredients. The joint reminded her of something she'd seen in one of Dean-o's Matt Helm flicks. There was only Frankie Degault's car in the curved driveway, but that didn't mean he was alone. A light was on in a front room. Chainey and Sixkiller parked a hundred yards away, down the slope leading to the house. They checked out the area.

"Do we knock?" Sixkiller nervously cracked his knuckles.

"Or wait till he comes out."

"And then what, Chainey? You gonna peel his dome? You don't think that's going to set you in solid with the board or his li'l sis, do you?"

She weighed his words. "You're right. But let's get out. I feel too boxed-in sitting in the car." They exited, both of them casting wary glances all around. Now the desert air carried a chill. The pre-dawn time was devoid of movement or sounds, save for the duo's feet making crunching sounds in the sandy earth. Across the lake was a recreation area replete with picnic tables, barbecue pits and hiking equipment rental booths. To the west was Hoover Dam. The mammoth thing was a wonder of will and engineering completed in 1935, two years ahead of schedule. The building of the dam, to siphon water from the mighty Colorado River, was responsible for the migration of blacks into the even then heavily Mormon-populated Nevada.

Enticing white workers to come work in the unforgiving heat on a rigorous deadline had been a hard sell for the companies responsible for erecting the dam. Especially in those years between the world wars, as the mining of magnesium, copper and other useful metals meant steady work for whites and the rise of their union power. The bosses who wanted Hoover Dam to be a reality recruited black labor from various southern towns to work longer and for less pay or benefits as they would have had to offer with an all-white workforce used to a certain standard.

After the dam was finished, the black laborers got jobs in the mines or work in the new Vegas that had concurrently come into being between the wars—and reached a new level when Bugsy Siegel opened the Flamingo in '47 after World War II. These men and their women became a staple of the service crews in the new hotels, eateries and casinos. But Nevada, which got its clientele from the Midwest through the South, practiced Jim Crow. So the workers had disposable income but few places to spend it.

This was a time when black entertainers like the Trenier Brothers, Pearl Bailey, Lena Horne, Nat King Cole, and a young Sammy Davis could pack 'em into the lounges of the white casinos but couldn't eat or stay there. But segregation has always been the mother in America, and thus this condition precipitated the rise of west Vegas as black Vegas. That was the area of town you could go, whether you were musician Earl "Fatha" Hines or the janitor at the Riviera, and rub shoulders and have a drink.

Chainey stopped reminiscing about the stories of her Grandfather Hiram and got back on track. It was lonely and quiet. "Molly's here," she said tersely.

"It would only make sense," Sixkiller agreed. "Degault's got to play the percentage and figure you're coming. And if that's the case, then I'd have my hired killer ready to rock and roll. Especially"—he grinned appreciatively—"since you took care of his number one."

"There's no way to sneak up on that house," she observed. Degault's place sat on a cleared parcel that contained low cacti and other desert plants to one side that weren't tall enough to hide an adult. The houses on this rim were spaced several hundred feet apart, with a fence or grass as the markings between properties.

"That also means your girl isn't in the immediate area either," Sixkiller concluded. "The closest she could be is in that brush." He pointed with the barrel of his gun. "And we can keep the house between us and there."

"Maybe she's inside, too."

"Want to smash the car into the house and see what happens?" Sixkiller was serious.

She glared at him. "I think subtlety is called for here, Vern."

"Okay, but keep it in mind, huh?" He crept forward.

"Oh, sure." She too moved off, alert to movement or sound from the brush. The two got about twenty yards on open ground, each ready.

"I wish something would happen," Sixkiller murmured, stopping and looking around.

"Careful what you wish for," Chainey advised. They continued on; then she tapped his arm with her pistol. He halted again, waiting, listening. Nothing.

"I can't take this," Chainey said. Crashing the car into the house was looking better to her.

"We're in it now, beautiful." They went forward again, this time splitting up, coming at the house from two different angles. If they were opened up on, then at least one of them might have a chance to run to safety.

The two were near the driveway as the motion detectors popped on security flood lights. And the front door swung open. Backlit, a man stood in the doorway with a rifle raised at shoulder level. The business end of the weapon was pointed at Chainey. "How much you want to bet I can cut her down then you, Sixkiller, before you can reach me?"

Chainey wanted to say something brave like, "Don't worry about me, Vern, gun him down after he shoots me." But that big bore hunting rifle Degault was holding would open her up like a Christmas package. And that was not a pleasant way to go. She didn't say anything. At least if Vern was going to tough it out, she wasn't going to beg for her life. *Take it like a woman,* she told herself grimly.

"Okay, Degault." Sixkiller put his gun on the ground and kicked it away.

Chainey did the same thing.

"Come on." Degault gestured with one hand for them to come forward, the rifle in the other. He stepped back as Chainey crossed the threshold. "You know why I picked the man, Chainey?" Degault was smiling. "Because the odds said he'd be chivalrous. How the hell could he explain it to the boys back home if he let a good-lookin' chick like you get blown away?"

Sixkiller had stepped in behind Chainey.

"That assumes he'd be alive to have such a conversation," she said.

"You, on the other hand," Degault continued, touching her shoulder with the rifle's barrel, "I wasn't sure what you'd do if I had the rifle on Sixkiller. You've proven to be tougher and smarter than I gave you credit for."

"Gee, thanks, Frankie."

"Not a problem," he said, as if he didn't catch her sarcasm. He kicked the door shut and jerked the rifle toward the light. The three marched into the tastefully appointed living room.

"Where's Molly?" Chainey expected her to suddenly walk into the room.

"I don't need that blood-hungry broad to clean up for me," he rasped. "Hell, it's her fault this all went haywire."

Sixkiller and Chainey had purposely stood in different parts of the spacious room. A matching set of suitcases was stacked in one corner. Off to the side was a Southwest-designed card table made of mahogany. There was a half-empty tumbler on a Riverhead coaster on it. The two had their hands up, and each was hoping that the other might still get a chance at the rifle when Degault opened up on the first one.

The big man said, "What the hell are you going to do with us, Degault?"

"Baker isn't around to be burying us head down like before," Chainey put in.

Degault had the rifle held low, part of it perpendicular to his abdomen. "That's okay, Chainey. Getting rid of you is going to bring me great personal satisfaction."

"And you leave Victoria to fend for herself?"

"Don't try to be clever, Chainey," the boss of the Riverhead challenged. "What you better get straight is who's the next of kin you want notified. I know your folks are dead." He laughed sharply at his bad joke.

"You just gonna leave our bodies to rot here in your house?" Sixkiller kicked at an end table. "How you gonna explain that, Degault?"

"Molly," Chainey guessed. "He's probably told her to stay loose until he calls her. He kills us, then calls her to come out here. He's also ratted to the cops, and they nab her or shoot it out with her, doesn't matter, does it, Frankie?"

He bit his bottom lip, smiling. "Like I said, you're sharp, Chainey."

Sixkiller got it. "He pulled her back so he could have one more fall guy just in case."

"Exactly." He brought the rifle up, sighting it on Chainey. "You ever read this book, Chainey? It's called *Shoot the Woman First.*" Degault held the instrument of her death very steady. "See, the book is about terrorism, religious sects, all that, right? So of course men being men, the cops think with their dicks and their reflex is to think a woman ain't as dangerous as a man. But you and me know different, don't we, Chainey?"

She hoped that Sixkiller would be able to get to Degault as her body hit the floor. It wasn't much to take beyond the grave, but it was all she had. "I thought you were an eight baller, Frankie," she suddenly blurted in a scornful manner.

"Getting me pissed off isn't going to help you much," he laughed. "But I guess you can't help yourself."

"Be a sport, Frankie," a new voice said.

They all turned to see Victoria Degault step through the door.

"Get out of here, Victoria," he barked. A look of uncertainty misted his eyes.

"I don't think so, brother dear." She was carrying a voluminous purse slung over one shoulder. "It's time I stopped being left out of the picture."

"This will resolve itself, Vic." His eyes flitted from his sister to the other two. "All you have to do is tell the board the truth—you knew nothing of the deals I made that went sour."

Derisively she said, "You mean the money you blew trying to get even richer quicker? Just like any mark?"

He put on a sheepish look, which was incongruous with him holding a rifle. "They seemed like good ideas at the time. And you know how it goes, once you're in the hole, you have to keep paying into the kitty just to protect your investment."

She stepped farther into the room. "The board's going to ream me, Frankie. They'll want to know why I didn't know what you were up to. Maybe, they'll reason"—she looked off toward the curtained window—"I was in on it, too."

"Now you know how Chainey felt," he remarked. "But it's covered, Vic. You give 'em these two and Molly on the slab, and you're set. I'll give you the source of the cash I hired Molly and her husband with"—he made a grand gesture with his hand—"all fingers point back to me. They'll buy that Chainey and Molly were in on it together."

"What about me?" Sixkiller piped in.

He lifted an eyebrow. "You were out for revenge for Smith and Delacruz."

"And you'll be disappeared." His sister ran a hand over her tired face.

"Give me two hours' head start, that's all I'm asking," Frankie Degault said.

She didn't respond. The only sound in the room was the hum of the electric clock over the red brick fireplace. "I will."

"Good." He brought the rifle up again, boring down on Chainey. Audibly, she drew in her breath, waiting for impact.

"You have to give her a chance, too," Victoria Degault said evenly. "I wouldn't know any of this if it wasn't for her nosing around."

Incredulous, Degault said, "So? She was out to save her own ass same as you and me."

"Still," his sister insisted, "you owe her a break, Frank. If you don't think so, I do."

"Fuck." He lowered the rifle. "So what am I supposed to do, let her and her boyfriend run around the lake outside, then I hunt them down like in that movie? I'm kinda on a schedule here, Victoria."

"Nothing that elaborate," Chainey said. It was a sucker's play. It was a goofball idea and was as likely to backfire as be successful. But it was fifty/fifty, and it was melodramatic enough to appeal to Frankie Degault's ego. And what the hell did she have to lose? "High hand, Frankie."

Everybody stared at her.

"Five card draw." Chainey indicated with a nod of her head the deck of cards and chips on a built-in bookshelf. "Victoria deals."

"I win, you die." He gave her a straight face.

"I win, we walk, and me and Sixkiller don't say shit."

"There's no guarantee."

"You got my word." She was about to add that it was worth more than his, but discretion prevailed.

"That's almost funny, Chainey."

"Why don't we find out?" Victoria Degault suggested.

"What are you saying?" he barked, irritated. "This is bullshit."

"I knew you were no gambler, Frankie."

"That psychic network psychology is played, Chainey. What's to say you won't rat me out?"

"Your sister will see to it," Chainey said. "I still have to do business in this town. It doesn't make sense to give any other story than she does. And if Molly should trip into a coffin, that's fine by me."

"It's in Chainey's interest to silence Molly," Sixkiller contributed.

"But what about your brothers?" Frankie Degault said. "I'm the one who ordered their hit."

"They were turncoats, out to fuck the tribe," Sixkiller said angrily. "They got what they deserved."

Fear of death was a great motivator for putting on an act Chainey reflected. "Well, you gonna be man enough or not?" It worked with Baker, would it work with him?

"Fuck you, Chainey. Let's do it. Only we're playing stud."

Men. "Fine," she said hoarsely. He won either way, the bastard. She sat at the card table. Degault sat opposite, the rifle resting across his legs. Victoria got a deck chair and sat between them at the table. Sixkiller stood near Chainey. Victoria Degault shuffled the cards. Sixkiller cut them.

Five card stud was usually played with at least four. The way it worked was, you got five cards down, and it might be a pair of jacks or better to open or guts. That is, you didn't have a pair or you might just have a pair of threes, but you bluffed and made an opening bet of a dollar or whatever. The other players either thought you were bluffing and bet into the pot or let you have your dollar back and the ante from the dealer by folding. If it was five card draw, the raise was matched; then you could discard up to four cards to see if you could get a better hand.

But this was different. It was the two of them, and it was stud. Each would be dealt five cards and that would be it. Victoria Degault methodically dealt the cards facedown. Each let the five slide in front of them before they picked them up to see the results. Neither gave away any emotion on their face. The whirring of the clock's gears were like the roar of a jet engine in Chainey's head.

"Pair of goddamn kings," Frankie Degault gloated. He flung the cards down triumphantly.

Chainey blinked at the cards in the middle of the table. "Yeah," she said. "A pair of twos." She rolled over the two of clubs and the two of diamonds.

"Good-bye, Chainey." Degault started to rise.

"And another for the kicker to make trips," she added, revealing the two of hearts.

"Damn," Sixkiller sagged visibly, clutching his face in his hands. "I damn near shit myself."

Frankie Degault was boiling. He bolted up, upsetting the table. Some of the cards floated to the floor as if in slow motion. "That's a bad sign, I tell you. Good luck for you means bad luck for me." The rifle was in his hands. His sister moved back. Chainey had the table between her and Frankie Degault.

"You motherfucker, you agreed." Sixkiller lunged.

"Fuck what I agreed to, Tonto." He shoved the stock of the rifle in Sixkiller's gut with great ferocity, causing him to gasp and fall to the floor.

"You triflin' chiseler," Chainey uttered.

"Yeah, well, you smart-ass cunt, you won't have me to worry about any longer." The barrel was aimed at her head.

Sixkiller was getting off the floor. Somebody screamed, and Chainey realized it was her as she scrambled and slid over the tabletop at Degault. A shot went off and Chainey distantly imagined how many seconds of consciousness she'd have till death claimed her. Or maybe her luck held and she'd just be a paraplegic the rest of her life.

Her body got to the other end of the table and collided with Degault's. She went over on top of him and found she was still breathing. Frankie Degault had a surprised look on his frozen face. He blinked rapidly, the weight of Chainey on him forcing air from his lungs. Hands grabbed her and hauled her off of him. The rifle was now held in limp hands.

"Vic," he whispered, his eyes shifting to peer at her.

"You'd fuck me on this, Frankie. You were going to leave me to take the heat and only came clean once I found out." She came forward and kneeled beside her brother. The gun she'd taken from her bag was in her hand.

"You'd do it again, Frankie." She put his head on her lap, running her hands through his hair. "You'd disappear for a while. Then, like I know you, you'd find it hilarious to come back here, probably Reno. Have yourself a new face, laser-altered fingertips, more weight. You'd try to work one of your scams or get at the money you and I have salted away from Dad, from the old days." She was talking tenderly, words only for him.

"Vic, I . . ." He didn't have the strength to finish.

"I know, I know, it's your nature. I've always known, baby brother." A change settled over her face. "But Daddy always taught us business comes first, isn't that right?"

He clamped his lips together as if tasting something bitter, and then he stopped living. Victoria Degault looked up, her eyes dry.

CHAPTER NINETEEN

Molly Zevonian stepped away from the entrance to the two-hundred-room Boomtown casino off I-15, south of town. The joint catered to the Iowa and trucker crowd and was a perfect spot to lay low while she waited to hear from Frankie Degault. Boomtown was actually a huge RV park with a grocery store, Laundromat, two pools—one for the adults and one for the kids—picnic area and rec room. It was a quarter past eight in the morning, and word from Degault had yet to arrive. And from the way he sounded on the phone, he was making to beat town before the sun was up, but the plan was, she'd be called to where she could come and finish off that amazon bitch Chainey.

She wasn't worried about Degault; he either called or he didn't. She wanted Chainey. Elwood and she had an arrangement, true. They were not the typical post-modern urbanites, or whatever the term was these days. Though it certainly could be argued that they were upwardly mobile. They didn't push marks out of this world for charity. She mentally patted herself on the back for having been the driving force in building up their careers.

When she hooked up with Elwood Porter he was content to be a sometimes enforcer and do an occasional snatch-and-grab or be a wheel man. She convinced him that together they could be effective as a man-and-woman shooter team. Not that such a pairing was particularly unique in the crime world, but given his family ties and the circles she ran in, they were bound to pull down some well-paying hit jobs.

And Elwood hadn't been adverse to her lifestyle, which was a big reason she could stand staying with him as long as she had. Zevonian stopped by a tree in the picnic area and cupped her hands to protect the lighter's flame. She lit a cigarette and puffed into the crisp morning air. She plucked a speck of tobacco off her tongue, watching the smoke drift upward.

Okay, maybe she wouldn't go to the ends of the earth barefoot to be with the guy, they weren't Ward and June, but who was these days? Goddammit, they'd had something. Fondly she remembered the shit-eating grin he'd get on his face as he sat and drank beer while she had the dildo strapped on doing another chick. Unconventional was what you could call their relationship. But it wasn't like when they did a job, did some wet work, that it turned them on or anything sick like that.

In fact, they'd be quiet and not talk too much about what had just gone down. But before a job, they made sure everything was lined up, that the target was in the box, as he liked to say. Zevonian pulled the cigarette away from her lips, letting a stream of vapor out. They'd brought along Elwood's second cousin on the Marin run. Break him in, her husband had said. A rough laugh from her released smoke through her flaring nostrils. They broke him, in all right, all the fuckin' way in. But he did know his electronics, compliments of a stint in the army. She wasn't much on luck or fate, but she'd had that tickle along her spine and she should have listened to it. She should have insisted to Elwood that their string was good with the two of them, a third was bound to stretch things. Hell, she was going to miss him.

She flicked the butt of the cigarette away from her and ground it on the grass. She stretched, put her hands in her jean's pockets and wandered about as she got her head around her business. For all intents and purposes Frankie Degault was out of the picture. Therefore, as far as she was concerned she was free to act in whatever manner she deemed appropriate. She was owed the balance on the job, but collecting from the sister was not going to be easy, she knew. Also, two other factors were at play. Zevonian walked between a row of RVs.

The board of the Riverhead might oust or cap Victoria because of her brother's bullshit. So if she was gone, who settled the bill? Not that she'd see it as her obligation anyway. The board was like any other corporation and would absolve itself of responsibility for the shenanigans of its renegade executive director. Plus, fucking with those guys would be a protracted mess, and in the end it would bring her more grief than she cared for. Best to let it go and keep her number-one goal in front of her—offing Chainey. Her continued existence was a stone on her heart and she was going to remove it.

She rounded the corner of an RV called the Wanderer, head down, lost in planning. From inside the RV she could hear a TV set going. She halted, listening. One of those goddamn game shows was on, and over that she heard a woman laughing. Zevonian was glad she'd never wound up like that, some hefty See's candy-eating chick in a mu-mu, living out her life watching other losers almost wetting themselves when they were touched by Bob Barker. Or ordering porcelain unicorns off the Home Shopping Network. One side of her face twitched. Whatever else, she had few regrets for what she'd done.

It had been a long way from Watchung, New Jersey. Her old man had worked himself to death running an auto salvage yard. He drank too many Pabsts and smoked too much, his only exercise bowling with his beer-guzzling buddies on Friday nights. Emphysema and a liver like paté had done him in. Her mother, who was still alive, had worked the jewelry counter at the Kress for more than twenty-five years, up until the day it closed for good. She had not been particularly careful at being hush-hush about some of the men she'd bop on the side. And her brother Gerry, hell, she hadn't seen or heard from that reprobate in years. He'd steal your eyes and sell them back to you for marbles.

Though when her dad was alive she didn't remember any of

their arguments being about sleeping around. And she and her sister didn't want for a new bicycle or the latest Donna Summer album, so there wasn't much to complain about. There just wasn't much to get excited about, either, in her hometown. Funny, Zevonian recalled, sitting on the picnic table and folding her arms as she smoked, it was her older sister who was the whorish one in high school. She was the one who blew both the quarterback and tackle sitting in the front seat of the QB's cherry '68 Camaro Super Sport.

At that point Zevonian had a crush on her gym teacher, Mrs. Gifford, who had one firm butt in her workout shorts. She was finally awakened to her bisexuality by the math dweeb Helen Kotais. She and her sister had snuck away with the quarterback—what the hell was his name?—to that party in East Rutherford. It was one of those end-of-the-school-year bashes, and the weed and hard liquor were in plentiful supply. And here was Kotais. Somehow she'd gotten there and, as usual, she was holding up the wall.

Zevonian was getting high, letting Owen Ramsey feel her up on the slow dance to the Chi-Lites "People Make the World Go 'Round." Kotais was looking at her, slylike. After the dance, Zevonian had gone over to her to tease her, but something about the way she glared back at her made her think of Mrs. Gifford. Before she knew it they were in the bathroom and Helen was going down on her. It was fantastic. The cigarette had burned down in her mouth and she threw it away. She got off the picnic table and headed back to clear out her room. That summer, after a few more times of naughty sex with Helen, and as her senior year loomed, the old man keeled over. She split town and kept going. She worked at square jobs, then did a few stripping stints.

She survived by doing the bump and grind, and offering some tail for extra dough. During that time she got a side gig running messages to the money collectors working for the low-level mobster running the strip club outside Newark. But those clowns were never going to let her do something real important, so she watched and learned. And when her chance came, she took it.

One of the regular collectors had gotten himself arrested on an old failure-to-appear warrant and she went in his place. She got the partial payment from a furrier who was an Auschwitz survivor and wasn't scared of much. But this slip of a girl who batted her eyes and got him to feel all fatherly suddenly holding a pair of shears to his gonads got his attention. And the attention of that slob of a club owner.

She walked inside and toward the elevator. Why was she dredging this stuff up? What the hell use was the past except for marking someplace you'd left? Next she'd be weeping about Zora. She never led her on, never promised her they'd go away together to Majorca or wherever the hell it was she wanted to go and tend goats. She was going to recover; she had nothing to moan about.

There was no room for sentimentality in her line of work. You went forward and you didn't look back. Why in the world was she dwelling on those times now? Must have something to do with Elwood's death. Well, that big bitch was going to pay. The elevator door opened. A sudden pop made her reach for her piece until she realized it was two kids running down the hall holding on to a couple of helium-filled balloons. Well, one was holding onto a balloon; the other now just had a string. Neither seemed to notice. Why the hell weren't those crumb snatchers in school?

She relaxed and unlocked her door. Coming at Chainey straight on was going to be hard on her home turf, but she'd get her. Yes, she would.

There was a shadow on the rug and she flinched, instinctively going for her gun again. Simultaneously she had to sight the target as her eyes took in the room. In fractions of a second she saw the white shoes, then up to the blue hem of the dress, the white smock, fixing on the maid's uniform. Too fuckin' early for room cleaning, some part of her brain registered as her gun zeroed in. Her father's face materialized in her memory.

Chainey shot Molly Zevonian once through the eye. The exit wound of the bullet was larger than the entrance hole. The spent shell bored into the cornflower-patterned wallpaper, bits of brain matter and blood journeying with it. Zevonian collapsed to the floor, arms and legs outstretched.

Calmly, Chainey got out of the stolen maid's uniform and exchanged it for the clothes in the Neiman Marcus shopping bag. She took the suppressor off the gun and tossed the pistol onto the bed. Closing the door, she removed the supple gloves she'd worn and added the suppressor to the contents of the bag, Unhurriedly, she went to the elevator down the hall and around the corner, the two kids zooming past her. She went downstairs and out into the parking lot. Absently, she touched one of her horseshoe earrings.

CHAPTER TWENTY

Chainey huffed her way to a stop around the track at the University of Nevada at Las Vegas. She'd pushed herself to do a five-mile run, then had completed the speed laps around the track. She bent over, crossing her legs at the ankles. She stretched her lower back, the muscles in her legs aching. But the burn was pleasurable, reminding her how good it felt to be healthy and in shape.

She straightened and a did a cool-down lap. Several male students were also out for their workout and gave her an appreciative appraisal. She had worn her running shorts. But starting a relationship with a younger man was not uppermost in her mind at the moment—or for the foreseeable future. That Stella action would have to wait.

She left the track and went to the Bally's near her house. There she did several sets with the machine and free weights. Again Chainey pushed herself, and for her efforts got a terrific strain across her shoulders. She ignored the pain and worked through fifty abdomen crunches. By the end, her teeth were cemented together and her head pounded from exertion and exhaustion.

Under the flow of the hot water, her body felt semirenewed in the shower. She let the water course through her thick hair and down her back. The muscles and tendons she'd maxed out were a different matter. But they, too, would regain their elasticity, they too would return to normal. Everything would go back to the way it was. It had been three days since the murder, since she'd done to Molly Zevonian what the hitwoman had intended to do to her.

The world kept spinning, and the dice in Vegas still rolled after she'd pulled the trigger on the woman. That night her sleep hadn't been fitful. The video of the woman with the hole in her head hadn't started to replay for Chainey until the following day. She was doing the laundry, an ordinary thing, when it overcame her.

Watching the soap powder drizzle from the plastic measuring cup, she became mesmerized by the particles. It was as if each bit was crystalized DNA. And here she was, casually letting the building blocks of life slip away. Had it been that way for Victoria? What had her days and nights been like as the enormity of killing her brother set in on her?

Like it had hit her on the street when Sixkiller drove up on her, the burden of guilt made her weak, disoriented. She'd propped herself against the washing machine and resolved to hold it together until . . . until what? As her clothes started to cycle, she'd gone out on her deck. The landscaping around her was serene, as if it was a 3-D painting. How odd it was to realize that dirt and plants would last longer than she would. Far longer. She turned off the water and stepped out of the shower.

Over the rise of low hills beyond her backyard, she could hear the swing and contact of golf clubs at one of the ubiquitous courses dotting the playland of Las Vegas and its environs. Hell, there'd be somebody on the links way after she was gone. Later, she wound up having a few scotches and sleeping on the deck, a blanket on her while she reposed on the padded Adirondack chaise lounge. Her house had felt too confining; it was too easy to be trapped there.

But trapped by whom? Zevonian's ghost? One of the Porters' kin come a'callin'? Or was it her own unease she was trying to get away from? But any fool could tell you there was no escaping your own skin. Humans couldn't shed their deeds like a snake does his scales. What you did in the past was yours to bear and was the bane of the present. She was getting downright philosophical for a gun-toting chick.

Chainey sat on the bench in the locker room in her underwear, drying her hair. Two other women entered. The pair were laughing and talking after their apparently rousing game of handball. One of them peeled off her glove and Chainey could see herself in that hallway, nonchalantly having tossed her gloves in the Neiman Marcus bag. She leaned her head back against the cool surface of the locker, one foot up on another locker door across the aisle.

Fuck it, she reminded herself one more time. Zevonian was gonna waste her. She was a coldhearted murderer and would not have hesitated to ambush Chainey. If there was a lesson you damn sure needed to take away from this, it was that only the schemers came out on top. They knew the odds were never in your favor, and every jackpot was prelude to a bust-out. The way to beat the system was to change the rules. Of course those homilies did nothing to assuage her mixed emotions.

She got dressed and drove toward home. Two blocks from her place she changed her mind and reversed direction, her new destination uncertain.

Frankie Degault had an electronic planner and on it was the phone number for Zevonian's hotel. The simple use of a reverse directory yielded the Boomtown designation. Finding out the woman's room number wasn't hard for Victoria to get either. All of it had been done over the phone. Ah, the modern age. Now the legwork, that had been all hers.

Chainey guided her car farther north, away from the city proper. There were a lot of places to go besides the Strip; Nevada was a big state. But getting away from her memory . . . that was entirely different. It didn't bother her that three people knew she had committed murder. Well, it wasn't murder really, now was it? The shooting had been self-defense, of the preemptive strike kind. That rationale worked in Nicaragua, Kosovo, Iraq and lots of other countries, right?

She found herself out in the desert, that long, flat expanse of Highway 15 laying before her with its possibilities. Where could she go and what would she do? She'd made that decision once she planted the slug in Zevonian. Even as Frankie Degault's body cooled on the floor of his cabin, as she and Victoria Degault exchanged looks, she'd put herself into automaton mode. She knew then that there was no way out of her situation save one patented method—the Las Vegas way.

Joe Williams sang "Can You Use a Big Man," on the CD player. Yeah, Joe, she could use a number of things. But there was no goddamn going back now. She'd begun on this journey more than twenty years before, when she got to town, tall and gawky, and lied about her age to get her first gig. And after all she'd been through, nobody put the Svengali on her to take a job on the wrong side of the law. Being a courier had dangerous possibilities.

Getting on in the showgirl trade, she'd taken the job because she wasn't going to wind up like all those stories anyone could recite verbatim about pretty and smart—and not so smart—girls who were fortysomething working bottom-rung strip clubs for the afternoon crowd, the pensioner bunch.

"Shit," she swore aloud, doing a doughnut on the near-empty asphalt. Chainey eased her foot on the accelerator. No sense drawing unwanted attention by speeding. She headed back to her place and a half-empty bottle of Cutty. She wasn't planning to drink her way to blackouts. But this bottle would get finished in the next few days and that would signal the end of this phase. She wasn't going to mope about what she'd done. There was no way for Chainey to function if she did.

She supposed the killing would eat at her; how could it not? Zevonian was a machine. She would have just as easily murdered her friend Rena or Mooch to further her revenge. She had no delusion that she'd been on an altruistic mission to rid the world of that viper. She'd done it for herself. There was no need to repeatedly beat herself up about that. No need at all.

Some time after one that morning, she lay awake in bed on

her back. Her head was fuzzy from the scotch but not so far gone that she was in orbit. Frankie Degault's death had been attributed to Vern Sixkiller. The sister and soon-to-be overall CEO of Riverhead Enterprises, would ensure that he got the best in representation. This would be done through intermediaries as no one was to know what actually went down in the cabin save for the ones there. Sixkiller fired a couple of rounds from the gun Victoria had used into the bushes in the back to make sure gunpowder residue was on his hand. Lizardo, the tribal cop had arrested Leopold and was making sure no one talked until the right time.

How the hell was Victoria coping?

From what had been pieced together, it seemed that Frankie Degault had for a period of years been losing money behind one loopy scheme or another. He'd siphoned off funds from accounts under his control to invest in several racehorses, a failed area football team, a NASCAR vehicle, and numerous chances on money and action. Here he was, the head of a casino, supposed to be a sharpie, and he couldn't stay away from gambling. Which is why he did it; the rush, the allure was too much for him to resist. He had to play the percentages like any mark from Montana.

The sums Frankie had lost weren't that significant in high-roller terms, but the fact that he'd essentially stolen the money from his own corporation was what would have gotten him removed as head of the businesses. Not killed, not broken up, just pitched out on the street. And his ego could not stand that.

So he was more than willing to arrange for the murders of numerous people to obfuscate his stealing and hide his misadventures. The seven large was just enough to run on and set up elsewhere. He'd had a ticket to Chile in his effects. Chile, for chrissakes.

It was easy to concoct the story that Sixkiller found out what Frankie Degault had been doing and confronted the security chief and Chainey in the cabin. That Sixkiller got the drop on Degault and the rest is Las Vegas folklore. One more tale to fascinate the rubes as the cabbie showed them the sights. And Rena got her cover on the *Express* and co-byline in a Newsweek piece.

Yet it wasn't those machinations keeping her awake in the gloom. And it wasn't worries over what she'd done to keep her own life. No, what suddenly occurred to her was the bomb that had been strapped under her couch.

Baker had said he hadn't done it and he'd sounded sincere. Zevonian was the only other candidate, but that wasn't her style. Now the third gun, he was the electronics guy. Of course there was the little problem of him being dead at that point. Okay, he could have made it before he died. But that would mean Zevonian and Porter had come back to Vegas, rigged the bomb, then split. And not wait around to see if their big surprise worked? Not hardly.

That fucked-up South African could have been lying. Certainly his former life indicated he knew about bombs, but still, she was unsure. Baker was gone, Frankie and Molly were dead, and the answer might go begging unless she was willing to hunt that sick bugger down to ask him again, politely.

Chainey rolled over onto her side, a tiredness finally enveloping her. Her eyes were fluttering when the phone rang. She plucked the handset free. There was only the sound of people conversing, and silverware clinking on plates. It was a dinner party in the background.

"Who is this?" she said.

"See you soon," a man's voice replied. There was more of the noise but she knew the man was listening. A woman could be heard saying 'ooops' and giggling. Then the line clicked off.

Without hesitation, she returned the handset and snuggled under the covers. The call was evidently meant to rattle her, but she was too beat to get worried about it at the moment. Her gun was in the nightstand, and she'd had a better alarm system installed. If whoever was on the other end was more than a crank, then she'd know soon enough. For now, she was going to get some rest. She'd earned it.

ABOUT THE AUTHOR

GARY PHILLIPS has been a community activist and organizer for over twenty-four years in Los Angeles. His op-eds and pieces on race, politics, and pop culture have run in publications such as the *L.A. Times, San Francisco Examiner,* the *Washington Post,* the *Baltimore Sun,* the *Miami Herald, Black Scholar,* and *Rap Pages* magazine. He has appeared on CNN, CBS network news, and "BET Tonight."

Phillips has published four Ivan Monk mysteries, a stand-alone crime novel, and several short stories. In addition to working on the next Martha Chainey book, *Shooter's Point,* he's working on a novel about blacks and the WWII years, and writing a direct-to-web film with rapper Scarface. And like everybody else in L.A., he's developing a TV show.

He lives in the mid-city area of L.A. with his wife, Gilda Haas, their children, Miles and Chelsea, and their semi-useless dog, Mitzy.